Illegal Woman

Illegal Woman

A Gypsy Love Story

4/4/2013

To MICHELLE —
THANKS FOR ALL THE SPECIAL
HELP AND ESPECIALLY GETTING
"THE SUCKER" WHICH MADE
OPENING DAY POSSIBLE. OUR
35TH CONSECUTIVE OPENING DAY.
HOPE YOU ENJOY MY
GYPSY ADVENTURE.
LOVE,
GABY

Ralph Gaby Wilson

To order additional copies of this book, contact:
Xlibris Corporation
1-888-795-4274
www.Xlibris.com
Orders@Xlibris.com
117357

It was one of the worst days of my life.

I was broke. All alone. And, five thousand miles from home.

No immediate prospects. No friends. Faint hope.

"Mama said there'd be days like this there'll be days like this my mama said."

I could hear The Shirelles singing that song. It was as if they had recorded it four years ago just so it would be embedded in my head, waiting for playback today.

"Mama said,
Mama said."

While it was one the worst, it was also one of the luckiest days of my life. But I didn't know that yet. Fate is funny that way. You may think she is dealing you one of the worst hands you have ever held—but you haven't seen the hole card yet. Fate springs things on you that way. She has an odd sense of humor.

So there I was a world away from home. Out of money. Out of luck. But not out of options.

As my Mom, Dad and Grandma used to say: "Never count yourself out. No matter how hard you get knocked down, you can always get back up." Everybody in my family shared a common trait. They were optimists. They had to be. There was never any way but up for them. But today, *up* looked like a very dim prospect.

"Mama said there'd be days like this there'll be days like this my mama said."

I was standing outside the American Express office in the European principality of Monaco. It was the spring of 1965. The early morning sun beat down hot. The air smelled salty from the nearby Mediterranean Sea. I leaned back against the pitted red brick front of the American Express building and tried to figure out what I was going to do next. I had expected to find checks waiting for me here. There were none.

Suddenly, things weren't going the way they were supposed to.

"Mama said there'd be days like this there'll be days like this my mama said."

I had come to Europe to become the next Hemingway. I wanted to be a novelist and I was working on my first novel. But I knew I had to support myself until I finished it. So, I decided to do what I knew best—write news and feature stories for the newspapers back home. That was Plan A.

Before leaving Kansas City in the middle of March, I had contacted the Kansas City Star and the Kansas City Kansan. I had covered the police beat, the courthouse and done undercover reporting for both newspapers. I had contacted United Press International and the Rocky Mountain News because I had freelanced feature stories and photos to them. I asked if they were interested in features from Europe—if I ran into anyone from Kansas. I had been told "yes" by all of them. I thought I had all my ducks in a row. Plan A seemed like all I needed. I'd figure out a Black Plan later if I had to.

Everything started off as if there were no need for a Black Plan. I got a job on a freighter and sold my first story while still at sea. It was one of those "right-place at the right-time" things. Although the outcome of the story was sad. I'll tell that story when I meet *her*. And, after all, this story is really about *her*.

Anyway, I was lucky. Almost every place I went I ran into stories. I sent them back to my contact newspapers in the States. They sent checks to me at American Express offices in London, Copenhagen, Düsseldorf, Venice and Florence.

Easy Money. The easiest money I'd ever made. I spent it just like you always do with *Easy Money*. "Easy come easy go." There'll always be more. Or, so I thought.

When I'd walked into this American Express building not more than thirty minutes ago I was on top of the world. But things can sure head south in a hurry.

The AmEx office was in a converted bank building. The inside looked just like every small town bank you've ever been in. Shiny marble. Black wrought iron. High-domed ceiling. Like I said, you've been here before.

The mail pickup area was downstairs. It had been the old bank's basement. Probably used for storage. Now, the coarse, pocked concrete walls were painted glossy white. The concrete floor was painted glossy green. Green and white were American Express' colors back then. Gold and Platinum hadn't been thought up yet.

There were six lines of people in front of three cafeteria type tables. Two lines to a table. Two alphabet cards hung above each table, indicating which line you should be in to get your mail. A-D and E-F above the first table. G-L and M-P above the second. And, at the last table, R-T and U-Z.

At the head of each line was a pretty young woman, who sorted through portable gray tin mail bins and retrieved your waiting mail. Naturally, the women were all dressed alike. Black slacks. White blouses. Green neck scarves with AmEx logos on them. AmEx's colors again. Some decorator must have thought he/she was clever with colors.

The cutie servicing the G-L line was an attractive brunette with a great smile. I spent my ten minutes waiting in that line trying to come up with something clever to say to her. You know, the clever comment that catches her attention. Something that makes you stand out. Something that might give me an opening to ask her to lunch or maybe out for a drink after work. An original clever comment that would break the ice. I mean, these women had to be hit on all the time. I didn't want to sound like a jerk—even if I was thinking like one.

When I reached the head of the line I said: "K. P. Kelly". I figured that she'd notice that most of my mail was from newspapers and say something. If not, I'd sort through the letters she gave me, and say something like: "Nothing from the New York Times?" Then I'd explain that I was a writer. Being a writer piqued interest in some women. Who knew where that might lead? Lunch? A stroll on the beach?

She dug around in one of the portable mail bins. Dug through a second bin. Then sorted through both of them again. She looked at me, shook her head sadly and with a sexy accent said: "Zorry, nozhing for Kell-Lee."

I couldn't believe my ears. I had been selling almost everything I had written. And, like I said, spending it about as fast as I got it. Now, nothing? I was speechless. I walked away in stunned silence. I even forgot to ask her out. Of course, I would have had to ask her out Dutch, wouldn't I? How cool.

Outside, I stood leaning against the old stained, red brick building, feeling the early summer sun beating down on me, smelling the sea in the air, trying to figure out what to do next. I was so lost in thought I didn't really see the pedestrians on the sidewalk or hear the traffic in the street. I had a problem. A major problem. My next drop point was Paris. Six hundred miles away. Six hundred miles between me and my next payday. I should say "possible payday." And, I only had thirty dollars in my pocket. Not enough money to take a train or a bus. Not if I wanted to eat.

On the other hand, if there *had* been checks waiting for me it would not have been one of my luckiest days. If there *had* been checks waiting for me I would have cashed them and taken either the bus or the train to Paris. And, had I taken a bus or train to Paris I would never have met *her*. Of course, at the time, I didn't know how lucky I was to be broke.

And, being broke, I really had only one option. Come up with a Plan B. And, until I came up with a Black Plan, there was only one thing to do. Start walking. Come to think of it, I guess walking was Plan B. It was Plan C that I needed to start working on.

I picked up my Samsonite suitcase and started walking. Walking and thinking about how I had gotten here.

Before leaving Kansas City, I had sold my one-year-old Ford Fairlane for $1,100. I had $400 in the bank. Also, I had secured a standby crew position on a New Guinea freighter headed from Montréal, Canada, to Bristol, England. It was carrying a load of raw bauxite from Dutch Guiana to Denmark.

I thought I had all my ducks lined up. I had fifteen hundred bucks, the most money I'd ever had. I had my passage to Europe locked in. What could possibly go wrong? Nothing. Unless you were arrogant and just a little too full of yourself. That could undermine your game plan, for sure. So, I was walk. Walking and hoping to get lucky."

Grandma used to say that luck was the result of hard work.

Well, walking and lugging that Samsonite suitcase was hard work. And, the hard work would pay off, and I would get lucky. I would meet a beautiful Gypsy woman and we would fall in love. But that was down the road. Literally.

Right now I needed to figure out a Plan C because Plan B sucked.

"MY AMERICAN COUSIN"

Plan C is another way of saying "time to improvise."

During the train ride from Florence, Italy, to Monaco, I had studied my road map to develop an overall plan of attack. If there were enough checks waiting for me I'd take the train to Paris and be there in a day. If not, I'd take a bus.

Well, I'd be taking the bus route—only now, it would be on foot. Six hundred and thirty-two miles to be exact. Only the rubber meeting the road would be my Keds.

As I left the American Express office, I walked west along what was probably the main street. All I knew about Monaco was what I had read in magazines. Grace Kelly had married Prince Rainier and they lived in the magical principality of Monaco. It was supposed to be a gorgeous fantasyland of the rich and famous.

In reality, it reminded me a lot of Minnesota Avenue, the main drag in Kansas City, Kansas, where I spent my early years. The wrong side of the Missouri river. Kansas City, Kansas, was the urchin half-brother of well-to-do Kansas City, Missouri.

The main street here in Monaco was lined with poor, run down, one-story shops. The new merchandise displayed in the front windows looked used. The sidewalk was cracked and pitted. Hungry storeowners were waiting in their doorways for any customer with money. Just like Kansas City, Kansas, the people on the street wore old or cheap clothes. Occasionally you saw a well-dressed man or woman. But for the most part they were people trying to get by and maintain as much dignity as possible.

I was seven years old before I crossed the river into Kansas City, Missouri, and saw how the other half lived. Until then I didn't realize how close to poor we were.

So, here I was walking down the main street of southern France's version of Kansas City, Kansas, trying to formulate a plan that was entirely flexible and I kept banging my Samsonite suitcase against my leg. Every half block I switched it to the opposite hand and banged the other leg for half a block. Every block I had to set it down and rest my arms.

Originally I had planned to travel with a beautiful leather suitcase—good thing I didn't because empty, that beautiful leather suitcase weighed more than the Samsonite packed. I'd gone to the Goodwill two days before leaving Kansas City, Missouri, and bought the Samsonite for five dollars. There had been a cheaper, lighter cardboard suitcase but it just wasn't cool. I mean, who would choose cardboard? I was sure Hemingway didn't set sail for Europe with a cardboard suitcase. Cardboard just wasn't cool. Now I was regretting that decision. And, come to find out, Hemingway did have a cardboard suitcase. I stared vanity in the eye and it was me.

I stopped in front of a shoe store to get some feeling back in my arms and as I looked up and down the seedy street I saw a backpack hanging from a storefront a half a block away. I trudged toward it.

As I lugged the suitcase down the street the storeowner stepped out. He was sleazy looking in his black polyester pants and black and white diamond-patterned rayon shirt. He surveyed the street, looking for prospects, saw me coming and went back inside his store. He was waiting just inside the door when I arrived, dribbling the Samsonite off my knee. I glanced up at the pack. Fifty francs. Ten dollars. A third of my money. I paid no attention to it.

"Bonjour," he smiled

"Bonjour," I said and began fumbling through my non-existent French. "Moi manque les legert bagage aller Paris."

The storeowner looked at me with arrogant disdain and shrugged—typically French. If you couldn't speak French fluently, they couldn't understand you. Naturally they didn't speak or understand English, unless there was money to be made. So, I perused the store lifting bags and suitcases to test their weight.

"Poids importance?" he asked.

It was my turn to shrug.

"Is weight important?" he asked. Ah, he was sensing a sale. Advantage to the tourist. I always thought of negotiations as a tennis match.

I nodded. "Oui."

"Let me see what I can do for my American cousin."

Interesting phrase, I thought. *My American cousin.* Normally, the French don't like us—and suddenly I'm his cousin. In tennis terms I was being drawn to the net and set up for a deep lob.

He guided me to a canvas suitcase, which I hefted. Lighter. "Better" I said. "Meillcur." I searched for the proper French words except I couldn't find them so I resorted to English, which I knew he understood. "It's not quite right. I will have to look somewhere else." I returned the lob to his baseline.

I started out of the shop, but did a double take on the backpack, and stopped and examined it. I sensed him following me. He took down the pack with a long wooden pole and held the dark green canvas pack out to me. I shrugged. He looked at the price tag.

"For you forty-five francs." He returned the tennis ball back over the net.

I took the pack—inspected it. It was perfect. Strong canvas stretched over an aluminum frame. Much like the one I had worn into the high Cascades with a childhood buddy in 1961. I should have been thinking pack from the beginning. I gave an unsure shrug. My volley ran him to the other side of the court.

"For you forty francs." He drove the ball into the net. Add-in!

I frowned and shook my head sadly. My best power serve.

"Twenty-five francs plus your Samsonite suitcase."

Ace! Game! Match!

I paid with a ten. He gave me twenty-five francs change. I transferred my things from the Samsonite to the pack and slipped it on. It felt comfortable and good. I smiled and shook his hand.

He pinned a United States flag to the back of my new pack saying it would make it easier to hitchhike my way to Paris. And, he gave me a better road map than the one I had.

Then I hit the road with ten U.S. dollars and twenty-five francs in my pocket.

I caught a free bus ride to the edge of town and studied my new road map. During the bus ride I found a better route. The map had kilometer markers between cities and the shortest route was five hundred and twenty-two miles. A hundred and ten miles shorter than the route I had originally planned to take.

I realized I had to stop converting kilometers to miles and start thinking in kilometers. This route was eight hundred plus kilometers, which made Paris seem much farther away.

At the end of the bus line I got off and started walking. It was seven kilometers to Nice Cote d'Azur, which took ninety minutes. It was noon when I arrived. Then I turned north on N202 and the walk *really* began. In the next six hours a couple hundred cars passed me. I thumbed at them all. None of them even slowed to take a look at the American hitchhiker.

*　　*　　*

Eventually, I made my way to a bed and breakfast hotel in La Croix de Fer, which cost five francs for the night. The five francs entitled me to two croissants and all the coffee I could drink in the morning. That left me with ten dollars and twenty francs—and just less than eight hundred kilometers to travel in what was now appearing to be a slim hope of finding checks at the Paris American Express. Hopefully, tomorrow I'd hitch a ride. I mean you have to look on the bright side.

The woman who ran the B&B was probably twenty years my senior with coal black hair and a hitch in her lanky get-along.

A fetching hitch it was, too. It was a hitch that allowed her to dust both handrails as she led me up the narrow staircase to the upstairs sleeping room.

It was a large room—empty except for a stack of about a dozen bare mattresses in one corner. She pointed at the pile of mattresses and left. I took the top mattress and dragged it and my pack to the opposite corner and was asleep the instant my head hit the mattress.

ON THE ROAD

When I awoke in the morning I discovered that I was surrounded by six occupied mattresses. Two attractive young women and four nerdy looking young men. The rest of the large room was empty. In the U.S., the mattresses and their occupants would have been spaced out around the large room. But this was France and the French herd mentality was in effect. Very French.

I studied the six sleeping people briefly. I wondered why it was that the French women are so beautiful and the men look like gene pool contaminants?

Then I shouldered my pack, picked my way quietly through the other mattresses and went downstairs.

It was a typical family operated B&B. The large dining area was a yellowish plaster with dark brown stained accent beams. The room had once been two rooms judging by the rough plasterwork where one wall had been removed.

There was a bar opposite the entrance. It was beside double swinging doors that, no doubt, led to the kitchen judging from the clatter of pots and pans within.

There was a long cafeteria-style table with seven plates and seven coffee cups on it. Each plate held two croissants, one pat of butter, one slice of cheese and an apple. At the end of the table were a coffee urn and a stack of paper cups and paper snap-on lids. The sign attached to an ashtray beside the paper cups said: 1f. cafe aller.

I ate one croissant with butter. I wrapped my other croissant and the slice of cheese in a paper napkin, and put that with the apple into my pack. I finished my coffee and got up to go. As I left I poured the to-go coffee in a paper cup, snapped on the lid, dropped one franc in the ashtray and hit the road.

It was probably the longest and most boring day I spent in Europe. Cars whizzed by ignoring the American hitchhiker. For ten hours I hiked uphill but made less than fifty kilometers.

At first, I passed the time singing hit songs from 1963. I had been in a hootenanny group in Kansas City. Actually, I was in the group because I lived in a place called Folk House. Folk House was an interesting phenomenon. It was a place where folk musicians lived in Kansas City. Then blues and jazz musicians moved in. All kinds of musicians traveling through town moved in. The music evolved. Soon we had folk-rock and all the lines between the styles got blurry. Blues guys rocked. Folk guys found jazz. Old stuff got contemporized.

It was a real happening place to be. This home for musicians on the road didn't happen by design. Places like that never do.

It started out simply enough. I had just gotten out of the hospital after a run in with Kansas City's mafia. I had decided to find a writing job where people wouldn't shoot at you if they didn't like what you wrote. Advertising seemed like a good idea. It even paid better.

So, after a successful job interview I had stopped for a celebration beer at the Castaways, a music club in Kansas

City's Country Club Plaza. The club's manager and bartender happened to be an old college buddy, Jim Gardiner. We drank beer and fought old wars. There was a three-man group on stage setting up for that night's performance. They joined Jim and me at the bar for a beer.

Jim asked me where I was living. I said I was looking for a new place. Jim said his Mom owned a four-bedroom house across the state line in Mission, Kansas, and she was trying to rent it. By the time we finished our beers, Jim, myself and the three band members had decided to rent his Mom's house. That was the start of Folk House. Just five people. March 1963.

By June there were a dozen of us living at Folk House. Jim, ten musicians and myself. The house had a full basement and newcomers partitioned off sleeping areas in the basement. The exciting thing was that they were all really good musicians and songwriters. And they were all on their way to "someplace."

By September there were eighteen of us. Jim and I were the only ones with day jobs. Which meant the two of us were the only ones guaranteed to come up with our share of the rent. The monthly rent was three hundred dollars plus utilities.

Sounds like an easy nut to crack, doesn't it? It wasn't. Even with eighteen of us there was always a shortfall. Somebody, or several somebodies, ran the phone bill way up. Several somebodies took long, long showers with girlfriends. Everybody left on the lights. Utilities killed us.

Jim Gardiner and I picked up the shortfall. Every month. And that was the reason for the formation of our Saturday and Sunday hootenanny group. It was payback for me from the guys in the House. A way I could recoup some of my shortfall. Stay a bit solvent.

And it wasn't a hardship for the guys at the House. No musician ever saw an empty stage that he/she didn't fall in love with.

We played somewhere every Saturday and Sunday afternoon. I played the guitar poorly and sang just as badly. One of the other guys, Gene Clark, a future Byrd, played quite well and ran off riffs to cover my mistakes. The third guy, Jim Glover, alternated between bass and banjo with great expertise. He became a Christy Minstrel. He's a dentist now. The other two members of the group were gorgeous young women with beautiful voices. Jay and Kay. Their job was to try to keep me on key.

Our pay for the hootenannies was all we could eat and all the beer we could drink. My date got a free pass, too. It really helped me put away money for this trip.

So, I killed time walking to Paris by singing. I sang our songs from the first year we hooted together. Songs like Jimmy Gilmer & The Fireballs' **Sugar Shack**.

"There's a crazy little shack beyond the tracks.
And everybody calls it the Sugar Shack.
Well, it's just a coffee house and it's made out of wood.
Espresso coffee tastes mighty good.
That's not the reason why I've got to get back to . . .
That Sugar Shack. Whoa, baby, to that Sugar Shack.
But that's not the reason I've got to get back.
There's this cute little girlie she's a working there.
A black leotard and her feet are bare . . ."

And I walked and walked, sang badly and loudly, but none of the cars whizzing by could hear me. Or maybe they did and that was why they didn't stop. Who cared, I was singing and having fun. It made the walking bearable. Like Jan & Dean's:

"Twoooo girls for eeeevery boy.

I got a '34 wagon and we call it a woodie

Surf City *here we come. here we come . . ."*

And of course I sang **King of the Road.** Maybe sang it a million times.

"Trailer for sale or rent

Rooms to let fifty cents . . ."

I can sing that damn song in my sleep. And often do.

"I'm a man of means by no means

King of the Road."

I walked and walked. And I got bored with my singing and drifted into what my Dad called a mental eddy. That's where you think yourself in a circle and the circling draws you in tighter and tighter to the point where you can never get back to the mainstream. Mental eddies can be both good and bad. Depends on your mindset going in.

Dad and I were trout fishing in southern Missouri when he first explained the concept of a mental eddy to me. I was about ten years old and I had no idea what he was talking about. Mental eddy? Fortunately, Dad was always more than willing to explain any concept to me.

He put down his fly rod, came over and hunkered down beside me. We were fishing Roaring River, a beautiful, clear, fast, wide stream in the V between two ragged Ozark mountains. We were just above one of its many waterfalls. It was early morning and the falls put mist in the air.

"Think of the river here as your mainstream of thought," he said. He loved allegories and similes and abstracts and such. He picked up a twig and flipped it out into the river. The current whipped it away and over the falls. "That's your idea or thought going from here to there."

He pointed to a spot in the river, this side of the falls, where water swirled around and around, never going over the falls. "That's an eddy."

He picked up a weed and crumpled it up and tossed it at the outer edge of the eddy. It spun around the perimeter, slowly being drawn to the eye of the eddy where it just spun in tight circles.

"Confusion. Indecision. Wasted time and effort." He smiled at me and got up. "That's a mental eddy. When you find yourself in one—Breakaway!" He turned away and started off. He did that when he wanted you to think a moment. Then turned back.

"But, Dad" I'd asked all those years ago beside that Ozark river, "how do you get out of an eddy?"

He had smiled. Picked up a big rock and heaved it at the eddy. It exploded in the water and blew the crumpled weed out into the stream and it was swept over the falls. "Breakaway," he said.

Breakaway. I went back to thinking about the hootenannies.

I thought of other songs that were crowd pleasers and I sang them. The crowd was generally made up of dating singles. Of course there were some married couples in their twenties and a few couples in their early thirties with little kids who would dance as we sang. It was fun.

The increasing uphill grade of the road was beginning to take its toll and leaving me breathless. So, the songs came further apart, leaving me with time for thoughts of home. Back into that mental eddy.

Back to my beautiful blonde ex who wanted to be a model and for whom I'd spent hours in the darkroom at school trying to make her photos look as intriguing as possible. Unfortunately she'd spent those same hours trying to intrigue art directors and ad managers. And, she did a better job of it than I did.

To get my mind off her, I started singing again. Of course there was *If You Want To Be Happy* by Jimmy Soul. It seemed apropos. And, The Angels' *My Boyfriend's Back*.

Finally I lapsed into silence, bored with my singing—too tired to think. Cars still whizzed by. I wasn't going to get a ride today—maybe tomorrow. As the sun sank lower and lower I focused on the countryside in the dimming golden light. Black trees, backlit, reached into a blue sky turning purple. Black cartoon car shapes sped by in the foreground. Black clouds of bugs and loneliness.

Just as the sun began to disappear behind the mountains ahead of me, I spotted what appeared to a campground. Turned out it wasn't. It was just forest. But it didn't matter. I couldn't go on any further. I'd just had to sleep. The ground was hard and cold. It didn't matter. Tomorrow would be a better day.

I lay down and sang my last song of the day. Nino Tempo and April Stevens' *Deep Purple* seemed fitting.

"When the Deep Purple falls
Over sleepy garden walls.
And the stars begin to twinkle in the night
In the mist of the memory
You wander back to me breathing my name with a sigh . . .
zzzzzzzzzzzzzzzzzzz.

A BETTER DAY

Morning. A pink sky with frosty air that I could smell. It had been cold when I drifted off to sleep but it was even colder now. Man, was I hungry and there was nothing to eat. I started walking to work off the chill, but my thoughts were focused on food.

A few kilometers up the road there was a small village—but none of the stores were open. It was too early. The sun was barely up. The village was medieval-looking and ghost-like in the long shadows. I'd seen this village before in a dozen horror movies. The villagers had fled it to escape an evil that even now lurked in the shadows waiting for unsuspecting travelers like me. I kept moving.

About an hour later I came to another small town.

Every store was closed except a coffee shop attached to a gas station. I had hoped to find a grocery store so I could save some money. But this coffee shop would have to do. I was too hungry to continue and who knew how far it was to the next town.

The coffee shop/gas station was a vintage version of an AM/PM Mini Mart—French style. That meant the interior of the coffee shop was yellowish plaster with dark brown stained wood beams. The French must have had a hell of a lot of yellow paint and dark brown stain left over from reconstruction after World War II.

I had a cup of coffee and the best piece of apple pie I'd ever eaten. Funny, how when you're hungry, whatever you're eating is the best food you've ever had. I made my feelings known in my broken French. The dumpy old waitress gave me a smile. She still had most of her teeth. And she proudly showed them as she kept giving me coffee refills. I paid her ten francs and left a two-franc tip.

She pushed the two francs back at me. "You need," she said.

"Merci," I said giving her my best smile as I started to rise.

She put her big meaty hand on my shoulder holding me in my seat. Then she flashed her random teeth and hurried off. She returned with the pot of coffee and a small slice of the pie.

"Merci, merci," I said and was rewarded with a sincere gap-toothed grin as she hurried away.

The coffee shop was beginning to fill up with its early morning regulars. Everyone spoke to each other by name. Made jokes. Called new arrivals to join them. This was a friendly, tight community. It was like home in that way.

I gobbled the pie, drank the coffee and while the waitress was in the kitchen, put the two-franc tip back on the table and hurried out the door. As Willie Nelson would later sing, I was *On the Road Again.* I was down to ten dollars and sixty-eight francs. It was painfully obvious that I was going to run out of money long before I reached Paris.

*   *   *

After about six hours my stomach began to growl. Well, it was just going to have to get used to being empty. I walked on.

About an hour later I came across a farmer's roadside vegetable stand. I stopped to see if I could find food I could eat raw since I didn't have a pot to . . . well, you know—cook in. Of course, the first thing I noticed at the stand was the farmer's daughter—a dishwater blonde. She commanded more of my attention than the food—so maybe I wasn't as hungry as I thought.

Like all French women, it seemed, she was pretty. Well, not just pretty—she was dazzling and she knew it. And she was a major flirt. Unfortunately, she was about fifteen—tops. Nevertheless she made it hard to concentrate. I settled on two asparagus stalks for one franc. A tomato for one franc, and two potatoes at a franc each. My funds had dwindled to ten dollars and sixty-four francs.

As I watched this teenage cutie bag my purchases I heard, in a mid-southern masculine twang: "She's a real looker ain't she?"

"Busted," I thought. But it was a twang I was familiar with.

I turned to see a smiling tall drink of water in well-worn jeans and a *Kingston Trio* style striped shirt and cowboy boots that looked like well-worn favorites. The gee-haw was oozing out of his pores. Flanking him on one side was a tall thin woman—obviously his wife—smiling with her buckteeth. She wore an expensive blouse, equally expensive slacks and a pair of very expensive cowboy boots. On his other side was his daughter, who was going to grow up to look like her mother, except for the teeth. She wore braces. Her clothes and boots were just as expensive as her mother's. They both knew how to spend money.

I smiled back. "What part of Oklahoma are you from?"

His smile faded. "Why, a ways outside Tulsa. How'd know?"

"I'm from Kansas City. Used to date a girl from Tulsa."

"Gol dern. Here we live two hundred miles apart and we have to come to France to meet up. Where you headed?" he asked.

"Paris?" I hoped the question mark I felt didn't come across in my response.

"We saw the flag on your pack as we passed," the wife said. "And we decided to come back and see if there was anything we could do for our *fellow American,*" she said dropping into a perfect LBJ imitation.

"Yeah," he added. "These frogs ain't so friendly even though my Daddy saved their ass in the war."

"You got that right," I said. "They only understand English when there's a buck to be made." I chuckled and smiled.

All three laughed. He stuck out his hand. "Billy Joe Collins." We shook. "Linda Sue." We shook. "Lila," the daughter said.

"It's Lila May," her mother corrected.

"It's Lila. I don't like two names. It's weird and outdated," Lila corrected her mother. She was about fourteen and, as they say in Oklahoma, she was beginning to twirl her own rope.

"Lila, you want to talk weird names?" I gave her my best smile. "Then, I get to go to the front of the line."

"It'll take some to beat Lila May," she said cocking a hip. She wasn't as dazzling as the farmer's daughter—but she had attitude. To be honest, I find attitude more appealing.

I cocked a hip right back at her. Mimicking her hip cock. What I was really hoping for was a ride and I figured a good story telling was my best shot at getting one.

"My father's family name is Kelly," I began. "So that part is a given."

"Dad had a slew of brothers. Uncle Tom. Uncle Bob. Uncle Roy. Uncle Jess. They all wanted me named after them. In fact they insisted.

"So, Mom and Dad named me after all of them. But it isn't Tom, Bob, Roy or Jess because Mom didn't want to play favorites."

"They didn't!" Lila was definitely the fastest of the three.

"The did." I nodded and gave her my best smile.

"I don't get it," Billy Joe said.

Lila started laughing. His first name is Kelly. Named after all his uncles. He's Kelly Kelly."

Linda Sue and Billy Joe started laughing, too. They were all busting a gut. "What do you prefer to be called?" Linda Sue laughed.

"You can call me by my first name or my last I don't care. A few people prefer my middle name, which is Pickett. Mom and Dad said I could choose my own name if I wanted. So they made my middle name Pickett.

They loved it and kept laughing.

Finally Billy Joe said: "We were just looking for a place to catch a late lunch. "Why don't you join us?"

I shook my paper bag of raw vegetables. "This is my lunch I'm sort of on a limited budget."

"We're buying," Linda Sue said. "We won't take no for an answer."

*   *   *

We traveled through two little villages, approximately twenty-five kilometers. But they didn't like any of the restaurants we saw. The ground we covered in twenty minutes would easily have taken me six hours. Maybe longer. Because the grade of the road continued to elevate. After another five kilometers, they spotted a little restaurant that met their liking.

It was the exterior sign that caught their eyes. A farmer and a chicken. Something rural they could relate to. *Le Cultiver et le Oeuf* or *Le Oeuf et Moi*. Inside it could have been a restaurant-pub in any country. Wooden tables with no tablecloths. Several of which were occupied. An elegant, white-haired lady occupied one table and sitting in the chair across from her was a very proud, white, standard poodle. A male of course. They appeared to be a very compatible white-haired couple. She talked and he listened as they ate their omelets. The specialty of the house.

The Collins ordered various specialties and I pigged out down home style. Bacon and lots of it. Three scrambled eggs. Fried 'taters and an English muffin. Who knew—I may never eat again.

As we chowed down, the Collins asked about me. And, being their guest, I felt they deserved an entertaining storytelling. I did my best to entertain them and they seemed to enjoy my story—maybe even a little impressed.

I told them about being in the newspaper business. But what interested Lila the most was my job on the freighter getting to Europe.

"How did you go about getting a job on a freighter?" she asked.

I could read between the lines. What she was really asking was how would she go about doing it.

"I was lucky. I went to the library to check on the prices on passenger liners because airfares were too expensive for me. Turned out going by ship cost even more. The librarian suggested I check the want ads in a shipping magazine. There was an ad for "standby crew" on a freighter from Dutch Guiana to Montreal. The ship was headed to Copenhagen with bauxite. I wrote and asked if they needed crew from Montreal to Europe. They sent an application. And, I got hired."

"Sight unseen?"

"Pretty much. They needed deckhands and kitchen help." I saw a light in Lila's eyes when I said kitchen help.

"I had to show up three days before they shipped out. Ready to work. It was a hands-on audition. So they could see if I could do the job."

"What was it like?" Lila asked.

"Well, it was hot, dirty, hard work."

I explained that bauxite, in its raw form, is a claylike rock consisting of aluminum oxides and hydroxides and various impurities. That it is the principle ore from which aluminum is derived. That bauxite was named after Les Baux, a small town in the south of France where it was discovered in about 1821. That it was a filthy, dusty, dirty cargo. That lots and lots of cleaning had to be done daily by the standby crew. And I saw Lila's eyes start to glaze over.

"There were three of us on the standby crew," I said, trying to get my audience back. "One was young, tall, lean, handsome and angry. He was from Boston and carried on his back the anger of the world's downtrodden. He had that animal magnetism that women can't resist."

"Where was he from," Lila asked.

I had Lila's attention again.

"Boston. Black Irish. He oozed outlaw."

"What was his name?" Linda Sue asked.

Funny what caught people's attention. And, because I had the attention of both of his women, Billy Joe was paying attention.

"Jack Dumas," I told Linda Sue.

"What kind of guy was he?" Billy Joe asked.

"A rabble rouser. You probably know the type."

Billy Joe nodded his head. He didn't like Jack already.

I continued, "Jack railed all day about how we were perfect examples of the have-nots who were being overworked and underpaid by the haves. How we had dug our own bottomless economic pits 'out of which we could never work our way.'

"Standby wasn't a very accurate job description," I said. "Nobody 'stood by.'

"The captain, sort of a Danish Jack London no-nonsense type, put us to work chipping paint before we left port. We chipped paint from sun up until the dinner bell. Then after dinner we cleaned up all the paint and bauxite dust until the sun set. The rest of the evening was ours. If we had any energy left."

"Tell me more about Jack," Lila said.

"Jack spent a lot of time lecturing about class wars. Haves and Have Nots. Sometimes it was hard to tell if he was lecturing or complaining."

"I know the type," Billy Joe said. "All mouth and no mettle."

"Actually, we hit it off pretty well. He talked. I listened. He liked that."

"Works that way with most boys," Lila smiled.

Linda Sue laughed. "You are growing up way too fast, young lady." Then to me: "What was he interested in? Or, was he all looks and wind?"

Lila didn't miss Linda Sue's meaningful glance.

"Two things." I said. "Money and the Boston Red Sox. He wanted to be a self-made man. Rich enough to buy the Red Sox. He said the key was stick-to-it-iveness."

"He seems like a first class dreamer-complainer," Billy Joe said.

I laughed. He sure had Jack pegged. "I'd never spent much time around complainers. Complaining always seemed like a waste of time to me. But when you're stuck in a tiny section of a small freighter, you don't have much choice but to listen."

"Borrrriing," Lila said.

"I tried to sidetrack his complaining by making bets."

"Like what?" Billy Joe asked. He was measuring Jack.

"Oh, he'd say 'I'll bet dinner's late. That's how they squeeze more work out of us.' And I'd say you're on for ten. I usually won."

"He ever pay?" Linda Sue asked. But she knew the answer.

"No. He always claimed they were make-believe bets."

I had to smile as I thought of Jack the day we made one real bet. He was so cocky and full of himself. He knew he just couldn't lose this one.

"But one bet he promised to pay off on. It was a race at the end of our Atlantic crossing. The first one of us to get from the docks in Bristol to the American Express Office in London, having spent the least amount of money, won. The first one there would leave a note for the other. Then we'd hook up and the loser would buy pints and kidney pies at a local pub. Fun idea.

"But it turned out that Jack wasn't much of a stick-to-it guy. After three days of hard work, he jumped ship before we left the docks. Too much paint chipping, too much paint dust and too much bauxite dust for his taste.

"It turned out that he wasn't a have-not either. His father was a Boston industrialist. Pipe fittings and flanges. Anyway, his father came to his rescue and offered him a first-class air ticket to London and Jack accepted. He got to London well before I did."

"And when you got to London there was no note," Billy Joe said. It wasn't a question. He had Jack pegged from the start.

"You didn't expect to find a note, did you?" Linda Sue said. Not a question.

"No."

"But you checked anyway. Right?" Lila the optimist.

"Of course. But enough about me. Tell me about you."

It turned out that Linda Sue and Lila were the talkers. Billy Joe just smiled and nodded for the most part. Women talk and men nod. Very Midwest.

"We were just dry land wheat farmers scratching out a living on three hundred and twenty acres," Linda Sue began. "Three hundred and twenty acres of dry land isn't enough to make ends meet. It was hard but we had each other. Billy Joe and I have been in love since high school."

Billy Joe nodded. "Since high school."

"I had a little vegetable patch," Lila said. "Beans, asparagus, tomatoes, like that. Tried corn but it never worked. Not enough plants to pollinate."

"She devised her own irrigation system," Linda Sue said proudly. Pumped water from the well that flowed directly into her garden. Then she got the idea that if we dug another well she could irrigate it from both ends. Really increase the size of her garden."

"But I didn't get water," Lila said.

"I can guess," I said.

"How?" Lila asked.

"'Cause dry land wheat farmers couldn't afford to be traveling through France in expensive clothes," I said. "And because I've seen that TV show that started a couple years ago."

Lila smiled. "Yep. Up came a bubbling crude."

The TV show was The Beverly Hillbillies. It came on the air in 1961 and would run ten years. The theme song for the show was written by two bluegrass icons, Lester Flatt and Earl Scruggs.

At the risk of driving away my ride, I broke into the theme song:

"Come listen to a story 'bout a man named Jed

They joined in singing on the first line and we harmonized like hounds on a hunt.

"Poor mountaineer barely kept his family fed
Then one day he was shooting for some food

And up through the ground came a bubbling crude
(Oil that is, black gold, Texas tea)"
And, we laughed ourselves silly.

"We couldn't spend it all if we tried," Linda Sue said.

Billy Joe laughed. "Believe me, these two Okies been trying."

When we were almost finished with lunch Linda Sue and Lila got up to go to the "little girls room." I thought they were giving Billy Joe and me some time for man-talk. That's exactly what it was. Good Midwest manners. You can't teach it. If you don't grow up with it, you don't get it.

Billy Joe and I talked wheat, weather and baseball. It was like being home. Then, in a handshake, he pressed a ten-dollar bill into my hand and gave me his parting advice.

"Keep walking. You will find more wisdom and beauty on the road than you can ever imagine."

Some of the best advice I ever got.

After lunch we headed north another five kilometers to where the road branched. They were headed to the left and Paris was straight ahead.

Billy Joe pulled the car over under a huge tree and parked. It had rough bark and strange purplish-green leaves. I'd never seen anything like it before or since.

"This is where we part," Lind Sue said. "But Lila has some questions for you if you don't mind."

It was obvious that their trip to the little girl's room wasn't just to give Billy Joe and me some time together.

I had no idea where this was going. "I don't mind, I guess." I looked at Billy Joe and he shrugged. This was new to him, too.

Linda Sue laughed. "It's not like she's gonna ask you to run away with her or something like that."

"Then, what's the point?" I laughed.

Lila looked me dead in the eyes. This was serious to her. "What's it like, being different?"

OOOUUUFFF! It was like having the air knocked out of me. It took me a second to regroup. When you aren't sure what someone means it's always best to clarify the question. "I'm not sure what you mean."

I looked at Billy Joe. He shrugged again. He was as lost as I was—or a great actor. This was "little girls' room" talk I guessed.

"Well, you don't have a job. You don't have a place to live. Your hair's too long. You're growing a beard." She paused a Moment to let that sink in. "Where I come from, and, I think, where you're from, too, that would be called different."

I looked over at Billy Joe. He gave me a well-it's-true shrug. Linda Sue's arched eyebrows said the same thing.

They were right. I'd never thought about it. But I was different. It wasn't that I had changed since I'd left home—although I had. The truth was: I was different. My whole family had always taught me to be myself. Not try *to be* different. Just be yourself. But Lila was right. Sometimes being yourself made you different.

One summer during college I had worked for a big farmer and one of the hands had a perfect way of expressing that. *"He hoes his own row,"* he'd say. In the Kansas City pool halls we called it: *"Shooting your own stick."* Or, like I thought about Lila: she twirls her own rope.

"You're right, Lila. On all counts," I said. "I don't have a job—now—although I've always had one since I was about eight. And what I'm trying to do now is get *the job* I want to have for the rest of my life. And, I'll just have to live where I can until I get that job and make some money."

Lila nodded and I think she understood.

"As far as my hair," I went on. "I got a haircut before I left Kansas City. I'll get the next one when I can. It's not a statement. Neither is the beard. It hurts to shave with cold water."

Lila and I studied each other. I knew what she was asking even though neither of us knew the right questions to ask or the right answers to those unformed questions. We were on the forefront of something. We could feel it but we didn't know what *it* was. Things were just different.

It used to be Pat Boone and The Kingston Trio. Now it was the Beatles and the Stones.

Comedians told the truth and the President lied.

Normal guys were like me.

Things were changing.

She probably had a greater sense of it than I did. Change was creeping up around me. It was in front of her. She had a better view.

"I'm just going for a dream," I said. "Who knows what I'll find."

Lila laughed. "I was going for vegetables and I found oil."

We all laughed. The kid really knew how to cut to the chase.

We said our goodbyes and Lila whispered four parting words to me. *"You need a bath."* And, despite my odor, she gave me a hug so she could mask slipping the ten into my shirt pocket.

"Keep twirling your own rope," I whispered to her.

I watched them motor off and I turned north toward Paris. Lila had left me full of questions but I was feeling the best I had felt in days. I'd had a good meal, good company and a good time. I was twenty dollars richer and, just as important as any of those reasons; I'd skipped at least two days of walking.

Oklahomans. Salt of the earth for the most part. I almost went to the University of Oklahoma on a baseball scholarship. But their journalism school seemed sub-par. But what did I know. My opinion was based on their dilapidated back shop.

I broke into songs from my second year of hootenannying. Gene Clark and Jim Glover had been signed to The Backporch Majority. Sort of a farm team for the Christy Minstrels. It took two guys to replace Glover. Pat Alexander, a far better guitar player than Gene, was still with us.

Good Ol' Buddy Pat, as he was referred to around Folk House, was a part time resident. He lived there Friday and Saturday, and spent the rest of the week in Paola, Kansas, as an engineering salesman. Interestingly enough he always kicked in a full rent share. Pat slept where he could find space. Generally that was wherever he was when he dropped his guitar and bottle of One Fifty One proof rum. People just walked around him. That took some walking. He was a big guy. Two-seventy. Ex All American footballer at Pittsburg State. He was the first of my many roommates to try to teach me to play the guitar.

So, anyway, I walked and I sang badly. I sang **Bread And Butter** and **Under the Boardwalk**. My Mom loved

Boardwalk and that's probably the reason I sang it a little better than the others. I tried to make her proud of me.

"Under the Boardwalk, down by the sea . . ."

With about an hour of sunlight left I came abreast of a field of hay that had been freshly mowed. I'd been smelling it for a good mile.

That unmistakable scent of fresh mown grass. Hay scent is just as unmistakable as the scent of grass—except it's a little rawer.

A four-foot deep ditch separated me from the fresh-cut field. I scrambled down into and up out of the ditch. I gathered five or six arm loads of the fresh hay and deposited them in the ditch. I lay down on the hay. Much more comfortable than last night's bare ground. In fact, my hay *"bed"* was extremely comfortable in comparison.

I gathered another five or six arm loads of the fresh hay and laid my *"blanket"* beside my *bed*, sat down on my *bed* and ate my asparagus and tomato dinner as I watched the sun settle behind the mountains and I dreamed.

One day, little Lila, I'd be a successful writer and eat what I wanted—not what I could afford. And I'd sleep in fine hotels. But tonight it was asparagus, tomatoes and the ditch. Tomorrow, maybe a haircut and a shave. Such is life.

I lay back on my *bed* and pulled my hay *blanket* over me. I was feeling pretty smug for a guy who was virtually broke. I had a comfortable place to sleep and I wasn't going to be cold tonight. As ditches went, this was the Waldorf Astoria of ditches.

"Look at the bright side," Mom used to say. "Most people don't have what we have. We are lucky."

I could picture Mom saying that. Her hands planted firmly on her hips. Standing tall at five foot two. Her blue eyes twinkling and looking for trouble.

"How do you get lucky?" I'd once asked her.

"You work hard, be honest, be true to your friends and be a man of your word. You'll see. Do that and you get lucky."

And she was right. It'd always worked for me.

Like now for example. I wasn't flush with cash—but I wasn't hungry. I didn't have a roof over my heard—but it wasn't raining. It was cold out—but I was warm in my Waldorf-ditch. I was lucky and doing well.

I laid back and watched the stars pop out. Brighter than I could ever remember. I was asleep in minutes.

THE FRENCH PHARMACIST

I awoke the next morning with the first rays of sunlight. *Awoke* was a very genteel way of putting it. I squirmed and thrashed my way awake. I was covered with chigger bites. I was all itches and every itch seemed to crawl. I was warm and comfortable last night. Today, I was going to pay for it. Chiggers hadn't crossed my mine when I was gathering the hay. Now I'd never see a hay field without thinking of chiggers.

Resisting the urge to scratch the bites was driving me crazy. Red welts on top of red welts. Lumps on top of lumps. The more I thought about them the worse they itched. But I knew better than to scratch them. Once you started scratching a chigger bite you can't stop until you've scratched it raw. Then it bled. Then you had scabs. And who would pick up a hitchhiker who looked like a leper?

I threw on my pack and started down the road.

About five kilometers down the road I came to a small town. Nothing was open this early. But as luck would have it, I saw the pharmacist entering his store. I rushed to the door and knocked on it. The pharmacist was only a few feet away, straightening items on a display shelf.

He approached the door and pointed at the closed sign.

I pointed at my face.

He studied me and then unlocked and opened the door a crack.

"Le chig-gair," I tried faking French.

He laughed and opened the door. "Chiggers are the same in any language, "he said in slightly accented English. "Close and lock the door please," he said walking away. I did.

"The best solution is also the cheapest. Rubbing alcohol. Applied frequently," he said. He took a sixteen-ounce bottle off the shelf. "Ten francs." He took a small box of cotton swabs off the shelf, too. "Five francs."

We exchanged francs for the cure. I was now down to ten dollars and forty-nine francs. Except I also had my Oklahoma money. What Billy Joe and Lila had given me. But I hadn't earned that. So, in my mind, it was emergency money. Your you-don't-use-it-until-you-absolutely-have-to money. Found funds.

"Take off your shirt," he said. "Let's see how bad it is."

I did.

"You are very lucky. Most of the bites are on the areas of your skin that were most exposed. Areas you can reach without help." He walked me back to the door. "Keep applying the alcohol—constantly. And in about two hours the swelling should go down and the itching should stop." He unlocked and opened the door. "Don't scratch. It will only make it worse."

I thanked him and walked outside, already dabbing alcohol on the bites.

"Oh, and one more thing," he smiled. "When a Frenchman tells you this, you should pay attention."

"Tells me what?"

"You need a bath." He laughed at the look on my face and closed the door.

THE LAST RIDE

Just like the pharmacist predicted, after two hours of hoofing it higher into the mountains, the itching began subsiding and the swelling around the bites began to go down. In that time I had only covered about six kilometers. The hike was getting tougher and together—the road steeper and steeper.

I was too winded from hiking uphill to sing. So, I went inside. A mind eddy. Mind eddies were great places to escape to when you wanted to avoid physical pain. My Dad had said it was sort of Great Plains Zen. It always worked for me.

Ever see Steve McQueen in The Great Escape? Remember how, when the Krauts threw him in the sweatbox for punishment, he escaped into himself by bouncing the baseball off the cramped hotbox wall? Concentrating on the ball is a Zen route to ignoring the pain. Baseball is a key to a lot of things Zen.

Growing up I'd wanted to be a baseball player. No doubt I got it from my Dad. He started me young. When I was about eighteen months old he propped me up against the sofa and tossed wadded up balls of newspaper for me to hit with a dowel-rod bat. Apparently I loved it. Couldn't get enough of it. I don't remember any of it. But that's what I've been told.

Anyway, it must have paid off. I could always hit and by the time I was in high school I had a bunch of major league scouts following me. I had a baseball scholarship offer from the University of Oklahoma and an appointment to West Point—baseball related. I was going to be a baseball player.

Until I hurt my left hand. During one game it went totally numb. Nerve damage. And who wants a catcher with a bad left hand? Makes catching anything hard. Makes swinging a bat even harder. The scouts evaporated like morning mist on a farm pond. *"You look familiar, kid. What's your name?"* Scouts had their own sense of humor and they never forgot anyone they'd followed. They knew your abilities better than you did. *"Ever play ball?"* They'd laugh and pat me on the shoulder. I'd want to cry.

"Hand getting any better?" They were just being polite. They knew the answer. The fat lady had sung.

After a couple hours of Great Plains Zenning about a baseball future long gone, a new VW bus pulled over to the side of the road in front of me.

I trotted up to the passenger window. A handsome driver and his gorgeous passenger beamed movie-star grins at me.

"We saw the U.S. flag on your pack," she said. "What part?"

"Kansas."

She looked over at the driver. "Cans-ass," she said.

He threw the van in gear and started forward. Their laughter rolled out of the car as it came to a stop.

"Hop in," she shouted.

I climbed in as they continued to roar.

"You should have seen the look on your face," the driver laughed.

She continued laughing. "Yeah. It went from surprise to hate in the blink of an eye."

"That's what I was feeling," I admitted.

We all were laughing as the van pulled back onto the road. They were laughing because it was a funny joke. I was laughing because I wanted the ride.

She turned in her seat and offered her hand. "I'm Amanda. This is Larry. And, we're from Cha-ka-ga."

As we rolled along I learned a little bit about them. Larry had recently retired from an ad agency in Chicago and they had moved to France. They had bought a villa in Charny, four kilometers west of Macon. They could take me as far as Macon where a friend of theirs had a bed and breakfast.

"I can't afford lodging," I explained and ended up telling my plight.

"Don't worry," he said. "We'll take care of it for you. I always wanted to be a writer myself. But I opted for the big bucks in advertising. Maybe when we get the renovation done I can try my hand at the fine arts."

"I doubt that it ever will end," she said to him, meaning the renovation. Then she turned to me. "Would you mind moving back to the third row? Not to be rude, but you stink"

"I'll ride on top just to get the ride." They laughed and I moved to the back row of seats and took a good look at them. I asked them some key questions so I could learn a little more about them. One thing I learned in newspaper was that if you asked the right questions people liked to talk about themselves.

Larry and Amanda Howard. He had been an Executive Vice President and account executive at D'Arcy Advertising in Chicago. He had supervised the Budweiser and American Oil (Standard Oil of Indiana) accounts. The two biggest accounts in the agency.

Larry was an extremely handsome man. Tall and dark with chiseled features. Even in his causal clothes he looked like he'd just stepped out of GQ. I could imagine how impressive he'd be in a suit. You always wonder how much looks contribute to someone's success and how much of it is due to ability.

After listening to him for a while I realized he was one bright cookie.

Amanda was stunningly beautiful. The perfect visual match to Larry.

Larry was sixty and she was probably in her mid-thirties. What today we would call a trophy wife. Back in 1965 we just called him lucky.

Amanda was a one-subject spokeswoman. Larry. Everything Larry. All of his accomplishments. His net worth. His big bonuses. His huge retirement package. His love for the Chicago Cubs. His love for the Chicago Bears. His love for the Chicago bars. His love for everything Chicago.

As we rolled along I listened to everything Larry. But what really impressed me was the number of kilometers that rolled by. Finally we topped the mountains. I couldn't believe that I had actually thought I could have made it over these mountains. It had looked so incredibly flat on the map. It would have been one hell of a hike.

Larry seemed to be getting a little embarrassed with "everything Larry." So, he shifted the subject to Amanda. She had been an account executive at D'Arcy working under him, so to speak. She had been in Playboy in a special pictorial called: *Women In Advertising In Chicago.*

"Damn if she wasn't the best looking nude in the whole magazine," Larry bragged and nudged her teasingly.

Amanda beamed a smile back at the smelly end of the van and I believed him. She was definitely hot.

"She also does stand up comedy," Larry continued. "Great sense of humor. Great personality . . ."

"Sews her own clothes . . . and all the girls love her." I said, completing the classic blind date description I'd heard a hundred times from women trying to fix me up with a roommate. I laughed. "She doesn't look like that blind date description to me."

They both laughed.

"I get my stand-up material from real life," she said. "Like one night, I was outside Mr. Kelly's waiting for a cab. You know Mr. Kelly's?" she asked.

I shook my head.

"Mr. Kelly's is the hottest jazz club in Chicago. Movie stars and entertainers don't need reservations there. All they have to do is drop in. Management keeps vacant tables in front of the stage for celebrity drop-in's.

"Anyway, there I was waiting for a cab and there was an empty one right in front of me. I was trying to talk and charm my way into it—but not having any luck because it was being held for some VIP. And out walks Frank Sinatra. The cabbie scurries around and opens the rear door and Sinatra hands him a hundred dollar bill.

'Gee, tankx, Mr. Sinatra,' the cabbie said."

She did a perfect Cha-ka-ga accent.

"Ever get a hundred dollar tip before?' Sinatra asked.

"One-st," the cabbie says and Sinatra hands him another hundred.

"Just curious," Sinatra said. "Who gave you the other hundred?"

"Y . . . yous did, Mr. Sinatra."

"Right then Dean Martin walks out of Mr. Kelly's. By now a small crowd has gathered and is celebrity gawking. Never one to miss a chance to entertain, Dean turns to the crowd and says: 'We're on our way to pick up my date. She's a magician's assistant. He saws her in half. With my luck I'll get the half that eats.'"

The three of us laughed. Amanda did a few more jokes. And the kilometers rolled up on the odometer.

The more time I spent with them the more I realized that they were a perfect match. He was handsome. She was beautiful. Actually, both were beautiful almost beyond belief. Both of them were smart, witty and quick. And most of all they were deeply in love. It made me feel lonely.

Finally we cruised through Macon. It was early evening—what filmmakers and painters call the golden hour. On the northern edge of Macon, we stopped in front of a gingerbread house. It was a pastel rainbow beauty. The walls were a light yellow. The shutters and gingerbread trim were pastel blues, greens and super light purples. Sounds garish but it was gracefully gorgeous. The colors had been applied with an artist's eye.

Larry went inside while Amanda and I waited in the van. He returned in seconds. I climbed out with my pack. He shook my hand.

"If you go back to Kansas City through Chicago stop at D'Arcy. Ask for Charlie Schuggart and tell him I said to give you a job. I expect you'll be broke and need one by then. Good luck."

Amanda smiled at me. "I'd give you a goodbye kiss—but you stink."

Larry laughed and turned to Amanda. "Mrs. Russet is drawing him a bath as we speak." Then to me: "Everything's taken care of. Enjoy." He started around to the driver's side of the van and stopped. "By the way, if you ever hope to get a ride from a Frenchman, take that U.S. flag off your pack. It's like waving a red cape in front of a bull."

As I watched them drive off into a pinkish sky all I could think of was "my American Cousin" luggage storeowner. He knew what he was doing to me when he gave me the U.S. flag.

How French.

*   *   *

I headed toward the gingerbread house wondering if Mrs. Russet might be a Brigitte Bardot type. My fantasy lasted about thirty steps. She appeared in the doorway. She was no Bardot. She looked like Charles de Gaulle in a skirt. Except maybe her nose was bigger. And she was haughtier.

She nodded with that nose toward the bathroom. It was like a railroad crossing arm pointing the way. I went the way the nose pointed.

The water in the tub was warm. Very un-French. Obviously, in response to Larry's instructions.

I eased into the warm water and my muscles seemed to melt off my bones. I scrubbed and relaxed for the first time in days. I have no idea how long I just floated there—but a loud, single knuckle knock on the door brought me back to reality. "Coming," I said.

As I crawled out of the tub I saw the huge black ring around the tub. It took nearly five minutes to clean the tub. Everybody had been right: I *had* needed a bath.

* * *

The dinner Mrs. Russert prepared was far from typical bed and breakfast fare. It consisted of a Rock Cornish hen, and a casserole of green beans, baby potatoes and spring onions. A spicy cheese sauce topped the casserole and everything was absolutely fantastic.

The dining room was small and dark. The only light came from candles. There was an upright piano, a couple of over stuffed chairs flanking a small coffee table, the dining table and little else.

Every time I looked at her I was struck by how much she looked like Charles de Gaulle. Younger. Much more svelte. A gorgeous, thick mane of hazel hair. Crystal brown eyes. But, in my eyes, she would always be *la* DeGaulle.

We started with small talk.

Mrs. Russert: "Larry, he's toll me tree zings about you. You 'ave no monet. You zleep in ze chi*gaar* blanket. And you vant to be next Hemingway." She laughed charmingly. "For I'm concern, Larry, he takes care of ze monet."

I laughed and took a bite of the casserole. "Delicious."

She smiled coquettishly and gave me a *but of course* shrug. "Larry sez you are hike-hitching."

"Not with much luck," I said. "I had a U.S. flag pinned on my pack. Larry said that was why the French wouldn't pick me op."

"The French," she explained. "Ve must dislikes zomeone. Is vat ve do bests." She laughed and I joined in. It was all very pleasant—and unusual. I'd never had dinner with de Gaulle before—especially when he was wearing a dress.

In our broken French and English we segued into U.S.-French relations—from Lafitte to the Statue of Liberty to World War I and WWII. We were politely feeling each other out about politics.

Then we got current. She asked me what I thought about Vietnam. Vietnam had become a major interest of mine. I already had lost a couple of close friends *over there*—at a time when most Americans didn't know where **there** was.

But mention Vietnam and the first image I always got came with a date. August 4, 1964. It was a Tuesday night at the Castaways. Open mike night. Between sets a bunch of us went outside to the parking lot to discuss the auditioning groups and generally shoot the shit. It was like any other night. Someone had snapped on a car radio and a "Special Announcement" suddenly interrupted the music. President Lyndon Baines Johnson made his Tonkin Bay address. "We have been attacked." And "We have responded." Johnson was sending more troops. Of the eight of us listening to LBJ's address that night four would go to Nam and two wouldn't come back.

"Vietnam," she said in a rich French accent that could make you forget her nose. "Vietnam *etait*, and still *est*, a French disgracement. And, it vill becomes an American disgracement, too," she almost shouted. Then she calmed herself with a deep breath. This was touchy ground. "I lose two brothers zair—both in villages zo small zhey are not on my maps." She sipped her richly bouqueted red wine. "And vhat dos you know of Indochina?" It was a challenge. *I've lost two brothers and what is your ante in this game, you arrogant young American twit?* It was unsaid of course—but I heard it loud and clear.

"I've lost two close friends there."

"Only two?"

"Two that I know of." Actually there were more than two at that point—I just didn't know it.

She gave me an *I'm sorry, I understand* look and nodded. "Eez all zo stoopeed. Good young mens with much lifes to live," she said. "But zat eez because politicians makes zee decisions. Zee French fights to retain our influenze in Indochina, as zeef we had any. Americans fights for dominos theory. Zee Vietnamese fights for zair home and family." She swirled her wine glass and gazed off into the future. "You tells me who wins." She shook her head sadly. "Influenze varsus dominos varsus family." She snorted coarsely and sipped wine daintily. "Politicians are zuch fools."

I nodded in total agreement.

She poured more of the ruby wine in our glasses and then raised her glass in a toast. Our glasses kissed and chimed in the dark candle-lit room.

"Fuck ze foulz."

We drank.

And we drank.

And we talked.

And we laughed.

And we drank some more.

And we talked some more.

And laughed and laughed.

The wine was really getting to me. But I was having fun.

The last thing I remembered thinking was that DeGaulle looked pretty sexy in a dress.

With that thick mane of hazel hair.

And those captivating crystal brown eyes.

THE COUNTERFEIT
& THE DITCH

I slept like a dog that night. A dog without fleas or chiggers, I might add.

Early sunlight and chirping birds woke me the next morning. I didn't remember going to bed.

I propped myself up on an elbow and looked around. My room was very small—a small bed, a tiny armoire and an end table at the head of the bed with a kerosene lantern on it. The room was only slightly larger than a jail cell where I'd once spent the night in Mountain Home, Arkansas—a story that is not part of this one.

On the end table, beside the lantern, a brown paper lunch bag sat on a thin, folded, faded, yellow and tan blanket. A folded note on cream colored cotton rag paper was propped against the lunch bag.

"*Monsieur Kelly,*

"*I have enjoy our dinnar and conversasions and such.*

"*Good lucks in your travails.*

"*Le foods are froms Larry.*

"*Le blanket es froms moi.*

"*Good lucks on becoming Hemingway*

—thou I think one is more than enough."
It was signed *Marie*.
I saved her note.

*   *   *

I hit the road early, exploring the contents of the paper bag. Two cucumber sandwiches and an apple. I hoped Larry had gotten his money's worth. I sure had. I should have left her a note in return. I still regret that I didn't.

Once again the air was crisp and clean. There was the sweet smell of flowers, which seemed to be blooming everywhere. The sky was bright blue and miles high. The sun was yellow-orange above dark green trees. Beautiful—truly beautiful. But best of all, the major crests of the mountains were behind me. Thank you Larry and Amanda.

Not having the U.S. flag on the back of my pack didn't make any difference. The French still cruised by. The difference was that no U.S. citizen stopped either. Maybe I needed to put the flag back on my pack.

I walked and I sang **The Little Old Lady From Pasadena**—but I was getting bored with my singing. After two days of meeting interesting people like the Collins and the Howards I was bored with me. I pinned my flag back on my pack—but that didn't help. But it was a shot.

A little after noon I chanced onto a wide spot in the road, as we say in Kansas. A gas station and a general store. A nerdy looking guy, whose facial features were asymmetrical, ran both establishments. But he worked at being pleasant and I returned the favor. We enjoyed each other's company and laughed as he butchered English and I fractured French. I chose a baguette and two kinds of cheese. When I tried to pay with a ten-franc note—all hell broke loose.

He slammed the bill down on the counter next to the cash register and glared at me. Suddenly, we weren't buddies any more. I didn't have a clue why. I shrugged. He shouted. I shrugged again. He screamed again and kept slapping the note with an open hand. What he screamed was in French and I didn't understand.

I looked more closely at the ten-franc note and then I saw what was wrong. Where the blue pastel picture of the helmeted Joan of Arc should have been on the ten, there was a picture of Adolph Hitler. It was a German occupation ten-franc note. The only place I could have gotten it was from my "cousin" the luggage storeowner. So, he had gotten full price for the pack by giving me the phony francs as change, plus my Samsonite suitcase. Sneaky, those French.

I pointed at Hitler on the bill and said, Ahhh." I quickly replaced the occupation ten-franc note with a real one and the proprietor calmed down. Suddenly I was down to ten dollars and thirty-nine francs. Plus the two tens from the Collins.

After profuse apologies I was back on the road in what was the most boring day of my walk to Paris. All I could think about was money. It seemed like I'd been thinking about money all of my life. Somehow when you don't have it, is when you need it the most.

Like in the first grade—if I took lunch money to school the older kids would beat me up and take it. If I didn't take any money they'd beat me up because I didn't have any money. Did I mention Kansas City, Kansas, was a rough neighborhood?

So, when I was about six I asked my Grandma about money. She was fixing dinner at the time. Rabbit, with gravy and potatoes and a green salad. She was slicing up the rabbit. I forget what I had named him.

"Why are you asking me?" she said studying me.

Grandma was half Irish and half Cherokee with long raven-black hair and ivory skin that turned a deep, dark mahogany in the summer. In the winter she looked black Irish. In the summer she looked Indian.

"I asked you because you always have money." I said.

"Well, you are observant," she smiled. She was one of the most beautiful women I've ever known. And, strong. She had to be to deal with Grandpa. Grandpa drank.

Grandma eyed me as she dumped diced onions, carrot tops and something else green into a big cast iron pot that already had water in it. "What about Grandpa?" She started quick-frying the rabbit parts and waited for me to go on.

"Well, after Grandpa gets paid on Fridays he goes out and spends a lot of his paycheck drinking."

"Unless he's playing handball. You know he doesn't drink when he's playing handball. He brings his wages home. And . . ." She waited for me to finish.

"And you put it in the sugar bowl—for when it's needed."

"Sounds like you already understand money." She put a rack in the pot and the fried rabbit parts on the rack and covered the pot.

"But Grandpa sneaks money out of the sugar bowl all week long."

"Of course he does. Grandpa Gene is Irish. He's got the curse." She turned the flame on low under the pot and started cleaning up the kitchen.

"But you're part Irish and part Indian. Aren't both cursed?"

"Some people think so."

"But you aren't."

"Sometimes one curse negates the other."

I didn't understand what she was talking about. So, I went back to the money. "But if Grandpa keeps taking money out of the sugar bowl, how do you get ahead?"

"I guess you aren't as smart as I was thinking." She laughed and grabbed her wide-brimmed garden hat. "You think I put *all* of it in the sugar bowl?" She laughed and headed for the door to the garden. She was always doing something. Never a wasted daylight hour.

She stopped at the door and looked at me. "Here's what you need to know about money. If you don't have any, better start figuring out how to get some—'cause you're going to need it. But if you've got it, you probably won't need it. So, the smart thing is to always have some on hand."

Grandma's Econ 101.

*   *   *

Funny what comes back to you when you've got nothing else to do but walk and think. I needed to figure out what I was going to do. Obviously, I was going to run out of money before I reached Paris. So, what was I going to do?

For the next two days I walked and thought about it. It was mostly downhill and that was nice. The terrain was beautiful but largely went unnoticed. I took the flag off my pack. I pinned it back on and took it off again. It didn't make any difference. No one stopped. Those two nights I slept in ditches and ignored the cold as best I could. Marie's blanket helped me to do that.

The third morning was clear and warm. Birds were singing. And so was I. It just felt like today was going to be special. It wasn't—but it was close. Little did I know that this was my last day of walking. That come tomorrow my life would change. That tomorrow I would meet *her*.

* * *

I kept walking that night long after the sun was gone. There didn't seem to be any place to sleep far enough from the road to be safe and there was no ditch for shelter—so I just kept going.

Finally I spotted a couple of faint campfires in the distance. I expected them to get larger as I got closer. But they didn't. The fires were dying.

The dying campfires were in a campground. But no one was stirring and the gate in the chain-link fence was padlocked shut. I could see out buildings and decided to sleep in the ditch and make use of the facilities in the morning. After all, I did need a shower. It was a simple decision. But one that would change my life.

I climbed down into the ditch, ate half my baguette and one of the cheeses, pulled Marie's yellow and tan blanket over me and gazed up at the stars for maybe thirty seconds.

HER

I awoke with the first rays of the morning sun. The gate to the campground was still padlocked. I decided to kill time until someone unlocked it.

I pinned the U.S. flag back onto my pack. It couldn't hurt—and I *was* proud of it. Then I broke out the half baguette and the remaining piece of cheese and started to eat it.

From nowhere children began gathering on the campground side of the chain link fence. Their skin tones ran the gamut from deep black to pale white. They reminded me of my old neighborhood in Kansas City. The kids stared hungrily at my bread and cheese. I held out the bread and cheese as a way of asking if they wanted some. They nodded in unison. I began cutting off pieces of bread and cheese and passing it through the fence. As each kid got a piece of bread and cheese he or she ran off.

I had one piece of bread and one piece of cheese remaining when the last kid ran off. Then I noticed her—one of most beautiful women I'd ever seen. Tall. Dark skin. Olive-gray in tone. Dark olive-gray. Long, glossy, raven black hair. She wore a frilly white blouse and an ankle-length red skirt. She smiled a heart-stopping smile. Apparently she had been watching the entire time that I'd been giving food to the kids. She had an aura about her that was heart stopping. I offered the last piece of bread and cheese to her. "Pain et fromage?"

She came over to the fence and said something in French which I didn't understand. Probably, in part, because I was mesmerized by her beautiful eyes. They were amber and loaded with flecks of green. I'd never seen eyes that color. I realized I was staring and she was amused by it. I shrugged.

She tried a couple more languages that I didn't understand. German. Italian. Spanish. Then she glanced down at my pack and saw the flag pinned to it.

"Oh, American," she said with an accent that wasn't French—but mysteriously sexy.

She took the piece of bread and cheese. "You have lots of bread and cheese?"

"No, that's the last of it."

"You gave the last of your food to the children?" she asked, surprised and intrigued.

"They looked hungry."

She smiled another heart stopper. "They are supposed to." She ate the bread and cheese and studied me. "Why are you in the ditch?"

"I was waiting for someone to unlock the campground so I could use the facilities." I nodded toward the out buildings. As I did, I noticed that both men and women were filing into the two out buildings.

"Are you hungry?"

"A little."

"You gave away the last of your food and you are hungry?"

"The kids looked like they needed it more than I did."

"Wait here, American sucker." She laughed and her magical eyes seemed to twinkle. She took another appraising look at me and strode away on long legged strides.

In a couple of minutes she was back, twirling a key on a green ribbon. She unlocked the gate and let me into the campground. "Do you like scrambled eggs?"

"Yes I do," I said. "My name's Kelly. And yours?"

She hesitated a moment. "Claudia. Claudia DeMore. Like in de more Claudia de better." She laughed. Her laugh was deep and musical.

I followed her across the gently rolling grounds with early morning light slanting in on us through ancient oaks. The smell of smoke and cooking food was in the air. I noticed more people moving around the campground now. Maybe it was my imagination but they all seemed to eye me warily.

"What state are you from?"

"Kansas," I said.

Claudia threw back her head and gave her melodious laugh. "Kansas! Dodge City! Wyatt Earp! Bat Masterson! The Dalton Boys! You are a cowboy! An American sucker cowboy!"

"To be honest," I said. "I've probably fallen off more horses than I've ridden."

She stopped and stared at me appraisingly. "An honest cowboy. Isn't that an anachronism?"

"No. An anachronism, in this case, would be a person who belongs to another age. Like, out of place in time."

"I don't understand. But I want to."

"Let's see. An example would be: I saw a caveman driving a car. They don't belong in the same time period."

She nodded slowly, absorbing the information. Then she smiled. "Amelia Earhart in a jet."

"Exactly!"

She clapped her hands once and did a little joyful hop. Obviously this woman loved to learn new things.

"I think the word you were looking for was: oxymoron. Meaning: contradictory terms. Like honest politician. Or, honest cowboy."

She smiled a heartbreaker. "A girl could learn from you. I like learning."

She turned and headed toward an old barbeque grill. I was happy to follow. "Lands-a-goshin," she said and laughed. "Isn't that what cowboy women say?" It really wasn't a question. She was just having fun. "What is a *Goshin*? I've always wondered."

"It's sort of like a henweigh," I said.

She stopped and studied me. "What's a henweigh?"

"About a pound and a half without the feathers."

Her eyes narrowed. Her lips almost smiled. She got it. She turned and started away. Over her shoulder she said: "Cowboy humor or Kansas humor?"

"Take your pick."

She gave me a sort of snort-chuckle without a look. It made me feel like an idiot.

Ever meet a woman who you feel an instant attraction to and get a little positive feedback and then do or say something idiotic? Well, I can't say it's uncharted territory to me—but . . . damnit anyway!

Just then, we reached the smoked-stained, redbrick barbeque grill and a good-looking, dark skinned young man in jeans, with thick, unruly black hair and a white dress shirt came out of a small green and silver trailer that was hitched to a 1958 Ford pickup truck. The Ford was mostly primer gray with patches of the original black paint showing here and there.

"Kelly, this is my cousin . . . a . . ." Claudia paused.

"Norman," he said, shaking my hand and patting me on the shoulder.

"And how are you this morning . . . a . . ." Norman waited for her to complete his sentence.

"Claudia," she said as she blocked his path before he could leave. "Give it back."

"It was just a joke," Norman said. "I wasn't going to keep it." He handed my billfold to me. "I'm practicing to be a magician." I looked in my billfold. It was empty.

"All of it," she demanded.

He handed me the ten and the forty-nine francs.

"All of it," she repeated.

He handed me the Collins' two tens, which had been in my shirt pocket.

How had he managed to take my billfold and take my money out of it and the Collins' money out of my shirt pocket without me noticing? He read the questions in my face, flashed a smile and walked off.

"What do you do?" she asked.

"I'm a writer."

"What kind? Letters? Diaries? To-do lists?"

I laughed. I'd never written a to-do list, nor had I kept a diary. "Newspaper reporter mostly. I've written a dozen short stories. Sold one. Now I'm working on a novel. I'd like to be the next Hemingway."

"You should set your sights higher. Steinbeck. Faulkner. Even Fitzgerald." She laughed that great laugh and shook her head. "You don't seem like the Hemingway macho, bullshit type to me." She laughed again. "But then what do I know? We just met."

She opened an aluminum ice chest beside the smoking barbeque grill. She took out a carton of eggs, some milk and a block of cheese. She cracked the eggs into a black iron skillet on the grill, added milk. Then, with a knife that came from nowhere, it just materialized in her hand, she began shaving cheese into the mixture in the skillet.

"Tell me more."

"If you'll reciprocate."

"That's cowboy for something sexual, no?"

"No," I laughed. And as I watched her scramble the eggs, they suddenly became an omelet as she added scallions and mushrooms. The scallions and mushrooms must have come from the same place the knife came from. It was an amazing piece of sleight of hand. She was at least as talented as her brother. Maybe better. Instinctively I patted my rear left pocket to check on my billfold.

"It's still there," she said without looking up. "Now are you going to tell me about yourself?"

While I talked, I watched this gorgeous woman with the incredible eyes and magical laugh scramble eggs for me. How the hell did I ever get so lucky!?!

I told her about my newspaper background. How I hoped to freelance my way around Europe while I worked on my novel.

I told her about getting a job on the freighter. About Jack Dumas. The same things I had told the Collins. A practiced story always tells better. You learn what to leave out and what to embellish.

"You are a good story teller," she said, dishing up the omelet. "We like that."

"We?"

"All my friends here. Telling stories is one of our favorite pastimes. Tell me more."

I told her that I had been selling stories but that I had almost run out of money in Italy. That I was headed for Paris in of hopes finding a few checks waiting for me.

"Italian women are really good at making foreign men run out of money."

"I know," I laughed. "They really cleaned me out. I hardly knew what was happening."

"They?"

"Sisters."

"You didn't stand a chance." And she started laughing.

I joined her with an embarrassed laugh.

*   *   *

"Quite a story," she said when we finished eating. "You're down to your last dollars and francs and you give the last of your food away. My people would say that you, Mr. Kelly Pickett Kelly, either have a good heart or that you're not too bright and are an easy mark." She laughed, the green in her light brown eyes twinkling.

"Of those two choices I hope 'good heart' is the one you chose," I said. "I've been doing all the talking. Now tell me about yourself."

She got up and started walking away. "My friends and I don't like to talk about ourselves. It's the way we were raised. Anyway, what's to tell? It's all so boring. I'm from a small town. My father was a traveling salesman. I traveled with him. I never knew my mother." She waved a hand in the air as she disappeared behind the green and silver trailer.

I stood there, watching the point where she had disappeared, inhaling the fresh country air when a motorcycle roared to life on the other side of the trailer. Motorcycle exhaust fumes overcame the country air and Claudia came back into view straddling an ancient, black, German NSU. She wore a black helmet. Another black helmet was on the black leather seat behind her. She had her red skirt wrapped around her, exposing long, well-shaped legs.

My heart skipped a beat. Above all, I was a legman.

"Want a ride to Paris?"

"That's a long way." I said.

"Not really," she said. "It's only a couple hours or so. Probably less as the bike flies. It would be much faster than hitchhiking. Besides, don't you want to find out if you have money waiting for you in Paris?"

I gave her my best smile. My luck was improving by the minute. Now a gorgeous woman was taking me to Paris.

"Hop on and hang on."

I put on the helmet and my pack and climbed on behind her. I put my hands on her waist trying to be gentlemanly.

"Never rode a bike before, huh," she laughed.

"A . . . not really."

"'*Not really*' that is cowboy wimpy for saying 'no,' is it not?"

She had called me out on that one. "I've never been on one before."

"Better hang on tight, cowboy. We Rom love our thrills!"

I slid my arms a little further around her waist. She laughed at me again, revved up the engine and popped the clutch. The bike stood up on its back wheel and I almost fell off. She dropped the bike back down on its front wheel and I scooted forward so that my chest was pressed against her back and I locked my arms around her waist.

"What did you mean by 'Rom'?"

"It's what my people call themselves. Other people call us Gypsies."

Shit! I'd fallen in with thieves. Good ol' honest, Midwestern me. I'd fallen in with thieves. Although it didn't seem like such a bad thing, considering that I was hanging onto Claudia. Actually, it felt pretty good. Maybe Gypsies were maligned. The victims of old prejudices. But, I didn't have time to rationalize further.

She revved the bike up again and we were off like a rocket.

*   *   *

As we flew toward Paris, Claudia conducted what I considered to be in-flight interrogation. She would turn her head and shout a question at me. I yelled the answer into the ear hole of her glossy black helmet. She either nodded or uh-huhed depending on my answer.

"Other than write, how do you make money?"

Fair question. But a tough one. Since college all I had done was write. Newspaper reporting. Advertising copywriting. Like that. There were the usual kid jobs through grade school. Delivering newspapers. Mowing lawns. Working in a pet shop. Sweeping out the back shop of the local newspaper.

In high school I'd flipped hamburgers, sold magazine subscriptions and mowed more lawns. I'd done anything else that would earn me a buck.

In college, my summer jobs had been construction laborer, railroad dock laborer, farm laborer, painter's apprentice and quality inspector on the Fisher Body assembly line.

"Nothing else?" she asked, snapping me out of my mental eddy.

"Bartending," I shouted, not wanting to tell the whole story.

She nodded approval.

The whole story was that one evening the owner of the Castaways, Frank Wilheit, informed me I was tending bar for the next two weeks to work off my bar tab.

"My bar tab!?!" I had shouted. "I don't have a bar tab!"

"Your girlfriend has been buying rounds at your table and signing your name."

She was the daughter of a frozen food mogul and thought money grew on trees. We broke up that night and I began tending bar.

But I left that part out.

"Writing and bartending," she said. "Soft hand work."

I didn't say anything. Construction laborer, railroad laborer, and farm laborer were all hard hand jobs. But I didn't say anything because these skills can be more impressive demonstrated than stated.

I just hung on and she drove her bike like a pro. She only knew one speed. Faster! And that was cool by me.

PARIS

One hour and forty-five minutes later, after passing every car and truck that was on the road in front of us, she slid to a stop in front of the Paris American Express office on Rue Scribe across from the *Opera National de Paris. Palais Garnier.* I just sat there for a moment holding onto Claudia and staring at the Opera's seven-arch palace with its weathered-copper green dome. The dome was topped by a copper-green goddess and flanked by winged goddesses above each end arch. It was a true beauty and marvel.

Claudia asked me what I knew about it. I said: practically nothing. She smiled and launched into a verbal history tour. I had no way of knowing that she was a history buff. I was really glad I hadn't said I'd seen pictures of it.

She told me that The Opera was designed by a relatively unknown architect named Charles Garnier and was completed in 1875 after thirteen years of construction. The delay was due to the discovery that the selected site was over an underground lake and spring, which still exists today. And the basement has never leaked. An amazing fact to a dry-land Kansas boy who thought all basements leaked.

I still have a hard time believing that the basement doesn't leak.

In fact, farmers in my area of the state had a saying: If you're looking for water, you don't need to drill a well. Dig a basement.

The Palace itself was 118,404 square feet, half of which was the auditorium with a vast stage with room for four hundred and fifty performing artists. The balance of the space was for logistical support and set storage. Interestingly enough, The Opera only seats two thousand two hundred patrons.

I couldn't believe it. I had made it to Paris! I was staring at The Opera with all its facts running through my head. Even better, I was holding onto the most beautiful woman I'd ever met. What next?

"You can let go of me now that we aren't moving." She laughed like music.

I dropped my arms and climbed off her NSU.

"Unless you don't want to." She laughed again.

I wanted to climb back on the bike and wrap my arms around her. But I was trying to be cool so I handed her my helmet instead. "I'll go check my mail," I said.

"Hurry. We have other things to do," she smiled. "And you still need a shower."

I went inside American Express. It was much the same as Monaco. The upstairs was ornate and downstairs, where the mail was, it was very utilitarian. There was only one person in line in front of me.

I had six letters waiting for me. One from UPI. One from The Rocky Mountain News. One from the Kansas City Kansan. Three from the Kansas City Star.

Claudia was sitting on a painted wooden bench when I returned. Of course the bench was green. It was outside the

American Express office and you know how they like green. Her NSU was on the sidewalk beside her. She was making notes in a blue, five-by-eight spiral-bound notebook. She closed it in her lap and waited as I sat down on the bench beside her.

The sun was warm and the air smelled of a mixture of exhaust fumes and dog shit. No one picked up after their dogs in Paris.

"Your life was in my hands for almost two hours," she said. "Were you frightened?"

"Maybe . . . a . . . a little."

"That's 'cowboy wimp' for 'yes,' is it not?"

"I was frightened to death. But I loved it."

"I love being frightened, too." Claudia looked me straight in the eyes and the green in hers seemed to sparkle. "Of course the degree of pleasure is determined by who you are holding on to."

"That had a great deal to do with it," I said.

"Open your letters." She elbowed me playfully. "Let's see if you are a writer—or what you *Gaje* call a wanta be."

"What's a Gaje?"

"A non Gypsy. Now open your mail."

I pulled out my multi-function, black, staghorn handle Boy Scout knife and slit open the UPI envelope. I pulled out a cover letter, a check and three Xeroxed pages of enlarged contact prints of pictures I had taken while on the freighter. Three of the contact photos were checked in red.

We had run into a major Atlantic spring storm. To make a long story short, another freighter was sinking and we had gone in to save any of the crew we could. We failed. But the rescue attempt had been undermined by greed. I had sent the story to UPI and AP along with photos, but I hadn't verbally told anyone about it. It wasn't a very pleasant story. In fact, every time I thought about it I got mad and then sad. And, vice versa.

I started reading the cover letter and glancing at the check. While I was doing that Claudia took the three pages of enlarged contact photos and was studying them. The pictures were of five seamen in a raft in the storm-tossed, icy-cold Atlantic. The men we had gone in to save. UPI had sold the pictures in a sequence of three to thirty-seven newspapers.

"What is this," Claudia asked. "You didn't tell me about this."

I put down the cover letter and looked at her as she jabbed the first checked picture. "What's this?"

"The surviving crewmen we went in to save."

They were smiling and waving, ecstatic that they were about to be saved. Moments ago they knew they were going to die. Now they were going to be saved.

She jabbed the second photo angrily. Three of the men lay crumpled on the bottom of the raft. One was in a corner clutching himself. The fifth was in the opposite, diagonal corner gripping the sides of the raft.

"Three are dead. The other two are dying."

She jabbed the third checked photo even more angrily. A huge wave was capsizing the raft. The five men, all dead now, were tumbling into the freezing sea

"You let these men die while you took pictures!?!" I saw a fury in her that I hadn't imagined was there. It was like she'd been betrayed.

"It wasn't a proud moment. Not one I like to think about."

"You let them die so you could take photos to sell!?! You let greed kill them!?!" She was on her feet. She tucked her skirt around her legs and threw one leg over the black leather saddle of her NSU. She was done with me.

"No! No! You've got it wrong," I almost choked on the words. "We tried to save them. But you are right. Greed did kill them."

Claudia studied me for a moment. Then she slowly climbed off her bike and sat back down beside me. She reached over and took the UPI acceptance letter from me, skimmed it. "Tell me about it."

"I haven't told anyone about it."

"You told United Press International about it."

"Writing it is not the same as telling it." I looked her directly in those magnificent eyes. "I cried when I wrote it. I don't think I could tell it without crying and I don't cry in front of people."

"Never?"

She had me there. "All of us on the ship that day cried. But that was different."

"Cowboys don't cry? Is that what you're telling me?"

"Something like that."

She reexamined the acceptance letter and the check. Then she focused on the Xeroxes of the three checked photos. "Tell me you tried to save them."

"We all did. Most of my crew was Danish. Our Captain was Danish. The freighter that went down was Danish. My crew knew half of their crew. We did everything we could to save them."

The images and pain of that day came flooding back. I could feel tears forming in my eyes. I shook my head and cleared my throat to chase away the feelings.

Claudia leaned into me. "You'll tell me sometime?"

I nodded.

She looked at the check. "One hundred and eighty-five dollars! That's nine hundred and twenty-five francs! You are rich!"

I laughed and opened two other envelopes.

The Rocky Mountain News and the Kansas City Kansan envelops each contained ten-dollar checks. I waved the checks at her. "For a story about the Danish beer strike this spring. It was two weeks old when I was there and the Danes weren't drinking any imported beer. They didn't even want to sell me imported."

"They are loyal to their beers."

"That was the point of my story."

Claudia grabbed the checks and put them with the UPI check. "One hundred more francs and three envelopes to go."

I opened the first K.C. Star envelope. "Voila," I said. "Twenty bucks for feature story about a Kansas City insurance man who was exploring the possibility of opening an office in Copenhagen for his company Kansas City Life." I opened the second envelope from the Star. "Another twenty! Another feature story. This one about Tivoli Gardens in Copenhagen."

"Feature stories pay better than news stories."

"Yes, they do!

"Why is that?"

"On a news story, everybody sees it. It's just who reports it first. But a feature story is different. It's there for everybody to see, too. But, it is all in the telling. Your own special way of seeing and telling it."

"Personality over immediacy," she said, getting the concept.

"That's why the columnists make the big bucks."

She took the two checks from the Star and waved all of them at me. "Twelve hundred and twenty-five francs."

She was amazingly quick with her math and dollars to franc conversions. Maybe it was a Gypsy thing

"Open the last one," she said.

I slit open the third envelope from the Star. It contained the coup de grace. A fifty-dollar check with a note paper-clipped to it. "This is your best writing to date. I want to see more of it." The note was from Mel Mencher, the city editor who had been a mentor.

"Wow!," Claudia said. "What is this for? A feature story, no."

"Yes. It was about my crewmembers sharing memories and feelings about the five men in the raft. Except it was only a half truth."

"You lied?"

"Not really. Everything my crew guys said is real. But it actually took place that night on our ship. I set it in a pub in Bristol the night we docked."

"Why?"

"Because it is easier for the reader to relate to the story. Most readers have been in bars. Not many have been in the crews' quarter of a freighter. And it allowed me to be a little detached."

"The man says it's your best and he wants more of it." She watched my reaction closely. I didn't think I reacted—but I must have. "Something is wrong?"

"I sold the story as the truth. And it isn't all truth."

"It seems to me that something is either true or not." She laughed. "*Part truth* seems to sell better that whole truth. We all take liberties with the truth. The question is," she honed in on the reality, "is that important to you?"

"I was brought up to believe that all you have in the world is your good name. And being truthful is how you maintain that good name."

Claudia studied me for moment and then smiled. "It seems newspapers pay better for half-truths than for whole truths."

I thought about that and nodded. She was right. My biggest payday was for a half-truth.

"It works that way for Gypsies, too," she said, as she took the envelopes from me and read the posting dates. "Mailed two weeks ago. It's a long process, no?"

"Two weeks for the story to get there. A couple days for a decision. Two weeks to get the checks back to me—if they buy it."

"You have other stories in the mail?" she asked.

"About a dozen. Why?" As I asked, thoughts ran through my mind. Why was she asking? Was this some sort of hustle? Was she trying to figure a way to separate me from my money? She was, after all, a Gypsy.

"You need to manage your money. You never know when your next check will come. That is right, no." It wasn't a question. It was advice.

I felt like a jerk. I was being suspicious of her intentions when her intentions were to look out for me.

"Yes. That's exactly right."

"So, you can't go wasting your money on flashy Italian girls."

I laughed.

"You are stuck with a cheap Gypsy girl, who spends her money on petrol to take you to Paris."

I started to respond but she placed her finger on my lips. "You are more worried about truth than money. And you've fallen in with a Gypsy who is more interested in money than the truth." She laughed. "Somehow I don't think this is going to work."

"I can be Gypsy," I said.

"That's pretty iffy," she said, handing me my envelopes.

"I can be anything I want to be," I said smugly, folding and stuffing the envelopes into my shirt pocket.

"Would *more observant* be one of those things?" It was her turn to be smug.

I wasn't sure what she meant until she handed me the checks, which I had assumed were in the envelopes. I smiled sheepishly and stuffed them into my pocket along with the envelopes.

Claudia got up from the bench and leaned against her bike. "You know, another thing, Gypsies take a little better care of their money than cowboys do."

A policeman strolled by and glanced suspiciously at Claudia. She stared back. For the first time since I'd known her she looked tough and defiant. She almost sneered at him. Then to me: "Cash your checks here. You will get a much better exchange rate."

When I returned with my wad of francs, Claudia wrapped her long red skirt around her great legs so she could straddle her bike and climbed on. "Hop on," she said. I climbed on behind her.

"I know a place you can stay that is cheap," she said. "Students live there. But it is mostly empty this time of year. Normally it is fourteen francs a week in the summer. I'll try to do better for you. Then, we go cheap for dinner."

She turned the key and revved the bike's motor.

"You don't have a typewriter, how do you write your stories?"

"I print by hand on a yellow tablet. Sometimes I rent a typewriter."

"Not very professional, is it. The yellow tablet."

But before I could respond, a well-dressed, middle-aged couple approached us and asked in Germanic-accented French directions to Les Invalides. At least I thought that was what they were asking.

Claudia gave them detailed directions in German with lots of hand movement. They thanked her in German. And we roared away from the curb on her NSU.

So, here I was in Paris, hanging onto this gorgeous woman from a Gypsy campground two hours south of Paris, who rode an NSU, who had taken me under her wing. She spoke English, French and German. She was familiar enough with Paris to know where American Express and Les Invalides were, and also to know a place where I could stay cheaply. And, did I mention that she was drop dead gorgeous? How did I get so lucky?

I hung on tight to her as we cruised through the streets and down alleys. Finally she rode up onto the sidewalk in front of an old six story gray stone building. It sat behind a gray stonewall with two huge, weathered wooden doors that appeared to have never known paint. The stones in the building and walls were square-cut. They were set so close together that they seemed to be held together by magic instead of mortar.

The building with its amazing wall was directly across a narrow, cobblestone street (Rue de Vaugirard) from Luxembourg Gardens. We pushed through the huge wooden doors and stepped into a courtyard that was entirely cobbled. Not one living plant anywhere. A couple of cars were parked there.

"Give me ten francs and wait here she said."

I watched her walk to the far end of the courtyard, knock on a door and enter. A few minutes later she came back smiling. She handed me a five-franc note. "Your rent is five francs a week due every Sunday night. Be late and you are out." She held up a key. "It's on the second floor. Let's go check it out."

She was full of surprises and I was loving it.

The room was small, a two-man study room with beds on opposite walls. Two small table/desks and two straight back wooden chairs completed the furnishings. I'd done with less. I tried the bed—a mattress over springs on a metal frame. Not exactly luxurious. But a lot better than the hard cold ground. Showers and toilets were at the far end of the hall one floor above. My room smelled a little musty and dampish—but what could I expect from what amounted to a stone cave?

"You have your castle," she tossed me a towel. "Now, go take a shower. I want you presentable when you take me to my friend's place for an early dinner."

"Why early?"

"Because, I'm hungry and because I need to get back on the road. I don't like riding alone at night."

I MEET ISABELLA

Claudia motored a couple of blocks down Rue de Vaugirard and up onto the sidewalk in front of a little bistro. The sign above the door said: Le Gros Chat Noir. As she padlocked her bike to a light pole she pointed to the bistro.

"The Fat Black Pussy Cat," she said. "The food is good and the prices are right. This is your neighborhood. You need to learn it. Meet the people. After today you will know Philippe and he will be your friend because he is my friend. You have any questions you go to him."

It was a quaint little bistro, probably built in the mid 1700's, with booths along one wall and an ancient bar running the length of the opposite wall. Four-top tables were organized in the space between the booths and the bar. There weren't many customers at this awkward time between lunch and dinner. A few late lunchers and a few early drinkers were scattered around the room. Claudia picked a table.

"Can you draw?" she asked.

"Cartoony type of stuff, why?"

"Down at the end of the block there's an art store. Pastel chalks are always good to have if you can draw." Claudia was cryptic. I questioned her with my eyes, but before I could ask . . ."You'll see why."

"Isabella!"

My attention was drawn from her to a waiter, who was rushing out of the kitchen with a big smile on his face. He threw his arms up in the air. "Isabella!"

I turned to see who Isabella was but there was no one behind us. I turned back and realized the waiter was headed for us.

Claudia stood. "Philippe!" she said holding out her arms and smiling.

Claudia and Philippe rushed into an embrace complete with cheek kissing and a rainstorm of French. They stood back and assessed each other. Another rainstorm of French was so fast I only recognized a couple of words. Then she pointed to me.

"Philippe this is my friend Kelly. He's a *good* friend. He's American. His French isn't very good."

"We can work on it," Philippe said holding out his hand. "You are very lucky to be a *good* friend of Isabella."

I looked at Claudia. Isabella? She nodded slightly.

"I certainly am," I said to Philippe. "And she says she's very lucky to have you as a friend."

He looked at Claudia-Isabella and beamed his appreciation. "Are you back for University?"

"In the fall I return."

Philippe nodded and smiled again, happy to see her. "I will leave you two alone. You don't need menus. Anything you can think of, I can prepare."

"Philippe," Claudia Isabella said. "I'm running short of time. How about the biftek et pomme frites?"

"Anything you wish. I will make a couple of sauces for dipping."

"I'm sorry to eat and run," Claudia Isabella apologized.

"Any time with you is a gift," Philippe said bowing away from the table.

When he had returned to the kitchen I said, "I thought your name was Claudia."

"It's Claudia Isabella. At first I didn't like Claudia—too common. So I used Isabella. Then a few years ago, Isabella began to sound pretentious to me so I started using my first name. It's more earthy."

"Whatever your name, Philippe was certainly happy to see you."

"A few years ago I fixed a problem he had. He's still grateful."

"What kind of problem?" I was curious—maybe a little suspicious.

"Of a personal nature." Claudia glanced around the room at the other patrons.

As she did, I studied her face, watching for some telltale reaction. There was none. It was an old newspaper trick I had learned. Look for a reaction before you look for what caused it. That way you don't tip your hand that you're trying to read someone.

Philippe returned with two large goblets of red wine. "Perfect for your biftek." He started to hurry away. But the door opened and he greeted his new guests. "Guisepe! Maria! Look who is here!" Philippe pointed at Claudia Isabella and hurried back to the kitchen.

A skinny, silver-haired Italian man of about seventy was holding the door for his wife who was about the same age. She could have been Sophia Loren's mother—seventy and very much together. Their eyes fell on Claudia and their faces lit up. "Isabella," they cried in unison and rushed to her. They jabbered in Italian and embraced Claudia, who replied in fluent Italian.

Claudia turned to me. "This is Kelly," she said to the couple. "He's an American writer and he claims to be able to draw some. He only speaks English." She reached for my hand. "Guisep and Maria own the art store that I mentioned." Claudia turned back to the couple. "I told him he needed to get some pastel chalks at your store. But I didn't say why. It's his first time in Paris."

Guisep winked at me. "She never tells you why. But, if you pay attention you'll find out."

Maria patted me on the shoulder. "Come by tomorrow. Your chalks will be ready."

"For Isabella's friend, no charge, of course," Guisep said.

"Of course no charge," Maria echoed.

"But that's not right," I said.

They both waved off my objection.

Philippe rushed out of the kitchen with our food on a tray.

"Eat, eat," Guisep and Maria said retreating to a nearby table.

Philippe set the bistro steaks and french fries with accompanying sauces on our table. He removed our check from the tray, shoved it quickly into his back pocket. He smiled at me and went to check on the other customers.

I made a quick appraisal of the other customers and then whispered to Claudia Isabella. "They all seem to be watching us."

"Not us. You." She took a sip of her wine. "They are trying to decide if you're good enough for me." She laughed. "They're the local shop owners around here. This was my neighborhood for a time. They are my friends. Now they are yours. Be nice to them and they will help you."

"Because I'm with you?"

"Partly. But more because they are good people."

We ate in silence for a while, as I thought about who she was and what was really happening here. I was drawn to this mysterious woman, and yet leery. It was just too much, too fast. I could see that she was amused by my confusion.

"How many languages do you speak?" I asked.

"Does it matter? I've traveled all over Europe from the time I was a baby. There are so many different languages—and yet they are so similar. It makes it easy. My father insisted that I learn the local language everywhere we were." She laughed and almost everyone in the bistro looked over at us and smiled approvingly. "Let's see. I also speak Spanish, Hungarian and Romanian. I would like to learn Japanese."

"Why? Do you want to go there some day?"

"Not particularly. But there are so many Japanese tourists here. Chip-chip-chipping to each other. I'd like to know what it is that they are saying that they don't think we understand."

Every time I thought I had a handle on her, I didn't. I was always about two steps behind. With her, I had to make no suppositions, hang loose and roll with the punches. She was truly an unexpected woman.

"Claudia, what are your plans?" I asked.

"Plans are a waste of time."

"You said you were going back home."

"Yes. I need to." It was almost a sigh.

"Will you be back?"

"Who knows the future?"

Was she being coy or letting me down easy? "I thought Gypsies were fortune tellers."

"We *tell* fortunes. It's an easy way to separate the *Gaje* from their money. But we don't believe in fortune telling. It's foolish to believe in fortune telling." She laughed her wonderful laugh and all eyes turned our way. Philippe was drawn by it.

She finished her last bite of steak. "It was wonderful," Claudia Isabella said to him. "Even better than I remembered."

Philippe actually blushed and I realized he was my age, twenty-five, or a little older, even though he looked a lot older. I looked over at Claudia and realized that I had no idea of her age. Originally I had thought she was my age, and maybe younger. Whatever her age, she was wise beyond her years. But I was brought up with the etiquette that it was impolite to ask a woman her age, so I didn't.

Claudia Isabella took Philippe's hands in hers. "Would you show Kelly your kitchen where you make such wonderful fare?"

"For you, of course. But is he really interested?" Philippe turned to me.

"I'd be honored," I said.

He smiled and led me to his kitchen. He was showing me his saucepots when I heard her NSU roar to life outside. I tensed and looked towards the door.

Philippe put a gentle hand on my arm. "You cannot control a wild thing," he said. "You can only let her go. If she wants, she will return. All you can do is enjoy the time she gives you.

Don't drive her away. Just enjoy what she gives you. It will be more than you think it is at the time, my friend." He patted me on the shoulder and guided me out of his kitchen.

As I crossed to the front door, Guisep and Maria smiled and waved at me. I waved and smiled back.

Before leaving Phillipe's I looked at the other patrons. I got smiles and waves, which I returned. They all understood what it was like to know and be left behind by Claudia Isabella. They must have understood the emptiness I felt. I smiled and nodded at them again. I had friends here thanks to her. I wasn't alone in France any more

I studied the ancient and beautiful neighborhood as I walked back to my room.

MY ARRONDISSEMENT

. I awoke around nine the next morning. It was the most restful sleep I'd had since Italy when I still had enough money to show off for the two Italian girls.

I walked the length of the sea-foam green hall and climbed up the old, dark stairway one floor to the showers. I showered in cold water. No hot water here. The plus side was that the mirrors didn't steam up.

I studied my face in the clear mirror and elected to let my beard grow. I felt like I was telling Lila that I was making a choice to be different. Whatever that meant.

I put on clean clothes and hit the streets to learn about my neighborhood. Or, as the French say: my "arrondissement," which was Number Six.

When Paris was founded alongside the Seine it was a river village. This original area would later be called Arrondissement 1. As the city grew, it expanded directly to the north, because there were no bridges south across the Seine. This add-on was called Arrondissement 2. Arrondissement 3 grew onto the east of A. 2. Then Arrondissement 4 grew south back to the river. And, in this spiraling clockwise pattern of Arrondissements, Paris was developed.

Arrondissement Six was mostly developed in the 1700's. It is directly south of A. 1. Bridges from A. 3. to the Ile de Cite made expansion south possible. Because Ile de Cite was the most defensible, it became the center of government in the 1500's and 1600's. The police, the trade commission, the hospital and, of course, Notre Dame were all located here.

Arrondissement 5., the Pantheon district, is just to the east of A. 6. It is where Boulevard St. Michel is located. After World War II and into the 1950's, modern construction began crowding, and replacing the old until the Parisians put a stop to it.

This modernization craze did not move west into A. 6. The original homes are scattered among the shops in a beautiful eclectic blend. My neighborhood was a collection of mostly ancient architecture with a few postwar rebuilds. Most of the streets are still narrow and cobbled. Walking these streets was like stepping back in time. You couldn't help but wonder who had lived in these gorgeous, ancient homes.

Eight-foot high masonry walls with large wooden doors surrounded the homes. They lined one side of an entire block with the exception of a shop on each corner with living space above the shop. Shops lined the opposite side of the street.

As I passed one home the wooden door was open and I could see inside to a colorful and beautifully maintained garden. It was a sharp contrast to the masonry walls and gray cobbled streets outside. An attractive woman in her mid-thirties was dragging a box of trash across the garden toward the street and I asked her, in bad French, if I could help.

"Yes," she replied in English and smiled.

"Oh, those French women," I thought. Her name was Margaux.

"You are American, are you not?"

I said I was and told her how beautiful her garden was. Margaux beamed. I asked her the history of the house. Margaux told me that once a famous painter and muralist had lived there in the 1730's. Francois Boucher. He also taught at the Universite. She asked if I would like a tour of her house.

"Would I!?! You bet!"

It was like stepping into a three-story museum exhibition of the 1700's. Her grandmother had begun the restoration around 1910. Her mother and father had continued restoring it in the 1930's.

The murals Boucher had painted on the walls had been damaged and over the years her father had enticed art students to help with the restoration. He thought Francois would have approved—although the Cultural Ministry had not.

When the Nazi's overran Paris in 1942, her father with the help of the French underground, had set off a bomb just outside the front door. The blast made the ground floor look like a wreck and uninhabitable. The Nazi's saw a semi-destroyed house and avoided it. The upper two floors were mostly unharmed and Margaux and her parents lived there unmolested throughout the entire occupation.

An hour later I was back on Rue Vaugirard, exploring my new neighborhood again. But, more importantly, I had a new friend. Margaux.

Philippe was standing in the doorway of the Fat Black Pussy Cat as I walked past. He invited me in for breakfast.

"Only if I can pay," I said.

"Isabella's friends do not pay."

I wondered what problem Isabella could have solved to warrant such loyalty. But I didn't ask. Back in Kansas prying into other people's affairs was considered rude. I had no reason to think it would be the any different here. So, we chatted and worked on my French.

After a delicious breakfast of *pancrepes,* I explored my way down the street to Tableau et Couleur. Canvas and Paint. Right to the point.

I went inside. The interior was a gorgeous blend of antique architecture and contemporary display. Guisepe and Maria had to be proud of it. Guisepe was nowhere in sight. Maria smiled and waved me over to her glass-cased counter. She handed me a 12 x 4 inch brown paper-wrapped package tied with string.

I started to unwrap it and was stopped with a barrage of "no's" and waving hands and a shaking head. Obviously this was not the time to open it.

"Isabella, she wants you to maybe walk along the Seine first. Take in the sights."

I thanked her and pulled out my billfold.

"No, no. Is Isabella's gift," she said and waved me toward the door. "Go and see what she wants you to see."

As I neared the door she said: "Kelly." I turned to her. "I think maybe Isabella . . . she maybe wants you to enjoy the Seine." She pointed in the direction I needed to walk.

I headed down Rue Vaugirard. The morning was brilliant. The walk through my new neighborhood was exhilarating. Everything was right with the world.

When I reached the Seine I understood Claudia Isabella's message.

THE MESSAGE

The Seine splits Paris in half. There is the Right Bank, where the original river city of Paris developed. And, there is the Left Bank, where artists have congregated for centuries. I was on the Left Bank. When I reached the Seine I turned right and walked along the westbound sidewalk going west toward Notre Dame. I walked past artists painting. Booksellers hawking used books from moveable stands. "Jewelers" selling used chains and rings and watches from the same type of mobile stands. Then I discovered what Claudia Isabella wanted me to see.

A guy was on his hands and knees. He had a bony butt and long brown hair that hid his face. He was reproducing a Picasso on the sidewalk with pastel chalks. A hat sat on the sidewalk beside the chalk drawing. It contained coins.

Several people were watching the work in progress. A guy in a business suit stepped forward and dropped a couple of francs in the hat. The sidewalk artist thanked the businessman with a smile—only the sidewalk artist wasn't a he. He was a she. A very pretty she. Funny how that bony butt became cute when the gender changed. I moved on down the sidewalk.

After passing more bookstands, a juggler and another painter I found another sidewalk artist. This one was definitely a *he*—unless *she* was a bearded woman. He had a picture of Brassai's Steps of Montmartre and was reproducing it with almost 3-D clarity. With my limited artistic ability, there was no way I could do anything that accomplished.

And yet, I got Claudia Isabella's message. This was a way of earning money while I was waiting for checks to come in for stories I'd sent back home. I didn't have to be totally dependent on my writing. Self-sufficiency was possible.

In all, there were eight sidewalk artists. Three were really good. The majority were at about my level of drawing ability and they were able to make some money—so, there was a chance. I decided that to make up for the difference in ability, I had to be clever with what I drew.

I wandered from one artist to another—back and forth. Studying their approaches, not so much their art, but their approach to what would earn them money. That special element that allowed them to separate the spectator from his or her coin. That special element that turned an artistic venture into a commercial one.

The sun warmed and then cooled slightly as I studied the artists. The smell of the Seine and the cry of the river birds were constants. The flow of tourists, too, was a constant. I was lost in this world of sight and senses until . . .

A violin playing a waltz caught my ear. I was drawn to the music and nestled into a crowd of people gathered around the violinist. He was an old man with a white shaggy beard. His face was heavily lined and smudged with various colors of pastel chalks. He was sitting on a folding wooden chair. His violin case was loaded with coins.

At his feet was a chalk drawing of a couple dancing on the beach in the rain with their butler holding an umbrella over them. It was misty and mysterious and made the viewer fantasize about the scene. Who were these chalk-drawn people? What was their back story? What had brought them here? He had done a superb job.

I watched for a while. He drew by far the largest crowd. And no other sidewalk artists were set up anywhere close to him. He was too much competition. I studied him. And I studied the crowd he attracted. They were mostly professional people and tourists. What I thought of as thinking people. People with money.

A little ten-year-old boy caught my eye. He wore shorts and a t-shirt with a Scotland crest on it. The little boy was making a copy of the violinist's drawing on a small sketchpad.

It was late afternoon before I headed back toward my rented room. I stopped at the Fat Black Pussy Cat for a glass of wine. I sat at the bar, nursed the wine and chatted with Philippe. The place was almost empty. Too late for the merchant lunchers. Too early for the after work crowd. Philippe was happy to have the company.

"Guisep and Maria gave me the chalks today," I told him. "And Maria sent me to the Seine because she thought that's what Isabella wanted."

"So she wants you to try your hand as a sidewalk artist. You should listen," Philippe said. "Isabella is very smart."

"Some of the artists are much better than I am."

"And, I'll bet some aren't."

I shrugged. "There was one old guy who . . ."

"Played a violin," he interrupted.

"You know him?"

"Old Rennie. He's a fixture. He draws the same painting every other day. Been doing it for a couple of years. Before that he just played the violin. Didn't do nearly as well just playing."

I finished my wine and asked for a refill. "I should ask how much first."

"For Isabella's friend, nothing."

"I can't accept that. It makes me feel strange. Uncomfortable."

"How 'bout for cost? Two francs?" he ventured.

"That I can get comfortable with."

It was a friendly solution and he poured.

"Isabella said you were friends because she did something for you," I said. "But she wouldn't tell me what."

"That's because it's my business and it is for me to tell—or not."

He went to check on the other customers. Outwardly being the proper host to his clientele. But I saw it as buying time. I had stepped over the line and he was trying to decide how to respond. I could kick myself. I was being too pushy after deciding not to be. It was another case of mouth over mind.

When he returned to his position behind the bar, he smiled and nodded. He'd made up his mind how to deal with me. He had decided to tell me. Now, I was glad I had asked.

"Isabella was in here one day. Her first time here. Sitting right where you are now. Two men came in. What you call bad men. They wanted me to pay them every week to make sure nothing happened to my place. I said I couldn't afford it. They said I should think about my answer and that they'd be back in a week.

"When they were gone Isabella asked me if I was the only one in the area these men were extorting or were there others? I said I didn't know. It was the first time the men had been here. But, I said, I could find out. I asked her why she wanted to know. She said she might be able to help."

Philippe paused to pour more wine for both of us.

"A week later she comes in with two nicely dressed men. One big and bulky. The other very trim. They moved the bar stools to create an opening on each side of where you are sitting now. Then they sat at the table right behind you. Isabella sat on the stool where you are sitting now, facing the bar.

She introduced them to me as her uncles. She asked if I had learned if those bad men were bothering other merchants, too. I told her many others. She ordered three wines. I served them but neither she nor her uncles ever touched the glasses. They just sat there.

"Every time someone entered, she glanced at them and shook her head slightly. Finally, the two bad men came in. They came to the bar and stood in the open spaces the uncles had created. Isabella stood up and asked where the toilet was. I pointed. The two bad men watched her rudely as she left. They smirked at each other and turned back to me.

"Suddenly the two uncles were right behind them. The big bulky uncle grabbed their heads and slammed them together. It sounded like knocking two coconuts together. The bad men collapsed to the floor. The uncles took two guns from the bad men and put them on the bar. Then they picked the men up by their belts and carried them outside.

"An old van drove up. They threw the men in the back, climbed in behind them and drove away.

"Isabella came out of the toilet and asked if I had a newspaper. I gave her a copy of Le Monde. She folded it, stashed the guns inside, put the paper under her arm and left.

"The bad men never came back." Philippe leaned against the back bar and smiled.

I shook my head. "Did you ever ask her what her uncles did to those two men?"

"I did. She said her uncles gave them a good talking to. 'Let's not talk about them again. It's too nice a day,' she said. And we never have since."

Philippe nodded and went off to check on the other customers again. I sat there thinking about Claudia Isabella. I finished my wine, waved goodbye to Philippe and walked back to my room, still thinking about her.

Claudia Isabella left a lot to think about. She was a Gypsy, which, by Midwest standards, meant she was a thief. Maybe a crook. Maybe even a gangster. Again, using Midwest standards, a crook was an individual; a gangster was a member of a gang. She certainly knew how to deal with the "two bad men."

Not that I was unfamiliar in dealing with bad guys. As a college intern I had worked the police beat for both the Kansas City Star and Kansas City Kansan. After graduating from The William Allen White School of Journalism at the University of Kansas I stayed on the same beat for the Kansan.

During that time I had met and gotten to know thieves, crooks, murderers, mass murderers and mobsters. Some of them I knew before they became infamous and others I came to know after their crimes. I never trusted any of them. Who in their right mind would?

But here I was, not only enamored with this beautiful Gypsy, but also trusting her. What was I thinking? Was I thinking at all? Was I thinking with the wrong head?

Back in my room I got my notebook out of my pack, sat down at my little table/desk and practiced drawing cartoon characters. The same characters I had first copied from my comic books in the third grade. There were the ducks: Donald, Daisy, Huey, Dewey, Louie and Scrooge. There were Popeye, Olive Oil and Wimpy. Batman and Robin. Superman. The Green Hornet. The Blackhawks' planes. Plasticman. And I roughed out a sketch of Claudia Isabella on her Harley, her skirt wrapped high on her exaggeratedly long shapely legs.

I lay down on my bed and tried to figure out how I could use my cartoon characters and how to use the clues Claudia Isabella had given me. I had one bright idea just before I fell asleep.

Did you ever notice that when you have a bright idea just before falling asleep, you can't remember it the next morning? That incredibly brilliant idea that you didn't need to write down because there was no way you'd forget it? Some times I think it's our self-conscious mind protecting us from the inanity of our last grasp at brilliance before the brain shuts down.

Our mind's way of saying: "Brilliant! Truly brilliant! You can shut down and rest now. Good boy," it says and scratches us behind our ears.

THE IDEA

The next morning I could not remember last night's brilliant idea. I looked at my sketches to see if they would jog my memory. They didn't. Finally, I decided to get out and move around. If it was a good idea, it would return. Like a homing pigeon or Lassie.

I walked in the opposite direction from the one I had taken yesterday, trying to learn a new area of my neighborhood. I spiraled inward toward the Seine along cobbled streets, flanked by ancient stone, brick and plaster buildings. I found Les Invalides, which is a complex of buildings containing museums and monuments dedicated to the military history of France.

Louis XIV commissioned the project in 1670 as a home and hospital for war veterans. Napoleon's gold-domed tomb, inside and out, is without question the most spectacular element of the complex. I stood, mesmerized by the interior for nearly an hour, overwhelmed by its architectural richness. Also, I was lost in thoughts that somehow always included Claudia.

A few blocks away was the National Assembly, where the Parliament's arguments led to the storming of the Bastille and the French Revolution on July 14, 1789. Every place I looked there were historical monuments and statues and other celebrations of the past. And at every site I wondered what history lesson Claudia might add.

I crossed the Seine and marveled at the Louvre Gardens.

I crossed back to the Left Bank and walked along the Seine studying the street scene that I wanted to become part of in order to earn enough between story sales to survive. For the most part it was a mobile commerce that could be set up and taken down in minutes. I realized that most of the vendors had bicycles with deep wire baskets on the front and/or deep saddlebag type wire baskets on the rear. Some even had carts attached. The vendors could pack up and be gone in minutes.

The sidewalk artists had it the easiest. Just box their chalks, pick up their proceeds and go. Their "canvas" would be washed clean by the night street cleaners and they would have fresh concrete to work on tomorrow.

THE FIRST DRAWING

I awoke early. Early for me these days, now that I had a bed. I grabbed my box of chalks and set out.

As I passed the Fat Black Pussy Cat I waved my box of chalks at Philippe. He motioned me inside.

"So you are acting on Isabella's guidance." He was happy for me.

"Yes, I am."

"And excited about it I see."

"Very."

"Have you picked a location?"

"Next to the violin player."

"Not a good place. He gets all the money there."

"Not today."

Philippe shook his head sadly. I could see it in his gray eyes. Isabella's friend wasn't listening.

"One thing. I need a cap. Where can I find one?" I asked.

"What color? What size?"

"It just needs to hold coins. If it fits and I like the color that would be a plus."

Philippe smiled at me and laughed. "Actually, if you set up next to the violinist, it won't need to be very big."

"I'll bet you I make almost as much as he does."

"A glass of wine?" Philippe asked.

I held out my hand. Philippe shook it and smiled.

He was amused and he had a hard time keeping a straight face as he said: "To get this *magic cap,* and it will have to be *magic* to earn you as much as the violinist . . ."

"Almost as much," I corrected.

"Almost as much," he agreed. "To get this cap, go down to Guisep's and Maria's store and turn right. Go a short block and turn right again. There's a used clothing store three shops down. If you can't find a cap, buy a towel and fold it. The towel is the second choice of the street artist."

At Guisep and Maria's art store I turned right. I saw them inside and waved the box of chalks at them. They both pointed in the opposite direction from where I was going. I could see Guisep mouth "Seine" as he pointed. I smiled back.

A couple minutes later I passed by their store again, this time wearing my two-franc gray tweed cap. I waved at them again and pointed at the cap. They understood. Maria and Guisep came to the door.

"Where will you be?" she asked. "We might want to see."

"Next to the violin player."

"Not a good place," she said.

"For me, it is perfect."

"No, no, no," she said, shaking her head.

"Want to bet?" I shrugged, arms splayed, palms up.

"A glass of wine?" Guisep ventured.

"You're on."

Guisep smiled and Marie went back inside shaking her head.

I could almost hear her thinking *crazy American.*

*   *   *

At the Seine, the violinist was putting the final touches on his "Couple in the Rain." He had already started attracting a crowd. People were dropping coins in his cap. I heard one American couple say to another American couple: "I don't know why he wasn't here yesterday. But see what I mean? Isn't he special?"

I saw the same little boy of about ten, who was here two days ago, watching the violinist drawing. Again, the little boy had a paper and pencil and was copying the chalk drawing. We all get our inspirations someplace.

The violinist finished his chalk art, picked up his violin and began to play. That was what I was waiting for.

I moved about ten feet to the left of his drawing and started mine. He had drawn the crowd and now they were watching me. Exactly what I was hoping for. I drew the outline of my first cartoon character. Moving to the left, going away from the violinist, I drew the outline of the second character. Continuing to the left, I drew the outline of the third character.

At this point there was no clue to what I was drawing. That was the idea. Keep the crowd guessing. This was street theater. Performance art.

I colored in my characters' clothing. Each of the three images had their arms sticking straight out to the side. But the arms ended at the elbow and the faces were blank. People were watching and wondering. Even the violinist was sneaking peeks. Keep them guessing.

Next I drew in the face of the first character. Popeye. He was grimacing. I drew in Olive Oil and Wimpy's faces. They were grimacing, too.

I drew music notes arching from Popeye toward the violinist. I heard a few chuckles. But better yet, I heard coins dropping into my cap.

Finally, I drew Popeye's ham hock forearms from his elbows toward his ears. I attached hands with his fingers were pressed in his ears so he couldn't hear the violinist's music. People started laughing. More coins started dropping. I completed Olive Oil and Wimpy with their fingers in their ears.

I turned to the crowd and drew applause and more coins. The old carnie nugget: Always keep them guessing and then leave them laughing. I learned that when I ran away from home at fifteen to join a circus. But that's a different story.

I spotted Philippe, Guisep and Maria at the front of the crowd. They smiled and nodded their approval.

"You did good," Guisep said in English.

"Merci beaux," I said.

Marie laughed and ruffled Guisep's hair. Philippe playfully punched Guisep in the arm and turned to me chuckling.

"We owe you," Philippe said. "Stop by on your way home to collect."

Then Philippe snapped a Polaroid picture of my drawings and the three of them walked off laughing.

The two American couples introduced themselves. One couple was from Denver and the other was from Colorado Springs. They asked about me. I asked about them and started taking notes. I decided to write little feature stories about them to send to their local newspapers to see if I could sell them.

It seemed promising. It was certainly worth a try.

Everyone seemed to be enjoying my "art work." Everyone except the violinist. But he'd get used to me. I had a whole squad of cartoon characters that I could draw with their fingers in their ears. I had a paying job.

The crowd thinned and I picked up my cap, sat on a bench across the sidewalk from my chalk drawings and counted my money. Twenty-seven francs. A little more than a week's rent and meals. Not bad. Not bad at all. Thank you, Claudia Isabella.

On the way back to my room I stopped to thank Guisep and Maria for the chalks. They invited me to join them at Phillipe's so Guisep could pay off the bet.

As we walked along the cobbled street Guisep and Marie kept stealing glances at each other and chuckling. I knew I was the butt of the joke. But I didn't understand why.

"What'd I do?" I asked.

"Back at the river," Marie began. "When you thanked Guisep for his compliment you said: 'Thank you, beautiful.' As if he were your sweetheart." And they both laughed.

"What I meant was . . ."

"We know," Guisep laughed. "We know."

Marie shoved both of us. "But you do make a striking couple."

When we reached the Fat Black Pussy Cat the after work crowd was there. We were greeted with a cheer. Obviously Philippe had spread the word about Guisep's and my "relationship."

Guisep and I were toasted. We were asked if we had set a date. Marie was offered condolences. Guisep and Philippe paid off their debts. Other patrons bought rounds to celebrate my success working next to the violinist. And, it was explained; Guisep and I should consider this our impromptu shower. The French do love to celebrate . . . anything.

It was dark when I left and I was feeling no pain.

I went back to my room. I was exhausted but too charged up to sleep. So, I wrote feature articles about the two Colorado couples I had met. Then I worked on my sketch of Claudia Isabella on her NSU. And that's about all I remember.

HUMBER

Two days later I drew Batman and Robin with their fingers in their ears. Then, today, I drew the seven dwarfs from Snow White—only this time with a twist.

I had the six dwarfs in the background grimacing at the music notes coming from the violinist. In the foreground was an incomplete Dopey.

One by one I finished the six dwarfs by sticking their fingers in their ears. I heard chuckles from the gathering crowd and I heard the clink of coins. Then I went to work on Dopey. I put his hands together and leaned his head against the back of one hand. I put a big dopey smile on his face. He loved the music. The crowd laughed. Clink. Clink. Clink.

After the crowd thinned, I went over to the bench opposite my chalk drawing and counted the day's take. Forty-seven francs. Almost ten dollars! Thank you again Claudia Isabella.

While I was wondering if I'd ever see her again, the violinist came over and sat down on the bench. He placed his violin and its bow between us and sat the violin case on his lap. He stared at my "art" for a minute and then looked over at me.

"You American?"

"Yes."

"No speak French."

"No."

He sat there a moment composing his English. "You I no like first." Then he smiled and shook his violin case. The coins rattled and I saw some pastel paper francs but I couldn't see the denominations. "But you good business. You come back?"

"Que sera sera." I said.

He held out his hand. "Humber."

"Kelly."

We shook. He snapped his violin case shut. It had a strap on it like a guitar case. He stood, slung the strap over his head and shoulder, positioned it so that it hung down his back, picked up his violin and bow in his left hand and extended his right hand to me again. "Kelly," he smiled.

I stood and shook his hand. "Humber."

He tucked the violin under his chin and walked off playing *"**Que Sera Sera**."*

*   *   *

Two days later, as we were counting our take from the day, Humber poked me in the shoulder and said: "People say you writer."

I smiled and nodded. So, he had been asking around about me and there weren't too many people he could have asked. "I'm trying to be."

"Come me. I show you place."

We packed up and walked along the Seine. Humber was humming happily. He was feeling so good it made me feel good. We stopped at a tiny park and he pointed at a store on the opposite side of the park, maybe fifteen yards away.

"English book," he said. "Only English. Owner famous." He gave me a gentle push toward the bookstore on the other side of the tiny park. I crossed the park and a little street called Rue de la Bucherie and found myself standing in front of Shakespeare & Company.

Inside was a mesmerizing world of books. Floor to ceiling bookcases in nooks and crannies that lead from every main room. And, carved in a beam over a passageway between two rooms was an unforgettable phrase: Turn not a stranger from your door least he be an angel.

JUST A PUZZLE TO BE SOLVED

The next morning I lay in bed, eyes still shut, thinking about yesterday. I was wondering when I'd see Claudia Isabella again. Or if.

All I had to do to get an answer was to open my eyes.

She was sitting straddling the chair from the table/desk, watching me and making notes in her blue spiral notebook. Behind her on the table was a little portable typewriter. She closed her notebook, smiled and waved my sketch of her on the Harley at me. "Did you plan to put my fingers in my ears?" She sailed Phillipe's Polaroid picture of my Popeye drawing onto the bed. "Or did you plan to put a stupid grin on my face like this." She sailed another Polaroid onto the bed. The seven dwarfs from yesterday.

"Neither," I said defensively. "The drawing of you was solely for me—in case I never saw you again."

"How romantic." She laughed. "But no such luck." She was wearing tight, faded jeans and a Sorbonne sweatshirt.

Then the *unasked* question hit me. "How did you get in here? My door was locked."

"What's a lock to a Gypsy? Just a puzzle to be solved."

"You really are an unusual woman."

"You haven't scratched the surface yet, Kelly. Now pack up and meet me at Phillipe's."

"You mean pack up—as in leave?"

"You can't go any place if you don't leave." She laughed. "See you at Phillipe's. Or not. Either way I leave in an hour or less. Probably less."

She picked up the little typewriter and strolled out the door looking fantastic in those tight, faded jeans.

I began throwing things into my pack. Of course I was going.

*　*　*

When I arrived at Phillipe's she was at the bar talking with him. She motioned me toward a table and then joined me there. She sat beside me—not across from me. I took that as a good sign.

I took her hand in mine. "I didn't know if I was going to get to see you again."

"I had to get permission to travel with you first," she said. "To get permission, we had to see if you were smart enough to make money at something other than what you normally do. Like a good Gypsy, you turned nothing into something by using your head."

"We?"

"My uncles and I. We watched you doing your chalk art."

"I never saw you."

"You weren't supposed to. A couple of my uncles are chaperoning us right now for my father and their other brothers. They'll be with us wherever we go—but do you see them?"

I looked around. "I don't see anyone one."

"See? You're not supposed to."

I shrugged. I guessed I would see them in due time. "Why did you have to get permission?"

"A Gypsy can't travel with the Gaje or, the Gaje with Gypsies, without permission from family."

"And your father and your uncles said it was okay?"

"Not my father. I haven't seen him in awhile." She smiled as she explained the Gypsy basics to me. "Your family consists of your relatives. They are the ones you are traveling with. And, the ones who care for you. It's always changing."

"So your family approved."

"With one exception."

"Do I want to know who?"

"My cousin. To him you are not good enough for me because you are Gaje." She laughed. "He won't get over it either."

When she said that I thought *'He'll get over it when he gets to know me.'* But I let that go and instead I said. "Well, since it's okay to travel together, can you tell me about yourself now?"

She nodded and smiled teasingly. "I will tell you a little." She thought for a moment. A smile flickered at her lips as she tried to decide what to tell me. Who knew if it was going to be the truth? She was Gypsy.

Finally: "I love to travel. I grew up traveling."

"I thought you grew up in a small town.

"I did," Claudia said. "But my father was a horse trader and traveled from town to town and I went with him. I loved it."

"Sounds like a hard way to make a living."

"It was and the business died out. Then he traveled and sharpened knives and mended pots and pans. I always got to go with him and I met so many interesting people. It got to the point that if we weren't traveling I felt like I was wasting time."

"When did you find time to go to school?"

"I didn't. Papa didn't believe in schools. Not formal ones. He always said the school of the road was the best education."

"But our first day here," I reminded her. "Philippe asked if you had returned to college."

"Universite," she corrected. "I taught myself to read and write. When I was thirteen, Papa died and I knew if I was going to make anything of my life I needed an education."

"Died? A few Moments ago you said you hadn't seen him for a while. You sounded like he was alive."

"That's my father. Papa Two."

I decided I could sort the Papas out later. "If you didn't learn to read and write until you were thirteen, you must have had to work very hard in school to make up all those lost years."

Claudia Isabella laughed. "Not really. Life offers unexpected prizes. You just have to recognize them and seize them.

I shrugged. "I don't understand."

"One day I read a newspaper story about a school in Lyon that was destroyed by fire. So, I enrolled in a school, wherever we were at the time, I told them my father had just died and I had just moved there from Lyon to live with relatives. I told them before papa died he made me promise to keep going to school. And I was there to honor my papa's wish.

"When they wrote for my transcript they discovered that all the records were lost in the fire. No one ever said another word about it."

"That was pretty gusty."

"Not really. What were they going to do? Throw an orphan out of school? I don't think so." She laughed her wonderful laugh. "Enough about me. What about you? Were you smart enough to skip any grades like I did?"

It was my turn to laugh. "No. I wasn't that bright. And, my story isn't that interesting."

"Come on, tell."

"Well, I was pretty much a jock through high school."

She shook her head and shrugged. "What is 'jock?'"

"Athlete. Basketball. Baseball. Football. Didn't want to do much except play sports. I tried for scholarships to college in all three sports. Football coaches said I wasn't big enough. Basketball coaches said I wasn't tall enough. A couple schools offered me baseball scholarships but I wasn't interested in them. So, I went to the University of Kansas. Turned out to be a good choice."

"What was your regimen?"

"Regimen? Oh, major. It was engineering."

"How did you get to newspaper writing from that. Engineering seems too rigid for you."

"You're right it was too rigid. Both my parents were engineers. They wanted me to be one. I didn't have any better ideas . . . so . . . Anyway I was dating a journalism student and went with her when she interviewed a professor who was doing research in macrobiotics. He was trying to make life forms last longer. I was fascinated.

"She told me that in the last two weeks she'd interviewed a paramedic, a bank examiner, and a woman training to be an astronaut. It was something new every day—not boring repetition like in engineering. The next semester I enrolled in journalism school."

"Because she was in journalism?"

"No, we broke up the week after she interviewed the macrobiotics professor. She was angry because I asked the professor more questions than she did. She thought I made her look bad."

"Did you?"

"Maybe. But she was overlooking some obvious questions that I was curious about. I thought other people would be curious, too, so, I asked."

"Inquisitive men are such a turn on to me." She studied me and smiled. "And to a lot of other women I'd bet." She laughed at the surprised look on my face. "How many women have you been with?"

I was speechless and she laughed again. I was on uncharted ground with this woman. She made me rethink everything. It seemed like she was always leading me into quicksand.

"How many?" An even bigger smile.

"I . . . a . . . don't know for sure."

"That's cowboy wimp for lots, is it not?"

"Yes. But I . . ."

"And you were married once, right." It wasn't a question.

I was definitely on uncharted ground with Claudia Isabella. "I thought you said Gypsies weren't fortune tellers."

"We aren't. No one can see the future. But an intelligent women can read the past."

"As in, 'the past is catching up with me?'"

She leaned across the table and whispered: "No. It's the present that's catching up with you."

She kissed me tenderly. Teasingly. I didn't resist. I liked the tender, teasing kiss. I liked it a lot. The kiss grew longer. Hotter.

Then she pulled back. "Right time, cowboy. Wrong place."

She looked out the front window. A gray Peugeot was pulling away. I followed her look and saw the car and the shapes of two men inside it.

"Time to go." She took my hand and led me out to her motorcycle. It had biker saddlebags on the back now. She lifted the flap on one bag to show me the little typewriter. Then she strapped my pack on over the saddlebags and climbed on.

"Mount up, cowboy." She handed me the extra black helmet.

THE BAD GUYS AND
THE UNCLES

Minutes later we were speeding down Highway A13, headed to who knew where. So, naturally, I asked.

"Where are we going?"

"I don't know yet," she said.

It didn't matter. I was in heaven pressed against her back my arms wrapped around her small and tight waist. After all, when you looked at the big picture I was just along for the ride anyway.

In less than an hour she pulled off the road at a little roadside café that offered yellow and white umbrella tables outside. She parked her bike beside one of the tables and we sat down in a lush setting.

Green trees were on three sides, screening out whatever lay between us and the distant, low, darker green, rolling hills. Multicolored flowers bloomed at the base of the trees. Overhead, a blue sky was paled by the thin stratus clouds. A gentle breeze brought the fragrances of the flowers and trees to us. Ah, a French paradise.

A red-faced roly-poly man with a sad, gray-haired comb over came out of the café drying his hands on a bar towel.

His facial expression didn't look like he has having a very good day. It looked like he was suffering from indigestion or domestic distress.

Until he saw Claudia Isabella.

"Rose!" he shouted throwing his arms in the air. He used his best fat-guy hurry-waddle to get to her, spouting excited French on his way. They hugged. He held her at arms length and studied her. "Belle!" He glanced at me.

Claudia Isabella, now Rose, spoke to him in French, occasionally gesturing to me. He threw me a beaming smile, sneezed, wiped his bulbous nose with the back of his hand and waddled back toward the café,

"Rose?" I said.

"What's in a name?" she asked. Her eyes twinkled green flecks.

"As Gertrude Stein said: 'Would a rose by any other name smell the same?'" I said.

She laughed. "'…smell as sweet.' And that was Shakespeare. Stein said: 'A rose is a rose, is a rose, is a rose.'"

"How many names do you have?"

"One for every different group of people I know. It helps remind me who I am, and who I'm supposed to be when I am with them. But to you I am now Rose."

"Until it changes?"

"Until it changes. And of course it will." she said. "What were your parents like?" she asked, changing the subject.

"I couldn't have been luckier. Open, honest, supportive and filled will good advice. Most of the kids in our little town came to Mom and Dad when they needed parental guidance because they couldn't get it at home. Most of the kids were older than

I was and I'd listen. Who knew? Some day I might be able to put that advice to use."

"Did the girls come to your parents, too?"

"They came to Mom mostly. Some wanted a man's view."

"And the girls let you listen, too?"

"The strong, confident ones did. That's probably why I like strong, confident women."

She glanced out at the road. A gray Peugeot was driving past.

"Our chaperons?" I asked.

"You catch on fast. A trait I like in a man." She gave me that glorious smile of hers. A real heart stopper. It also stopped my brain from functioning. I suddenly realized she knew a hell of a lot more about me than I knew about her. I was the investigative reporter and yet I was being out-interviewed.

To be more precise, I was running off at the mouth to impress her. She asked and I told. I wasn't asking enough questions.

The roly-poly man came out of the café carrying a tray with two iced teas, a sugar shaker and two spoons on it. As he reached the table, a black car pulled into the gravel area in front of the café. The occupants just sat there in the car.

The roly-poly man smiled at Claudia Isabella I mean . . . Rose, yakking at her in French as he set the iced teas and sugar dispenser on the table. Then, as he kept up his running dialogue, he polished the two spoons with his bar cloth and sat the spoons in front of us.

I reached for my spoon and Rose laid her hand gently upon mine.

Roly-Poly noticed her loving gesture, smiled, backed away and sneezed. "Pardon," he said wiping his nose on the bar towel. The towel he had just wiped our spoons with. Then he headed back to the café.

I withdrew my hand from the spoon.

"A lot of friends have foibles," she said.

I glanced back at Roly-Poly. He was about half way to the café when two doors opened on the car that had just pulled into the lot. Two men got out. Roly-Poly froze.

"Oh, oh," Rose said, more to herself than to me.

"What?"

"Bad men."

"Like Phillipe's bad men."

She looked at me and raised an eyebrow as if to say 'how did you know?' She glanced at the highway. No doubt looking for the Peugeot. It was nowhere in sight.

I took the old portable typewriter out of the motorcycle's saddlebag and sat it on the table in front of me. It was a way of getting a good look at them without looking suspicious.

Roly-Poly was waving his arms now, his voice getting loud and shrill. The two men looked over at us to see if we could hear. Their attention went back to Roly-Poly. Then one of them did a double take back to us. He elbowed his buddy and pointed to us. All three looked at us.

The two bad men took a step in our direction. Roly-Poly stepped in front of them. They shoved him backwards over a table and onto the ground. They approached us smiling. The smiles were mean smiles. They stopped in front of us.

"Mr. Kelly," Rose said. "Would you leave us? This doesn't concern you."

The one closest to me said: "Yes, Mr. Kelly. This doesn't concern you."

I got up. Picked up the portable typewriter and clutching it to my chest took a step away from the table. A measured step.

They both pulled switchblade knives. There was no subtlety here.

"I think we should give her a wider smile," the one closest to me said.

He must have had good peripheral vision. He was turning toward me, as I was in mid-swing with the typewriter, swinging it as if it were a discus. The typewriter caught him in the eye. Blood sprayed. Typewriter keys flew. And he went down.

The other one turned his attention to me.

I still had the typewriter and I held it in front of me like you'd hold a basketball with two hands. Only I was using it as a shield. I blocked two knife thrusts. On the third thrust I twisted the typewriter. I heard the blade snap. More keys flew through the air. He stepped back. No longer armed. Confused. This wasn't going as planned.

I swung the typewriter like a sidearm fastball and let it go. It hit him square in the chest, knocking the wind out of him. I leaped forward and hit the guy with my best punches. Not too much effect.

I realized there were running footfalls crunching across the gravel behind me. Suddenly I was gripped under each arm and lifted off the ground, struggling for all I was worth. I was pivoted around so I could see Rose. She was slipping a pocketknife into the hip pocket of her jeans.

"Kelly! Quit fighting! It's okay."

I quit struggling and was set down. I turned to see who had grabbed me. It was the big bulk uncle. He smiled at me. I heard a heavy crack and looked over to see the thin dapper uncle shaking his right hand as the remaining bad guy collapsed.

Rose went over to the bulky uncle and kissed him on the cheek. "Uncle Ollie." Then she kissed the other uncle on the cheek. "Uncle Stan." She walked past me on her way to her motorcycle.

I studied her uncles. Uncle Stan and Uncle Ollie? They both smiled at me. It was obvious where she had gotten their names. They looked like Laurel and Hardy. Both uncles nodded at me and pulled up chairs in front of the unconscious bad guys. I couldn't take my eyes off them. How had they gotten here so fast? And from where?

"Kelly." Rose was pulling on her helmet as she climbed onto her Harley. She patted the seat behind her.

I grabbed my helmet and glanced at the ruined typewriter.

"I'll get you a new one," she said.

I climbed on the bike behind her and pulled on my helmet. "What are your uncles going to do to them?"

"Convince them to find a new line of work."

We roared back onto the highway. Heading west again. Holding tight to Claudia Isabella Rose.

"Still no destination?"

"West."

MONT SAINT-MICHEL

Two hours later we skidded to a stop at the shoreline of the Bay Mont Saint-Michel in Normandy. The wind was blowing off the ocean and there was a fine mist in the air. Gulls circled overhead, black *V*'s against a white cloud sky. About a mile out from the shore, completely surrounded by blue-green water' stood Mont Saint-Michel, the famous Gothic abbey and fort.

"It used to be surrounded by water like this all the time," she said. "Now it only happens a couple times a month. I thought you should see it like it used to be."

"Truly beautiful," I said. "And amazing. I've seen pictures of it, probably on calendars. But I don't know much about it."

She leaned back into me and I maintained my grip around her waist. We were both very comfortable. That made it even nicer.

"The original abbey was founded by Saint Aubert in 708. King Philip II destroyed it in 1203." She pointed at the abbey. "This abbey was built sometime in that century I don't know exactly when. I need to find out." She nodded as if making a mental note. Then she reached back past me and got her blue spiral notebook from her saddlebag. The mental note became a written reminder.

"During the Hundred Years' War," she continued, after making her note, "the English attacked it again and again. They always failed. They lost a number of frigates trying to circle behind the fortress. But the passage was too shallow. I've heard, but don't take this for fact, that the English figured tide levels and the draft a ship needed in order to circle behind the fortress. I've heard, again I don't know for sure, that they were building those boats when the war ended." She nodded to herself again. Another mental note? "I need to find out for sure." Again, she made an entry in her notebook.

"You sure know a lot about it."

"When I am interested in something, or someone, I try to find out all I can about it, or him." She pushed back against me as she said the word *him*. Maybe I was just being paranoid about her knowing more about me than I knew about her. Then she scooted forward and kicked the bike back to life. "We need to find a place to spend the night."

That sounded promising.

We roared off in search of a place to spend the night. I wasn't sure why we were looking now because it was just a little after noon. But I didn't ask. I figured I was either being trained or learning when not to ask questions that weren't going to be answered anyway. Learning or being trained? Who cared? I was right where I wanted to be. Holding tight to Claudia Isabella Rose.

HER REAL NAME

About a half an hour later we motored up to the gate of a campground that looked very much like the one where I had met Claudia. But I knew it couldn't be the same one.

"This looks like the campground where I met you."

"All of ours look alike." She turned on her bike seat and looked me dead in the eyes. "We know what we like." I barely heard the words. I just saw *eyes*.

Two little boys in bright colored shirts ran up to the gate, waving at Claudia. Isabella turned around on her seat, waved back and they opened the gate. Rose motored into the campground as the two boys closed the gate behind us. It was getting crowded on the motorcycle. Claudia, Isabella, Rose and I. Two dogs trotted up and flanked all of us as we motored deeper into the campground.

Three large oak trees dominated the rolling terrain. Picnic tables were scattered around. Some in use. Some not. Two concrete block outbuildings were off to the right just like at the other campground. At the far end of the grounds were some tombstones and crosses. I hadn't noticed any at the other campground—but that didn't mean there weren't any.

There was an old Airstream trailer pulled by a newer black Mercedes station wagon. I noted a pop-up trailer, now folded down, behind a battered primer-painted pickup truck. There was a newish white and green VW van with a small pop-up trailer attached. And, there were several European-made cars that I couldn't identify. Each one had a small pop-up trailer hooked to it. The pop-ups were certainly popular.

When I pointed this out to Claudia, she just nodded and smiled as if saying: Don't you get the obvious? Then, aloud: "Cheap privacy for the young family with few possessions."

About a dozen men and women and an equal number of small children came toward us smiling and waving at her. When she climbed off the NSU, they saw me and stopped. The smiles disappeared. But two of them kept coming. One was a short, solid man about forty with salt and pepper hair and a very serious look on his heavily lined face. His nose belonged on a much bigger man.

Trailing him was a tall strikingly handsome man with raven black hair and an olive complexion any woman would kill for. He was about my age. As he got closer I decided he was younger than me. Very muscular. He was obviously the older man's backup.

I climbed off the bike, not knowing what to expect. The two weren't acting real friendly.

The older man said nothing, just worried his big nose angrily until he was about twenty feet away. Then he started spouting angry words at Claudia in a language I couldn't identify.

She raised her hand to silence the man. "In English. He only understands English."

"Kalina," he said. "You don't bring Gaje here." He motioned toward the tombstones. "This is special ground."

"Kalina?" I murmured. Had I actually discovered her real name? I hoped it was. It was the best name of them all.

She nodded at me. "Yes, my name is Kalina."

The older man looked embarrassed. "You hadn't told him?"

"I was going to. I just hadn't decided how or when. Now I don't have to worry about how or when." She planted her fists on her hips. "Do I!?!" It wasn't a question. There was not only anger, but also authority in her voice.

"I apologize," he said. His eyes dropped to the ground. "But he is still Gaje."

Kalina slid her arm around my waist. "Two bad men were going to cut up my face. He stopped them. He's not just Gaje. He is *my Gajo.*"

A smile broke out on the older man's face revealing several missing teeth. And several of his remaining teeth looked like they were at the departure gate.

"Old Jumpy, this is Kelly." She hugged Old Jumpy to her. "Kelly, this is my uncle, Old Jumpy."

Old Jumpy stepped forward and shook my hand. "Welcome to Romani."

The younger man shook my hand. "I'm Mateo. Welcome, Kelly."

A serious look elbowed its way onto Old Jumpy's face. "Are the bad men still looking for you?"

"No," Kalina said. "Uncle Stan and Uncle Ollie are discussing matters with them."

Mateo laughed. "Well, then that's settled."

Old Jumpy laughed, too. "We were just getting ready for the road. You, Cinderella, Mateo and his family will travel in our caravan." He motioned at the Airstream. "Kelly and I will ride up front in the Mercedes and get to know each other a little."

"Old Jumpy." The way Kalina said his name it sounded like a warning.

"I won't tell him anything he shouldn't know."

"Jumpy." This time it wasn't a warning. It was a threat.

"We will travel in silence. A boring way to travel when making friends." He turned and started toward the Mercedes. "But I do it for you because you are my favorite niece." Then he came back and spit on her motorcycle.

I looked at Kalina. "How many uncles do you have?"

She shrugged. "I'm not sure how to explain that to a slow learner."

I was beginning to realize that to the Rom truth was elusive and limited to what you believed at the moment. If you believed anything.

Man, Kalina had nailed it. I was a slow learner. What a dumb question: *How many uncles do you have?* How many uncles can pick pockets on the head of a pin at the same time?

I BECOME GAJO

We were on the road about thirty seconds when Old Jumpy broke the silence.

"Tell me about yourself," he said.

"I thought we were supposed to travel in silence."

"That's what you promised Kalina," said a melodious voice from the back seat.

I hadn't been aware that there was anyone in the car besides Old Jumpy and me. I looked in the back of the Mercedes. There was someone lying on the backseat completely covered with a blanket.

"You promised Kalina silence," the voice said. "And, I need silence so I can get some sleep. I'm certainly not going to get any sleep in the caravan with Mateo and his kids cavorting."

"They are your kids, too," Old Jumpy said.

"Maybe." Cinderella flipped the blanket off and sat up. She was in her late thirties. Dark skinned like Kalina. Raven black hair and, yes, beautiful. Only her hands showed age.

Old Jumpy motioned at the back seat with his head. "That's my wife, Cinderella. Cinderella, Kelly."

"I know who everybody is," she said, rummaging around in an overnight bag. Then to me: "So you rode here from Paris with Kalina. She goes so fast your nerves must be shot." From the overnight bag, she produced a clear bottle with brown liquid inside. She jabbed me in the shoulder with the bottle. "Here. Drink."

"What is it?"

"It is an old Romani secret. It will make you relax and sleep. Then it will be silent in here and I can sleep."

I looked at the brown liquid but made no move to accept it.

She took it back, unscrewed the lid and took a big swallow. "See, it's not poison. Gypsy women don't poison their men—except in movies. In real life we screw them to death. Drink big."

I took a big swallow. Gag! But there was nothing to do but swallow. Gag!

"Some day I will make a better tasting one. Now drink more."

I did. It wasn't as bad as the first swallow. Still bad, just not *as* bad. "Tell me something."

"Anything in particular?" she asked.

I laughed. "When I first met Kalina she called me a Gaje. Then she introduced me to you as 'her Gajo.' What's the difference between Gaje and Gajo? Or is there any difference?"

Old Jumpy laughed and Cinderella snorted and ruffled my hair.

"The Gaje," she said. "They are anyone who is not Rom. A non-Gypsy. But by calling you 'her Gajo" she put you in a different category. It means that you are a non-Gypsy who has helped her in a special way. And that all of us could count on you for help, too. Consequently, you should never be bothered, or tricked or taken advantage of in any way. Now go to sleep so I can get some sleep."

Whatever that brown liquid was it was working. I could hardly keep my eyes open. Cinderella kissed me on the cheek and said something about making babies tomorrow. Old Jumpy laughed and that was the last thing I remembered.

PAPA TWO

The slamming of the Airstream doors woke me. It was night. I'd slept the day away. I must have needed the rest. I saw Mateo and his two boys opening the gate to another campground. Old Jumpy drove in. Two vans and about ten trailers with their towing vehicles were scattered around. Old Jumpy picked an open space and parked.

Kalina tapped on the passenger's window with her blue notebook and signaled for me to get out. "I need to introduce you around."

I climbed out into cool, damp, night air. Campfires speckled the night—looking warm and inviting.

She took me from campsite to campsite introducing me as "*my Gajo.*" I was greeted with smiles and warm handshakes. At one site I was told that my deeds preceded me. At another I was referred to as "the American hero." Each site had a campfire surrounded by dancing shadows in the flickering light. Wine was being shared. Children and dogs were everywhere. There was soft music on portable radios. Occasionally there was a guitar player strumming softly.

At most of the sites someone was enthralling the children with tall tales while the adults just smiled at the outrageousness of the stories.

136

At one campfire, a tall thin man acted out his tale as he spun it for the children. Kalina nestled into me and subtly nodded her head at the man. His eyes flashed from child to child from beneath his black, flat brimmed hat. He gestured with fluid movements that made his bones seem liquid.

When we returned to our campsite Mateo and Old Jumpy were just getting a fire started. Cinderella came over to Kalina and whispered: "Old Bohemius is here. Did you see him?"

"No. How is he?"

"Not well. And he refuses treatment," Cinderella said, rolling her eyes. "He's going to Lourdes instead."

"I'll talk to him," Kalina said.

"You're the only one who can."

Mateo and Old Jumpy looked expectantly at Kalina. Old Jumpy pantomimed taking a drink. Kalina walked to the rear of the Airstream where her bike was mounted and took a bottle of scotch from her bike's saddlebag and handed it to Mateo. He bowed and he and Jumpy wandered off toward guitar music. "See you in awhile," he said.

"Oh, great," Cinderella said. "Now I'll have to keep them away from the young women." And she marched off after them.

I looked at Kalina. "Looks like you made her mad."

"It's an act. A game they play," she said. "The Rom love playing games. But the greatest game is fooling the Gaje."

"Like picking his pocket. Or, telling me a wrong name."

"Sure. Why not."

"What's the story behind Cinderella and Old Jumpy? At first I thought they were married."

"They are."

"But she said Mateo's boys were hers."

"They are sort of," Kalina smiled. "Mateo's wife was killed in an auto accident. Cinderella helps raise the boys. She's their Momma now. It's only natural."

"Why is it natural?"

"Cinderella is Mateo's mother."

"How old is she?"

"Who cares?"

I thought about that for a few seconds. "How silly of me to ask."

"You are catching on."

"So do we have a plan?"

She laughed at me. "I thought you were catching on. Gypsies don't make plans. We just do." She walked over to the Mercedes station wagon's tailgate, opened it, dragged out a mattress and a double sleeping bag. "It will get cold tonight. But I guess you know that, he-who-sleeps-in-ditches." She smiled and winked.

Kalina put the sleeping bag on the mattress and sat down on it. She patted the sleeping bag beside her. I sat. "So what's it like growing up a Gypsy?" I asked. "I mean, I've heard stories about Gypsies stealing things and stealing children."

"Stealing is the license of the road. But stealing *children*!?! Look around. We've got too many as it is. But it makes the Gaje watch their children when they should be watching their billfolds and purses."

We both laughed.

"Actually," she went on. "It was fun growing up. Always on the move. New towns. New sights. New marks."

Kalina's face brightened as a memory came back to her. "I remember one Sunday I had to baby-sit my cousin. I was eight. She was one. We were in Lyon. I heard church bells and it suddenly occurred to me that Roman Catholic priests gave money to a baby after baptism to start the baby out in life." She laughed, delighted with her cunning. "I hit eight churches that Sunday and had the baby baptized eight times. After that I begged baby-sitting jobs every Sunday. I made a bundle."

"How did you get interested in languages?"

"Well, there are four major Gypsy tribes. The *Lowara*, *Kaldaerasha*, *Matchvaya* and *Tshurara*. Each has its own traits. Old Jumpy and his family are *Lowara*. Mostly a matriarchal society. They are generally stocky people who wear bright colors. See the guitar player over there. *Sinti*. They are another story. Sort of Rom sort of not. Short and short tempered. A lot of musicians. The women usually dress in black. And see the tall, thin, mean-looking guy over there? He's *Tshurara*. Generally, they are dirtier than most. And watch out for their women. Very seductive."

I was sure I knew before I asked. But I had to ask. "And which tribe are you?"

"*Tshurara*. But you guessed that didn't you."

"I did," I said.

Kalina laughed that magical laugh of hers. "Anyway, I was maybe ten when I realized the different tribes, who are from different places, spoke the same language but it is made up of many different foreign words. I was fascinated. I taught myself the language of whatever country we were in."

"Is any of that true?"

"Sure. You're my Gajo now. I can't lie to you."

Suddenly, a tall, tough-looking man appeared out of the
night. He wore an iron gray suit, a faded red dress shirt
buttoned at the neck and a fedora pushed recklessly back on
his head. He was about fifty. A knife cut on his chin made him
look dangerous. He had the eyes of a devil. He glared at me,
obviously sizing me up. Then he knelt and embraced Kalina
for a long moment before standing up again.

"So this is your Gajo."

"That's right."

"Not a very tough one it seems.

"There were two of them," Kalina said.

"Just two? And he needed help?"

"I did okay." I told him. "They had knives and I had a
typewriter. They didn't stand a chance."

"So I heard." The old man laughed explosively.

I held out my hand. "Kelly," I said.

He just stared at my hand and made no move to shake it.

I slowly let it drop to my side. He extended his hand. I
reached for it and he let his hand drop to his side.

"Gaje are so easy," he said and this time shook my hand.
He exploded into laughter again. But this time it turned to a
hacking rattle.

Kalina stood and hugged him again. "I want you to get the
treatments."

"I'm going to Lourdes."

"Why won't you take your treatments?"

"I wouldn't be . . . being me."

Then I saw a new side of Kalina. Hair-trigger raging fury.
"God damn it! You better do what I tell you!"

The old man turned away laughing and disappeared into the night. But his voice came back to us. "Watch out, Gajo. She's just like her mother."

"You old fool!" Kalina shouted at him.

"See you later." He called back.

We could hear him laugh. I looked over at her and saw tears flowing down her cheeks. She wiped them away quickly. Brusquely. Angrily.

"I take it that was your father?"

"Who else could make me so angry?" She said scooting a little closer to me on the sleeping bag.

Just then four young boys appeared out of the dark. Each was carrying an armload of wood. Kalina smiled at them and pointed at the fire pit. None of them said a word. They just went to work setting up a campfire and left without lighting it.

But they didn't go far. I could hear them whispering although I couldn't make out what was being said. I glanced over at Kalina and discovered that she was studying me. She gave me a Popsicle grin. At least that's how my uncle described that type of grin.

When I had asked him what he meant by it he said: "Picture a little girl running through a yard sprinkler in her good dress. She knows she shouldn't be doing it. But it is just too much fun to resist. That devilish light in her eyes and the mischievous grin, that's what makes a Popsicle grin. Now, when you see a woman grin that grin, you are in for trouble—and you have no idea how bad. Just keep your mouth shut and be leery."

Unk knew a lot about women. He had lots of experience. He was married to six different women. Two of them twice.

So, I kept my mouth shut and waited to see what was going to happen. I could tell she was a bit surprised that I wasn't asking questions. But occasionally I learn from past mistakes.

About a minute later a couple in their early thirties came out of the gloom and sat opposite the fire pit. They smiled at Kalina and nodded politely at me. They were just the first. More just kept coming. Twenty-five, thirty, maybe forty of them. They sat in a semi-circle around us.

The boys returned and this time they lighted the campfire.

I'd glance at Kalina and she'd give me her Popsicle grin and I tried to anticipate what I was about to encounter.

It was a test. What else could it be?

Then Old Bohemius returned out of the dark carrying a new bottle of scotch and three glasses. He smiled at me and sat down with Kalina between us. He opened the scotch; poured a drink, handed it to Kalina. He poured a second and handed it to me. As he poured a third, I heard wine bottles popping in the dark and bottles clinking against glasses as drinks were poured. Old Bohemius raised his glass in a toast. "To new friends."

"Bahtalo drom," the crowd responded.

We drank the toast.

Kalina got to her feet. "Most of you have heard of my American Gajo. Kelly is my Kansas cowboy. He writes for newspapers with some success because I've seen the checks." There were murmurs of approval. "But he wants to write books." No response to that. Interesting.

"I don't know if he is any good at making money with that type of writing." Smiles. "But he is good at making money drawing cartoons with chalks on the sidewalk." Light applause. It was obvious that making money was important to these people. It had to be. Most of the standard employment routes were out of bounds for them.

"Another thing I can tell you about him. He's a good storyteller." Enthusiastic ahhs. "That's the reason we are here tonight." She gave her Popsicle grin. "He started telling me about why and how he got here and I told him to wait and tell everyone. She gave me that grin again. "Kelly."

So, that was it. Sort of a trial by fire. I took a slug of the scotch, sat the glass down and stood up.

I really hadn't expected this. Wasn't ready for it. But, what the hell.

I looked out at the faces lighted by the flickering flames of the campfire. They were smiling. It was a lot like being on a stage in a club. The audience wanted you to succeed. They wanted to be entertained. It was story time and I did love telling stories.

"I wanted to come to Europe for as long as I can remember. My Dad's two sides of the family came from Scotland and France. Mom's relatives came to America from Ireland and the other half were already there."

That got frowns and cocked heads, trying to figure that out.

"The other side of Mom's family was Cherokee Indians."

Ahhs and smiles. They got it.

If you wander in storytelling, you can lose your audience in the blink of an eye. So, I set up my story about my trip over on the freighter as quickly as possible and got to the point.

"Three days out of port we hit a huge spring storm. We started to sail south around it. Then we got a distress call. Another ship was going down. A freighter with forty-seven crewmen." They were interested now.

"The freighter was breaking up in the heavy seas. It was carrying Volkswagens from Hamburg to New York. And unlike the claims made in Volkswagen ads, VW's don't float.

"The heart wrenching reality was that half of our crew were friends with half of their crew. We had to go save them. Our captain threw caution to the wind and headed directly into the storm in an effort to save his friends."

I could see that I had them hooked.

"When we first caught sight of the freighter, it was several miles away and listing to the aft. The closer we got the more infrequently we saw the ship because huge waves were blocking our vision. But each time we caught a glimpse of it the bow was higher out of the water. It was sinking fast.

"When we arrived, the freighter was gone. There were only five men in a raft being tossed about by huge waves. Everyone else had been lost. Unfortunately, a Cunard passenger liner had arrived first.

"According to the 'The Law of the Sea' the first ship to arrive at a disaster is in charge of the rescue. That put the Cunard liner in charge. But, it was riding too high in the water to make the rescue. Its deck was a hundred and fifty feet above the ocean's surface. There was no way they could reach the men in that raft. Our Captain told the Cunard captain that we were riding so low in the sea that we could wash the raft up onto our deck. However, if Cunard allowed that, they would be giving us *lead ship rights*, which translated into *salvage rights*. Cunard refused.

"It was a stupid issue. There was nothing to salvage. The freighter was on the bottom of the Atlantic. The VW's were on the bottom of the Atlantic. Most of the crew was on the bottom of the Atlantic. The only things to be salvaged were five lives. Still, Cunard refused to give up the salvage rights.

"The Captain called me on the ship's echoing intercom and asked me to come up to the bridge. 'Be careful. Time the waves,' he said.

"There was a steel ladder with round rungs from the first deck to the bridge." I pantomimed climbing the ladder. "My timing wasn't so good. I got hit by a wave half way up the ladder. The force of it was amazing. It ripped my right foot and arm off the rungs." I threw my right arm and leg out at an angle and swung around as if hit by the wave. I got some "Ooos." My left hand was stretched back as if gripping the ladder.

"The ship rolled on its side and suddenly I was dangling in mid-air with the angry ocean below me." I twisted and grabbed the imaginary ladder with my right hand. "I was a high bar gymnast in high school and college and I knew how to hang onto a round bar. And, I hung on for dear life. When the ship rolled back upright I scrambled up the ladder and into the bridge just as the next wave crashed over the ship.

"I was wet and freezing cold. I couldn't imagine being in that raft.

"The captain brought me up to date in a hurry. 'You're a smart kid,' the captain said. 'Got any ideas? Those men are going to die if we don't do something.'

"At first I didn't know what to say. The only things I really knew anything about were sports and newspapering. Those avenues didn't seem to offer much hope. Then I got an idea.

"What if we say to hell with the law of the sea and just go get them?"

The Gypsies liked that idea.

"But the captain looked down at the deck and shook his head. "I would lose my license." The radioman said something to the captain and the captain said to me: "My entire crew would lose their licenses,"

"I thought through the myriad of part-time and summer jobs that I'd held in college but none of those offered any hope either. Then I got an off-the-wall idea.

"Maybe a long shot."

"Anything."

"Can you patch me through to UPI New York? Maybe we can put some media pressure on Cunard," I suggested, naïvely.

"The radio operator, a gaunt Norwegian with silver hair, went to work with his telegrapher's key. In seconds, he was in contact with UPI. "I have them Captain," he said.

"Tell them our situation. Tell them we have a reporter on board."

"Seconds later I was dictating the story to UPI through our radio operator, who remained expressionless through it all. My words went in his ear and out his fingers as fast as I could talk. The UPI editor responded that the story would be on the wire in a matter of minutes and maybe that would put pressure on Cunard to let us go in. I told him I was taking pictures, too, but had no way of developing them at sea. The editor said he wanted the story and photos. He didn't ask for an exclusive. So, after we disconnected, I asked if the radio operator could patch me through to AP in New York.

"Again, the captain set up the scene and I dictated the story.

"Both large wire services contacted Cunard and asked why we weren't allowed to make the rescue. Both services were pushing the corporate greed angle. But Cunard held firm to its position.

We waited.

"We watched huge waves toss the raft around like a tennis ball. We watched and waited and prayed that Cunard would let us go in and save those five men. Cunard never called.

"We watched the five men freeze to death in the raft. Even though we were sure they were dead, we continued to watch, hoping for a miracle. Hoping for a sign of life. Finally, a wave capsized the raft. And, the five men joined the rest of their crewmates on the bottom of the Atlantic Ocean.

"Our hard as nails captain cried.

"The impassive radio operator cried.

"And ol' tough-guy-me cried.

"I had sold my first stories since leaving the States. I would have done anything to have taken those sales back."

There was a mass exhalation of air, followed by sighs and groans and the Gypsies began getting up. Some came forward to shake my hand or put a comforting hand on my shoulder. Then they drifted off into the night.

I walked over and sat down beside Kalina on the unrolled, green sleeping bag. "I guess I didn't go over very well."

"Are you kidding?" She kissed me on the cheek. "You were great."

"But it is such a sad story."

"Gypsies expect real. They appreciated honesty. There can be no heroics. That would not have been real." She kissed me on the lips, lingering. "I was proud of you."

She kissed me again. Longer. Our tongues flirting. It lit me up.

She drew back and winked at me. "Of course they will expect more stories from you. Word travels."

She held out what looked like that medicine bottle Cinderella had given me. "Drink your medicine. It will help ward off the cold. You'll sleep out here tonight. I'll sleep inside."

She caught the disappointed look on my face. "What? You thought you were getting lucky? On a first date? What kind of girl do you think I am?"

I took a sip of the medicine and didn't gag. "Is this the same stuff?"

"Cinderella likes you. She mixed in mint so it would taste better and who knows what else. She wanted to be a pharmacist and now she is one," she laughed. "Of sorts. We all appreciate the things she can do. She is sort of our own Merlin."

She laughed again as she walked over to the trailer, opened the Airstream's door and looked back at me. "Get some sleep, Gajo. Tomorrow there will be a wedding here. You'll need your energy."

I took another slug of the medicine, crawled into the sleeping bag. Alone. I looked up at the stars and thought about the evening and the storytelling. How I might have made the story better. I thought about the things that I might have added to the storytelling that would have made it a fuller experience for the listeners.

As I lay there looking up at the stars, they seemed to get brighter.

Then I heard Kalina's words again: "Of course, they will expect more stories from you. Word travels."

My mind started spinning. More stories. I had more. Lots more. I thought about the day I spent with Senator Jack Kennedy, his brother Bobby, and the future governor of Kansas. Just the four of us joking around and having fun.

And there was the time I met Martin Luther King, Jr.

And there was the time I had dinner with the head of Kansas City's mafia. At his home. Only three years after he tried to have me killed.

And the time I went to interview an inmate on death row at Leavenworth. A guy I knew. And as the guard was leading me to his cell I hear "Hi, Kelly." Three guys on death row and I know two of them. What are the odds!?!

The stars were getting brighter and brighter. Neon like. Taking on colors where there were no colors before. They began forming constellations that were faces from other stories.

Like the couple who set fire to their house with their baby inside so they could collect on the baby's life insurance.

Like the out of work, in-debt father, who killed his wife, his 11-year-old son, his 15-year-old daughter and himself so they wouldn't have to suffer through the disgrace of his financial ruin. It was my first violent crime scene. The daughter was still alive when the two detectives and I got there.

"Why did Daddy do this?" she asked, blood bubbles coming out of the holes in her chest. We didn't have an answer. "Am I going to be okay?"

"Yes," we lied.

They were the last words she ever said.

Thinking about her still makes me want to cry.

Damn it, I had a thousand stories to tell them and they were all playing out against a sky of pulsating stars. And I was running all these stories through my head simultaneously. I needed to think of something lighter.

Like the night in Copenhagen when the three-month beer strike ended and the whole city went crazy. So many people were wandering through the streets carrying six-packs and cases of beer that the police blocked off the streets and joined the party. And I could see it all in the sky above me.

Man, I'd never experienced anything like this. It had to be a combination of nerves and exhaustion and fear of failing in front of Kalina's friends and relatives. And yet it was all so vivid and colorful.

It had to be a dream. Or was I still half awake?

I had learned a long time ago that when you were having a strange dream, one that could border on a nightmare, the best thing to do was lie back and enjoy it.

So, that's what I did. I lay there in my sleeping bag, focusing on the stars and the stories. Some of the people in the stories began smiling and waving at me. As if they were beckoning for me to follow them.

I remember thinking that seemed like a pretty good idea. And I just sort of fell into the sky and the remembrances of those stories.

NO THANK YOUS, PLEASE

When I awoke in the morning Kalina was sitting on the sleeping bag right beside me. The bright, silver, early-morning sun hung in a transparent blue sky behind her and turned her into a glossy black silhouette.

All colors were extremely vivid this morning, almost as overwhelming as they had been in last night's dream. The trees were myriad shades of green. The cars and trailers in the campground glistened as if they had all been hand washed and waxed during the night. Everything was so vivid that it was strangely unsettling.

"Good morning, Gajo," she whispered. "Sleep well?"

Kalina leaned forward and gave me a gentle kiss. It made my lips tingle.

I tried to return the kiss but she pulled back. Same game as last night.

"Now that I have your attention, I need to tell you a few things," she whispered. Even though she was whispering, her whisper seemed to have an echo. "As long as you are traveling with my people you need to know that there is a *Gypsy way* of doing things. Yesterday you thanked Cinderella for her medicine. Gypsies don't thank people until we are ready to leave. And then we don't say thank you. We say: Bahtalo Drom. It means: "Lucky Road." Thank yous are embarrassing."

"Okay."

"In the morning we don't look at each other or make eye contact or talk to one another until we are finished eating."

"Why is that?"

"Since we live so close to each other, this is how we give each other privacy. And show respect."

"Interesting," I whispered back. "I'll probably drive you crazy with questions about these things."

"You expect to be given answers?" She laughed her laugh, softly. "Save your breath." She swatted me playfully with one of the two towels she was holding. "Pay attention. All answers are there to be seen."

"What was I thinking?"

She laughed again. It was such a great sound to wake up to. Last night's extraordinarily vivid dreams seemed to be carrying over in sounds and colors into this morning. It was really strange.

"You see the two buildings over there?" She pointed at the two concrete block structures. Yesterday they had just been gray concrete. Today they appeared almost glossy. In fact, everything seemed glossy.

I nodded yes. And blinked my eyes. They were still glossy.

"The one on the left houses the showers. Men and boys enter on the left side. Women and girls enter on the right. The building on the right contains the toilets. Same deal. Men enter left side, women on the right.

"As you enter the shower building there is a small dressing room. On the walls are hooks for your clothes and your towel."

She tossed me one of the towels she had been holding. "Inside, it is just one big room. Men shower on the right hand wall, which is the one nearest us. Women shower on the far wall. There will be some beautiful women showering while you are. Do not look or stare."

"That will be hard."

"Yes, but you are a stranger and you are being accepted as my Gajo. Don't screw that up. Honor our ways. Live Gypsy ways. Not Gaje. Be true to me. Don't embarrass me."

"I promise."

"Good. Time to shower. No more talk."

"Until after we eat," I said.

"Shhhhh."

We were up and strolling toward the showers. I smelled old smoke from last night's campfires and fresh smoke from this morning's cook fires. I smelled coffee. The camp was alive with smells that I had not noticed last night. I could almost taste the foods I smelled. But food wasn't all I smelled. I smelled leaking gasoline and oil from the old cars and trucks. I smelled lingering exhaust fumes from vehicles that had already departed. And, I smelled me.

All my senses seemed to be working overtime. I heard birds in the trees and the hiss of tires on the road outside the Gypsy campground. I heard an occasional dog whimper or bark. But they were good Gypsy dogs for the most part. They whispered their barks and whimpers.

The thought made me start to laugh but I quashed it into a soft snicker. Not soft enough apparently and Kalina gave me a sharp elbow to the ribs.

The glossy, gray concrete-block shower building loomed ahead. A test? A threat or a treat? Funny—there is only a one-letter difference between *threat* and *treat*. An *h*. I fought off a snicker. Everything seemed funny to me.

I just wasn't hitting on all cylinders this morning—or maybe on a couple too many. It was hard to tell.

Kalina gave me a warning glare and veered off to the right. I veered left. Two older men entered the building several yards ahead of me.

The entry room of the showers was exactly as she had described it. A dressing room with several dozen hooks on the walls in groups of two. More than half of the groups of hooks held clothes on one and a towel on the other.

The two men who were in front of me were undressing as I entered. They moved to the back of a short line of naked men. I hung my towel on a hook and began to disrobe. As I did a man came out of the shower area, got his towel and began drying off. The guy in the front of the line went into the main shower room, which I still could not see.

Two more men left, the two in front of me entered and I could see the shower room. It was exactly as Kalina had described it. One big open oblong room with about a dozen showers on each of the two long walls.

Having played lots of sports I was used to showering with other men present. But I wasn't used to a bunch of naked ladies on the other side of the room. And, they seemed to glow. I didn't look. What I mean is, I tried not to look. I mean, glowing naked women!?! Some gorgeous. I really mean gorgeous. Even the older ones were hot. What was wrong with me? I was trying not to act crazy. But what I wanted to do was rip off my clothes and race across the room and . . . But I didn't have any clothes to rip off. I tried not to look. Of course, I wanted to. But I didn't. Much. I hoped Kalina wasn't waiting for me with a baseball bat.

When I came out of the showers Kalina was waiting for me. She wore a black leather jacket with a frilly white blouse under it and faded jeans she'd been poured into. Jeans that were guaranteed to make my jeans fit tighter—and they did.

She took my hand and led me back to our campsite. I couldn't believe how weird I was feeling—but she didn't seem to notice.

Cinderella was scrambling eggs when we got there. She was even prettier than I had first thought—and maybe older, too. She wore a low-cut frilly white blouse that you could practically see through. An ankle-length purple skirt clung to every curve of her body. It was hard to take my eyes off her—and she could tell.

Old Jumpy, Mateo and his boys were eating, eyes downcast as if each were alone. Cinderella dished up two plates, piled on biscuits and handed them to us. She gave me a wink and a sexy smile along with the plate. I resisted saying thank you and ate in silence.

The food was exceptionally tasty. Hell, it was fantastic. I shoveled it down like a starving man. I noticed that Kalina was giving me a strange look and I slowed down, trying to eat more gentlemanly. But, damn, it tasted great!

When I finished eating I glanced around the campground. Yesterday I didn't know what I was seeing. Today, what I was seeing had new meaning. It was the Gypsies' morning ritual in progress. Although today I wasn't sure I was seeing what I was seeing. Everything seemed so exaggerated.

Cook fires and grills were burning. Light smoke was hanging in sun-dappled air that was still slightly moist from the night before. People were flowing into the shower and the toilet buildings. People were moving about in silence, eyes downcast. Respecting each other's privacy.

It was a close look at a microcosm of society that most Gaje never experience.

At the same time, it was like watching a movie with heightened colors, distorted sounds and permeated with the odors of everything. The leaves, the food, the smoke, the dogs, the autos, the people. Truly everything.

Cinderella slipped up behind me and gently placed her hands on my neck and shoulders. I almost jumped out of my skin. Then she began to massage my neck and shoulder and the meat damn near fell off my bones.

If she asked me to run away with her, I was ready. I was so turned on I couldn't think straight.

I stole a glance at Cinderella. God, she was looking hot this morning.

I shot a glance at Kalina and she was seething.

Kalina gave a sharp hiss and Cinderella chuckled and backed away from me. What was going on?

Kalina scooted over to me and stared into my eyes. One second I was ready to run away with Cinderella and now I was tumbling into Kalina's gold and green, bottomless eyes. She smiled and hugged me. "Poor baby," she whispered into my ear. "Cinderella's been playing games with you."

"I don't understand," I whispered back.

She placed her forefinger on my lips. "Only the teacher is allowed to speak." Then she pointed at two reddish brown squirrels chasing each other through a gnarled old oak. "Study them," she whispered.

I watched the two squirrels chase each other through the oak freeway system, the sun glistening off the red hairs in their coats. Tails pumping. One hundred and eighty degree spins. The same one was always in the lead. The other always the pursuer. What was the chase about? Was it territorial? Had one invaded the other's nest? Stolen nuts? Stolen the other's mate? What else did squirrels steal from each other? Maybe it was a game. Squirrel tag? Kick the can?

I started chuckling at that idea. Even though it really wasn't that funny.

"What do you think they are doing?" Kalina asked in a whisper.

"Too many possibilities to hazard a guess." I started chuckling again. Trying to keep it as quiet as possible, which only made me laugh a little louder. "How am I supposed to know what a squirrel is thinking?" I started chuckling again. Although I didn't know why I thought it was so funny. It just seemed like everything was funny.

"I like the way he thinks." Cinderella whispered. She was back, standing right behind Kalina, trying to keep from smiling. Whatever it was that I thought was funny, was obviously funny to her, too.

Kalina spun around and snapped something in whispered Romani at Cinderella. Her face was pinched and angry. I started to laugh, but knew better.

Cinderella fired back in silent, mouthed Romani, a smile on her face. She shrugged at Kalina with a palms up gesture.

Kalina snarled a couple more words in Romani, without raising her voice above a whisper.

Cinderella smiled and held a forefinger to her own lips to quiet Kalina. It only made Kalina angrier.

"Girls. Girls," I whispered through my chuckles. "You are supposed to speak English in front of me. It is only polite." I started laughing again. "At least that is the way I understand it."

Kalina transferred her glare from Cinderella to me. Then her glare turned into a smile. "I called her a bitch," she said softly.

"And, I apologized," Cinderella said so softly I had to lean forward to hear her. "I did not know that you were not sleeping together."

"And, I said it was none of her business."

I looked back and forth between them. I was missing a whole lot here. I wondered how long I had been missing out on whatever was going on. And, there was no doubt about it, I was not thinking straight. It was like a hangover—except it was extremely cool.

Cinderella winked at me. Then she turned, started walking away, but came back to whisper: "I trust you had wonderful dreams last night, Gajo. Just think what it might have been if you weren't sleeping alone." She patted my cheek and walked off.

I looked at Kalina. She smiled at me. "How are you feeling this morning," she whispered.

I didn't know what to say. "A little . . . unusual." I thought about how things seemed so intense this morning. The colors brighter. The smells . . . The sounds . . .

"What was in that stuff she gave me last night?"

"Only Cinderella knows for sure. Probably some ancient aphrodisiac. Maybe cactus flowers. Maybe lysergic acid diethylamide. Her potions often carry over to the next day before wearing off." She motioned with her head to my left.

I looked. Cinderella was leaning sexily against a twisted pin oak ten or fifteen yards away. She blew a kiss our way and smiled.

Kalina laughed softly and blew one back.

Cinderella pointed at Kalina, frowned and shook her head. Then she pointed at me, blew another kiss and subtly and suggestively flexed her hips.

Kalina got to her feet. She was no longer smiling. I had no idea where this was heading. One second they seemed serious. The next they were joking. Then they were serious again.

I knew that I wasn't running on all cylinders. Whatever Cinderella had put in that medicine still had me in deep left field. So, I couldn't really be sure what was going on between them.

Kalina took my hand, pulled me to my feet and gave me a push toward Cinderella.

I felt like a peace offering.

Cinderella raised both hands and waved them at Kalina as if to say: You keep him. Then she turned and walked away showing plenty of "sashay."

I couldn't take my eyes off her.

Kalina tapped me on the shoulder, getting my attention. Then she motioned with her head for me to follow her. I realized that Gypsies communicated as much with gestures, head nods and looks as they did with words. Words let the Gaje know what was going on. The unspoken communications went by the Gaje unnoticed unless he was really paying attention.

I wondered if this whole thing had been a demonstration for my benefit. They did love playing games and playing jokes on each other. And they both knew they had me at a serious mental disadvantage.

Kalina led me to the Airstream, opened the door, reached in and withdrew a pile of men's clothes. "For you to wear at the wedding." She thrust the clothes into my arms.

'Where did you find them?"

"Here and there."

"You stole them?"

"It's the license of the road. And Mateo found you a new typewriter." She laughed. "It's fun finding things. If you didn't sleep so late you could find things, too. Early morning is the best time to find things. Or late night. Or in the bright sunlight. It depends on what needs to be found."

"How do you know they'll fit?"

"I checked you out in the showers."

"I didn't think you were supposed to look."

"A good Gypsy woman needs to check out her Gajo . . . to make sure the 'found' clothes will fit. We may have to take the pants in a little in the crotch," she laughed.

She patted the clothes that she had handed me and head-nodded toward the Airstream trailer. I went inside. I didn't find the clothes to my liking. A gray, coarse wool suit. A bright yellow shirt. A screaming red scarf.

I came out of the trailer and spread my arms as if modeling. "Somehow it isn't me," I said.

Kalina stepped forward and buttoned the top button of my shirt.

Damn, I knew that. Funny what observations never make it from your eye to your brain. I'd never seen a Gypsy man who had an open throat on his shirt. But I hadn't thought about it.

Kalina stepped back and appraised me. "At least now you don't stand out like a sore thumb. Now you look Rom." She muffled a snicker. "Sort of." Then she adjusted my red scarf. "That's how you wear your *diklo*."

"I feel silly dressed like this."

"You've got to do your best to look and act Rom. You'll never fool the Rom. But you might fool the Gaje. You don't want to draw attention to yourself. I'll coach you along."

"Sort of 'My Fair Gajo'?"

"Everything means something." She took the lapels of my gray suit. "This is *Tshurara*. For me." She flipped the collar of the yellow shirt. "This is *Lowara*. For Old Jumpy and his family."

"And the red scarf?"

"It means you are available and looking. And I will take it from you before the night is over." She smiled. "I told you last night that today you'd need your energy."

My heart skipped a beat and she laughed at me. Then she reached into the Airstream and pulled out a gray felt fedora and handed it to me.

"I'm really not the hat type," I said. "Unless it's a baseball hat."

"Look around. All Rom men wear hats all the time. They only take them off when they are sick."

"What's the custom behind that?"

"No one knows. It's just the way it is."

As I put on the hat, which actually felt good, Old Jumpy shouldered his way by me with an armload of things. He put them in the trailer.

He looked me in the eyes. "We go." His black eyes were hard. Angry. His left eye twitched.

I didn't blame him. I'd be pissed, too, if my woman had come on like Cinderella did with me. But Kalina was reading me like an open book.

"It's not about you," she whispered.

Cinderella grabbed my shoulder and moved me to the side. "You are in the way, Gajo." She climbed into the trailer with some cooking utensils. Mateo followed her carrying some other items. I didn't see what they were.

"What is happening?" I asked

"Be quiet," Kalina said softly. "It is time for you to be Gypsy."

I took another step out of the way as Mateo's two boys entered the Airstream carrying camping and cooking stuff. Then Mateo and Cinderella climbed down out of the trailer. Mateo stepped up to me and gave me an appraising once over.

"Get more sun," Mateo said. "Your skin needs to be darker to pass as Gypsy." He flipped the brim of my hat and patted me on the cheek. "Take good care of Kalina, my brother." And Mateo climbed back into the Airstream.

Cinderella stepped forward and threw her arms around me. She was stronger than I expected and she crushed me to her. She kissed me passionately, her tongue everywhere. She ground her body against me. I heard Kalina laugh. But Cinderella didn't let up until she knew I was totally aroused. Then she stepped back, winked at me, patted my crouch and said: "Good Gajo."

I felt like a dog being told "Good boy."

Kalina still found it funny. She laughed again.

Cinderella climbed into the Airstream, started to draw the door shut behind her and stopped. "When you get tired of her, and you will, there is room in my caravan." She closed the door.

I realized Old Jumpy was standing only a couple of feet away while his wife had been sticking her tongue down my throat and grinding her body against mine. I didn't know how he'd react. I didn't know what to expect. I glanced at Kalina and she didn't seem concerned.

Old Jumpy stepped in front of me, hooked his finger in the pocket of my yellow shirt and ripped it. Oh, boy! I was obviously in deep shit. A thousand thoughts were racing through my mind. This man had been good to me. And . . .

He smiled. *"Te khlaion tai to shingerjon tshe gada, haj tu te trais sastimasa tai voyas a."* He patted my cheek, flicked the brim of my hat and started for his Mercedes. "Bahtalo Drom," he called over his shoulder.

I looked at Kalina she was moving her lips, like I should say something. "Bahtalo Drom," I said.

He nodded, climbed into his Mercedes station wagon and drove off hauling his Airstream trailer.

I looked at Kalina. "What just happened?"

"A number of things," Kalina said. "When he ripped you shirt pocket he said 'May your clothes rip and wear out, but may you live on in good health and in fulfillment.' He gave you his blessing. Mateo said you are his brother. And, what Cinderella was saying I'm sure you got."

"Why are they leaving? I though there was a wedding."

"Old Jumpy and the bride's father are not on good terms. It would be disrespectful to stay."

"Why aren't they on good terms?"

"Not your business." She shook her head at me like she was saying 'you ask too many questions.' "Come, Gajo. We have a wedding to attend. But, before that we have to exorcise whatever Cinderella put in you."

EXORCISING IS FUN

I really didn't have any idea what form Kalina's exorcism of Cinderella's special mixture might take. I was hoping it would be working it out of my system in the way it was intended. Too much to hope for? Maybe. But a guy can hope, can't he?

My hopes soared when she took my hand and smiled at me. They sank just as quickly as she said: "I've got some people I want you to meet."

As she led me over to the closest campsite, I noticed that more cars were coming into the campground than were leaving. Generally the morning was an exodus period.

I was watching the influx of cars, campers and caravans and not where I was going. Kalina stuck out an arm and stopped me just before I stepped into an empty guitar case. The couple in front of me stared at me like I was an idiot. I felt like one.

She was short, dark and dumpy but a big friendly smile crept over her face. He was light skinned, lean, mean and angry looking. He stood up like a snake uncoiling. I had the feeling he'd seen "The Magnificent Seven" too many times.

He had probably studied every move James Coburn used to transfer his knife from one hand to the other. I could tell by the way he spun his guitar in his right hand as he transferred it to his left. He glared at me and nodded at my automatically offered right hand—but he didn't shake it.

"Kelly," Kalina said, smiling at the pudgette. "This is LeRosa, my cousin. A magnificent cook and a truly dependable friend in time of need."

I knew better than to offer a woman my hand. I'd made that mistake before. So, I gave her my best smile, a proper bow and felt like a fool. I saw "James Coburn" roll his eyes, which told me I had a right to feel foolish. Everything seemed to be moving in slow motion and I felt even more awkward.

"Cinderella gave him one of her potions last night," Kalina said, by way of explaining my actions.

"Poor boy," LeRosa said throwing her arms around me and rocking me in a motherly hug. "There's not much we can do about that. But we can try"

Then "Coburn" gave off something between a hoot and a laugh and offered his hand. We shook. "You tell a good story," he said. "Ever think about writing lyrics?"

I nodded to him. Naturally I had thought about it when living in a place like Folk House. I tried to think how to explain it to him but could not come up with the right words.

Kalina and LeRosa began talking about the upcoming wedding while LeRosa tossed what looked like tea leaves into a pottery mug, added boiling water and honey. She sampled the tea, added some more tea leaves from a different bag and sampled it again. She smiled and offered the mug to Kalina, who took a sip, nodded and handed it back to her. LeRosa poured the contents through a strainer into another mug.

All the time that I was fixated with LeRosa's project, the "Coburn" was yammering away about music.

"Call me Picker," the guitar player said. "You'd never get my real name right."

"I can try."

"Utamahaquasm."

"Picker works for me," I said. Then I laughed. "It'll certainly be easy to remember. My middle name is Pickett."

"Hey," he said smiling. "I like that better than Picker. Why don't you just call me Pickett, too?"

I studied his loopy smile and blood shot eyes for a brief second and said: "Is that Pickett, too? As in also? Or Pickett Two, as the number?"

"Take your pick," he laughed. "Pick it."

It wasn't all that funny but I couldn't keep from laughing with him. What was wrong with me?

I glanced at Kalina and LeRosa. They were smiling slightly and shaking their heads in unison. Then LeRosa started over to me with the mug. The smile on her face said it was something special.

And it was. It was hands down the best mug of steaming tea I'd ever had. I nursed it while Picker and I talked music. I gave him a shortened version of Folk House and how it formed. He was familiar with and impressed with the names of my ex-roommates.

He gave me the names of up and coming groups in Europe. Names that were strange to me at the time.

I told him about trying to write lyrics for my roommates and about how that had been a total failure.

"Did any of them try to put music to your stories," he asked.

"No. They usually started with an idea or a thought of their own and they started hearing their own music. Although one buddy and I wrote some parodies of existing songs and a couple of groups used them. Short comedy stuff."

"Humor is always a crowd pleaser," Picker said.

As we talked music and how to please a crowd, I noticed the increasing flow of cars into the campground. Visually things started to adjust to normal, as did my other senses. My thought process seemed to become more organized. I could hold a thought from one minute to the next.

But Picker seemed to jump from one subject to another as fast as his mind moved. Maybe Cinderella had visited him, too. One second he was talking about how to generate a crowd on an empty corner. The next, how to read an audience. Then he was expounding on how to add music to lyrics. And, how Cinderella could come up with so many strange potions.

About the time I was finishing my cup of tea, Kalina was giving LeRosa and Picker hugs, telling them we would see them at the wedding and leading me to another campsite.

I have no idea how many people we visited, nor do I remember their names. It was just a parade of friendly faces, most of them complimenting me on my storytelling. But most of the conversation focused on the wedding and who would be coming and who wouldn't be. Everybody was really getting charged up for the wedding.

They were like children the day before Christmas.

Eventually, along about noon, we ended up back at our camp.

Kalina sat down on the sleeping bag and I joined her. She kissed my cheek and laid back. I lay down beside her. She whispered a few things into my ear. Like how much her friends had liked me and such.

I was lying there staring up at the blue sky through the massive over-hanging branch of an oak, feeling good about what her friends had said. I know I must have had a smile on my face when she asked:

"What are your dreams?"

I immediately thought of the weird dreams I had had last night. It must have shown on my face because she laughed and said:

"Not last night's dreams, silly. Your life dreams."

Wow! Life dreams! She had caught me completely off guard again. I mean guys don't talk life dreams in the middle of the day. Maybe late at night. But . . .

"For example I want to do something special for my people," Kalina said. "Something I'll be remembered for."

That put my mind racing. Remembered for? When I was a kid I wanted to grow up to hit thirty home runs and drive in a hundred runs every year. People remember that sort of thing.

"And, I'd like to visit your country. I've seen pictures and it is beautiful. So many different types of terrain. So many different types of living spaces. Some crowded. Some desolate. It is so many things." She rolled quickly onto her side facing me, her head propped on her hand. The sunlight filtering through the giant oak made her green and gold eyes shine like reflectors.

I was mesmerized but she was too excited to notice.

"Just think about it," she said. "France is five hundred and fifty three thousand square kilometers. Western Europe is . . ."

"Hold on," I interrupted. I could tell I was frustrating her by butting in. "You are talking to a kid from Kansas with a Cinderella addled mind. Square miles I understand. But doing the five-eights thing is . . ."

She cut me off with a deep enjoyable guffaw. "Let me give it to my simple cowboy in simple terms. France is roughly two hundred and ten thousand square miles. A little less than eighty percent the size of Texas but two and a half times bigger than Kansas."

"How did you do that? Or are you pulling my leg?"

She laughed again. "Numbers are easy for me. They stick in my head. And I can do most math without trying." She stared at me for a moment. Then: "May I continue?"

"Please."

"Well, the United States is eighteen times bigger that France. Can you imagine how many miles of roads that is? Can you imagine what that means to a Gypsy? All those roads to travel? It is mind-boggling! That's why I want to visit your country."

She started laughing and I was with her. I couldn't help myself. It was mind-boggling. Especially if you were a Gypsy.

We lay there chuckling and cuddling for the longest time.

The afternoon slipped away as we shared our dreams.

Because Gypsies were distrusted, disliked and discriminated against, Kalina didn't believe there was one big thing that she could accomplish that would change their overall standing in the European community. She believed she could do a number of smaller things that would add up to something important.

I told her that the stories I was interested in telling would give people a better understanding of other people.

Ours was the type of sharing of ideas that usually takes place late at night, not during the day. And it was exciting and the afternoon just got away from us.

THE WEDDING

She took my hand and led me across the camp. I was duded out in my newly acquired Gypsy clothes and feeling good about it. She was gorgeous in her . . . how do you describe old, love-worn clothes that fit like she was born in them. They were so cool you couldn't wish for better.

She wore a full, white, ruffled, low-neck blouse that clung to her waist, accentuating how small her waist was. And, a full length purple skirt that clung to her long legs and made me stare.

I felt proud to have her arm entwined in mine as we strolled across the campground in the late afternoon.

A lot of people were heading in the same direction. They were smiling. They were jostling each other. Joking. They were having fun. It was a total party atmosphere. You could tell by their reactions that they were going to get exactly what they were expecting. And they knew it.

More vans, campers, trailers and trucks were turning off the highway, pulling into the campgrounds and parking.

The number of people was increasing minute by minute. I couldn't believe what was happening. Everyone was headed in the same direction, like lemmings with an extra purpose.

I was totally taken in by the festive air, the spontaneity, the excitement that was building and the oneness of the crowd. It was a stunning late summer afternoon with blue skies. Blue with a hint of purple in the east. Warm breezes. Evening songbirds somewhere, although I didn't see them.

Kalina was watching me, reading my reactions. She hugged me and kissed my cheek and whispered. "Gypsies live from *patshiva* to *patshiva*. From ceremonial celebration to ceremonial celebration."

"Well," I said. "You certainly couldn't ask for more beautiful weather."

Several people turned to see who had said that. They focused on me and looked me over. Then they glanced at Kalina and shrugged at each other as if to say: "What do you expect from a Gaje," and continued on.

"What'd I say this time?"

"Rom never talk about the weather because it is too self evident. It is what it is. It is to be enjoyed, not commented on. You gave yourself away, Gajo."

"I'll try to do better."

"Pay attention," she whispered. "The wedding starts *NOW*."

Ahead of us was a family of five sitting around a campfire. The father was a distinguished-looking burly guy with a time-ravaged face. His long black and silver streaked hair was pulled back in a ponytail. His mustache and goatee were a singular black unit. Next to him was the mother. She was angular and gorgeous with dark satin skin. Her face was chiseled beauty. Beside the mother sat the oldest son. He was lanky like his mother and ruggedly handsome like his father.

Beside him sat two step-stair burly brothers who were spitting images of their father. All of them were very dressed up. They sat quietly and paid no attention to the people who were arriving and encircling them. The growing crowd of people sat a respectful ten yards away, speaking only in very low whispers.

Kalina indicated a spot next to a family of six or seven and we sat. The family members all nodded and smiled at us. Although the kids took second glances at me.

Kalina subtly pointed toward the family around the campfire and whispered to me: "That's Uncle Bias. His oldest son is Bahtalo." She head-motioned toward the back of the crowd. "And here comes Ithal Lee and his daughter, *the lovely Reservoria.*"

I looked in the direction of her Rom nod and saw a tall, dark, handsome man, in his mid to late thirties with a silver and black handlebar mustache, making his way through the seated crowd as if they weren't there. He was followed by a very pretty, very young girl. She was dark and lean. Truly lovely in any gathering. And she, too, paid no attention to anyone. It was as if they were the only two people there.

I whispered to Kalina: "Bahtalo and Reservoria look so young."

"He's sixteen. She's fourteen. Not too young for Romani."

Ithal Lee wove his way through the hundred and fifty, or more, spectators as if they weren't there. And I realized the crowd was still growing.

Ithal Lee stopped about fifteen feet from Uncle Bias and pointed at him as if he hadn't seen him until now. He shouted a Romani greeting. There were murmurs from the crowd.

The two men were truly pleased they had chanced upon each other.

Kalina whispered a translation to me. "What a surprise! He is privileged and pleased to see his old friend Uncle Bias."

Uncle Bias shouted back a greeting, rose and offered Ithal Lee a seat beside the fire. Ithal Lee sat and Reservoria stood shyly behind him. She stole glances at Bahtalo. Quick glances. Both smiled a lot. They could not, even if their lives depended on it, have kept from smiling.

That's when it hit me. I leaned over to Kalina and whispered: "It's a passion play."

She pinched my cheek. "Good, Gajo," she whispered.

Her whispered breath was so hot and sensuous against my ear that I lost track of what was going on for a few seconds.

Uncle Bias poured a cup of coffee and offered it to Ithal Lee, who accepted it with a bow of his head, his long straight black hair sweeping forward like it was bowing, too.

Kalina whispered: "They are showing what good friends they are by sharing."

Ithal Lee raised his coffee mug in salute. "Bahtalo drom." They clinked mugs and sipped the coffee.

The crowd sighed.

"He wished him a lucky road," Kalina whispered.

Uncle Bias extended his hand asking for the return of the coffee mug. Crushed, Ithal Lee gave the mug back and hung his head.

The crowd groaned.

Uncle Bias pitched the coffee from both mugs into the fire.

Again the crowd groaned.

Uncle Bias turned to Bahtalo and said something I couldn't hear. Bahtalo got up and left the circle. Reservoria followed him. They touched hands briefly. Shyly. Lovers stealing a moment away from their fathers.

It drew "ahhs" from the crowd.

Bahtalo climbed into a beautifully carved and ornately painted caravan that was mounted in the bed of a pickup truck.

Uncle Bias leaned over to Ithal Lee, whispered in his ear and patted him on the back. Ithal Lee straightened up smiling.

"Ahhs" from the crowd.

Kalina leaned over and whispered: "Uncle Bias told him that coffee was not good enough for his fine friend Ithal Lee. He has sent Bahtalo to get his best whiskey out of his caravan."

I whispered back, "His son is named Lucky?"

Kalina winked at me an smiled.

Bahtalo came out of the caravan carrying two bottles of whiskey. The crowd "Ahhed" its approval as he returned to the circle and gave one bottle to each father. Then Bahtalo looked over at Reservoria who was still standing by the caravan. Other girls began to join her, surrounding her, teasing her. He winked.

The two fathers nodded to each other, uncorked the whiskey bottles and exchanged them. Each poured whiskey into the other's mug, toasted each other and drank.

"Ahhs."

"They have agreed that they are good enough friends to philosophize," Kalina whispered. "Who knows? If they are equally brilliant, they might consider pairing their oldest children in order to insure having brilliant grandchildren."

"Te na khutshos perdal tsho ushalin," Uncle Bias said.

Kalina translated: "One should not try to jump over his own shadow."

Ithal Lee nodded wisely, agreeing. They toasted and drank again.

"Ahhs."

"Yekka buliasa nasti beshes pe done granstende," Ithal Lee said.

Uncle Bias nodded thoughtfully, agreeing. Again they toasted each other and drank to a chorus of "Ahhs."

Kalina continued to tanslate for me. "With one behind you cannot ride two horses."

"Tshattshimo Romans," Uncle Bias said.

"The truth is expressed in Romani," Kalina whispered.

Ithal Lee nodded, agreeing with Uncle Bias' wisdom. Again they toasted and drank.

"Ahhs."

"Si khohaimo may patshivals sar o tshatashimo," Ithal Lee responded.

"There are lies more believable than truth."

"Ando gav bi jurlisko shavi piraved o manush bi destesko," Uncle Bias said.

"In a village without a dog a man can walk without a stick."

The two fathers nodded agreement, toasted and drank.

"Ahhs."

Then they leaned together and began talking quietly.

"They are discussing Reservoria so no one can hear them in case there are shortcomings to be made known."

Uncle Bias got up and walked over to Bahtalo and whispered to him. His son nodded. Uncle Bias looked him in the eyes, shrugged and returned to his seat at the campfire. Then he whispered to Ithal Lee, who motioned Reservoria forward. He pointed to the ground behind Uncle Bias. She stopped at the indicated spot. She kept her eyes downcast.

Bahtalo and his father exchanged comments, which I couldn't hear. I looked questioningly at Kalina.

"Bahtalo is asking if his father doesn't want to see her. And Uncle Bias said: 'One should select one's daughter-in-law with the ears not the eyes.'"

Uncle Bias asked her a question and her response drew "Ahhs." And he nodded in agreement.

Kalina whispered to me: "He asked which is greater the oak or the dandelion? And she said 'whichever of the two achieves fulfillment.'"

The two fathers leaned together, whispering.

"They are negotiating the price," Kalina whispered.

"For her?" I asked.

"For both."

Suddenly the two fathers stood up and held their mugs high. "Reservoira! Bahtalo!" they shouted and drank to a chorus of "Ahhs." A violin and a couple of guitars began to play. Reservoria sprinted off, chased by the other girls. Bahtalo strolled, almost a strut, back to the caravan and climbed inside. The two fathers poured whiskey in each other's mug, sat down and continued to drink.

"Friends for life," Kalina told me.

There was one last chorus of "Ahhs" and the crowd arose en masse and hurried off.

"Where's everyone going?" I asked.

"To prepare the banquet for tonight," Kalina said. "And we must go too, so the fathers can have their private time."

As we walked away I asked a question that had been bothering me. "Why aren't there anyone but Gypsies in these campgrounds?"

"They aren't public campgrounds. You see, in France Gypsies aren't allowed to stay in a town more than forty-eight hours. We have to sign in and sign out with the police. Unless we are staying on our own land."

"Why would they make a law like that?"

"It's Nazi law from the war. The French find it convenient to continue it. It's so the police can keep track of us. So they know where we are." Kalina laughed. "Keep track of Gypsies!?! Never! We own land all over Europe and we keep moving. Usually staying on our own land. No sign in. No sign out."

I laughed with her. There was no outwitting these people.

"I have a number of questions about when the Nazis were here."

"Another time. This is a *patshiva*.

THE WEDDING BANQUET

From nowhere, Kalina produced a bottle of wine and two glasses. We lay down on the grass, drank the wine and cuddled. There were other couples doing the same thing. It was as if the wedding were an aphrodisiac. But of course, all weddings are.

"Do you want to take my *diklo* now," I whispered.

She arched her eyebrows about as sexily as I'd ever seen and matched it with a smile. "I'm thinking about it. Give me time. The day is young. Who knows who else might show up. I might find someone better."

And, looking at the handsome young Romani men strolling about, it was entirely possible that she would. After all, as we would say back in Kansas, I ain't no Cary Grant. My nose had been broken five or six times and wasn't exactly a pretty thing to behold. Nor was it structurally sound. Often times in the morning I would look in a mirror and discover my nose leaning more to the left or right than it should be. By placing my hands on either side of my nose I could realign it. It hurt like hell. But it looked better.

Kalina saw me straightening it one morning and laughed. A couple mornings later she asked if she could do it. As always, it hurt like hell. But it didn't matter as long as she had her hands on me.

As we were finishing the bottle of wine, people started flowing past us. They were carrying picnic tables, folding tables and chairs, food, and drink. They were all heading toward Uncle Bias' camp.

"You need to help," she said. "Be Gypsy."

I strolled to a picnic table being carried at one end by a woman a couple years older that me. On the other end were two boys about twelve years old. I took the boys' place at the back end of the table. The woman, whose back was to me, sensed the weight shift and looked over her shoulder at me. She dropped her end of the table and marched toward me. She looked extremely angry. Beautiful and angry. I didn't know what I had done wrong. But, based on the look on her face, I expected that I was about to have my throat cut. Or at the very least my nose would be broken again.

She stopped an inch or two in front of me and thrust her face toward mine and spouted Romani at me. I just shrugged. She stared hard at me for a couple of seconds then she opened my suit jacket. She flipped the torn pocket on my yellow shirt and smiled. "You are Kalina's Gajo."

"Yes, I am."

She hugged me and kissed my cheek. "Welcome. I am Asperia."

I looked to my right and Kalina was standing there smiling.

Asperia flipped my red *diklo* over my shoulder. "If she does not treat you right, come see Asperia."

I realized this was all tease and temptation. It was all a game just as it had been with Cinderella. I was the new guy being made sport of. Fine. It was part of being accepted. It felt good.

Asperia and I carried the table to Uncle Bias' camp. There it became part of a big U made of other picnic tables and folding tables. The bride and groom were at the head of the U. Each was flanked by the other's parents. Bahtalo wore a black suit with a bright blue shirt. Reservoria wore a simple red dress. Men began to seat themselves around the table. No other women were seated.

The women and children put the food and beverages on the table. They retreated a respectful distance, sat down and waited.

Next the men sat down at the tables. Ate. Drank. Partied. Sang along with the violin and guitar music.

Kalina sat down with the other women and pulled me down to sit beside her. "It is a special celebration," she said. "You should realize they are honoring you by letting you be here. Still you aren't allowed to eat or drink with the men."

"Does that mean I'm a second class citizen?" The minute those words cleared my mouth I knew I had screwed up big time.

"Just shut up and pay attention, Gaje."

With one dumb eight-word sentence, which was meant as a joke, I had gone from '*her Gajo*' to *Gaje*. The verbal demotion wasn't easy to take. But I shut up and paid attention.

And it was an amazing event. The passion play was still happening. I realized that it was going to continue the rest of the day and probably all night.

I reached over and took Kalina's hand. It was not responsive. She looked me in the eye with those gorgeous tan eyes flecked with green and it was not a forgiving stare. I had stepped over a line that I didn't know was there, yet it didn't matter whether I knew or not, I had transgressed. I withdrew my hand and paid attention.

After about an hour the men finished eating and got up from the tables. They took the wine and booze with them as they began singing and dancing to the violin and guitar music. They were shouting, celebrating and repeatedly praising the two fathers.

As the men began singing and dancing their way away from the table, the women and children began to poise themselves like sprinters in the starting blocks.

"You wait here," Kalina said, as she moved from a sitting position to a crouch. "You wouldn't stand a chance."

The two fathers motioned at the remains of the banquet on the tables. There were grand sweeping gestures to the women and children. And the women and children charged the tables. Playful fighting and arguing over the food. It was reminiscent of an old movie depiction of Apaches looting a wagon train.

While I was waiting, a very dark skinned young beauty with long black hair walked by and winked at me. She locked eyes and smiled. I smiled back. All this flirtation was fun.

Kalina rushed back with an armload of food, smiling.

"Nice table manners," I laughed.

Kalina glared at the beautiful young woman who had just winked at me and spit at her. "Dugnata!" she sneered, and spit again.

Whoa! I'd missed something there.

The gorgeous young woman tossed a chuckle over her shoulder at Kalina and a sloe-eyed wink at me. Gypsy flirting sure was exciting—and obviously it could be dangerous.

"Dugnata" wasn't the exact word Kalina used. It's just as close as I can come to it.

"What's *dugnata* mean?" I asked.

"It's a warning to keep her hands off your *diklo*."

I had to stifle a laugh.

*   *   *

As the sun slid below the horizon, the celebration heated up. Everyone was singing and dancing. Drinking. Laughing. Making out. Lots and lots of story telling. *Swatura*, tales of experience told among the men and women. *Paramitsha*, fairy tales told to the children. It was a visual circus of people and colors in the dancing firelight. Hundreds of colors popping out of the blackness of the night. I was totally mesmerized by it all.

"Not many Gaje have seen this," Kalina said, snuggling up to me.

"This is truly incredible. Where do I sign up?" She felt good next to me. Her skin, silky, warm and fragrant. Her breath a sweet tickle on my neck.

Kalina laughed and kissed me. Long and hot. Our hands explored each other's body. Then she broke away. "Come."

She led me over to where I could see the bride and groom. People kept going up to them and handing them envelopes and saying: "Das dab ka I roata le neve vurdoneski."

"It means: To give a push to the wheel of the new wagon."

"Beautiful," I said.

The Gypsies had such beautiful ways of expressing things. The more I heard and saw, the more I loved their ways of communicating. Nods and gestures when words were superfluous. Word-pictures when words alone weren't enough. To me, it was a strange and magical world.

"Do you see what the bride and groom are being given?" she asked.

"I see money. But there are envelopes, too."

"Cash. Gems and jewelry. And gold. Traveling wealth." She pulled a necklace from under her blouse. It was made of gold coins. "My *galbi*. My inheritance. I never take it off."

"It's beautiful," I said. "But I've never seen it before."

"We don't wear our wealth to be seen. Gaje advertise their wealth with cars and clothes, and watches and jewelry. It's a signal to us that says: Steal from me. I can afford it. And we say, 'If you insist.'"

The mother of the bride and four or five young girls, the same girls who had been hanging around the bride earlier outside of Uncle Bias' caravan, came dancing through the crowd with a white dress. White satin shift-like, but what do I know about dresses? To me, it looked like a traditional, simple wedding dress. They danced around the bride, showing off the dress to the crowd. Then they slipped it over the bride's head, over her red dress.

"Now what's happening?"

"The wedding day is the one exception to the rule that red is never worn by an honest Gypsy woman."

"But you were wearing a red skirt the day I met you."

"Exactly."

"But I've seen lots of women wearing red."

"Of course. But not today. Today everybody is pure."

It sounded like a verbal anomaly to me—but I kept my mouth shut for a change.

Reservoria's parents and friends led her in one direction and Bahtalo's parents and his brothers led him in the opposite direction.

"Shouldn't the bride and groom be going off together?"

"Later tonight Bahtalo will abduct Reservoria." Kalina winked at me. "It's more romantic in the darkest of night."

"Silly me. Of course it'd be better if she were stolen in the dark of night."

"You are slow, Gajo," Kalina said. "But you do get there. Occasionally." She laughed her best deep wind-chime laugh. "And now it is time for me to steal you away."

"Is it dark enough?" I asked, being flip.

"It's dark enough for this point in our relationship."

I should have kept my mouth shut. But that was nothing new.

She grabbed my red *diklo* and led me away from the firelight. And into a dark section of the campground, closer to the highway. Away from the festivity. She slid her arms around me and we kissed. Long. Hot. Intense. Our hands exploring each other's body. Unable to get enough of each other.

My kisses drifted downward. Across her throat. My fingers found the buttons on her blouse. My lips found her breasts.

"Kelly."

"Huh?"

"Work your way back up."

"What?" Had I just flunked some Rom sex test?

"Work your way back to my lips. And listen." There was urgency in her voice.

I was alert. Ready for what, I didn't know. But I did as I was told, rebuttoning her blouse. When my lips reached hers she said: "Look over my shoulder. See the black Morris parked on the shoulder of the highway?"

"Yes." It was there and I could make out the shadows of two occupants.

"Police," Kalina whispered. "They always try to ruin a celebration by watching."

"Just when I think I'm getting lucky, I get unlucky," I said.

"I know exactly how you feel," Kalina said. "But, we have work to do."

She took me by my *diklo* and led me back to the celebration. At the edge of the celebration she let my *diklo* drop like you do with the reins of a horse when you want it to stay put. I stayed put. She moved through the crowd, whispering and nodding toward the highway.

The crowd's attention became focused on the black Morris. Almost as one, the Gypsies stood up and marched toward the police car. Kalina took my hand and we joined the migration. We stopped at the campground fence and stared at the two men in the car. They acted like they didn't see us. Now the watchers were being watched.

A pebble *pinged* off the hood of the Morris. I looked over and saw a little boy about six years old throw another pebble. It *clicked* off the windshield. The Morris' engine rattled to life and the cops drove away.

A cry went up from the crowd, two words in unison.

Kalina leaned in close and translated: "Celebrate life."
Everybody did.

"*Patshiva!*" I said.

She laughed. "My Gajo learns." She took my *diklo* and led me toward a yellow 1960 Citroen ID station wagon—one of the world's ugliest cars ever made. There was a small campfire burning. I hadn't seen her start it or gather the wood. But there it was and it was very romantic. The smell of the burning wood and the night wind. The sounds of music and celebrations in the dark. A quarter moon in the cloudless sky.

She opened the tailgate of the station wagon and pulled out a mattress and a double sleeping bag that looked familiar. She put them near the fire. And she began to dance suggestively to the guitar and violin music that haunted the night.

Okay, I have to be honest. My heart was racing. My blood was racing. Everything about me was racing full tilt. Except my brain. It had disengaged hours ago.

She continued to dance to the music and began unbuttoning her blouse. She danced out of her blouse and twirled it in the air around her. Then she threw the blouse into the fire. "So there is no record of my humiliation tomorrow."

She was gorgeous. She had a lean, hard body with beautiful breasts. They weren't big. They were smallish. But proud and firm.

Her gold *galbi* sparkled in the firelight, a lighter gold than her skin tone. It was mesmerizing.

Then she began to undress me. My red *diklo* went on top of the Citroen. My gray suit coat and pants were almost ceremoniously folded and set aside. That left me in my yellow shirt and boxer shorts. She took off my shirt and threw it in the fire.

"So there is no record of my humiliation tomorrow," I said.

She laughed. "Good try Gajo." She put her arms around me and drew me to her. We kissed. Long and hard. Her skin was silky to the touch. I could spend the whole night just touching and stroking her. Her skin was magic.

"Gajo," she said. "In Gypsy tradition the woman is unclean below the waist. You have to remove my skirt and under garments. That makes me clean and then I can remove yours."

I did and she did.

Patshiva!

It was the best sex I'd ever had. It could have been partly because of the celebration. Partly the situation. But it was mostly Kalina.

She had an incredible way of making love. We kissed and explored each other's body for a long time. Like I've already said, her skin was magic to touch.

Finally she rolled over on top of me, grabbed my wrists and pinned them to the ground. And somehow, without using her hands, she drew me inside her. She laughed at my surprised expression. "Something new, Gajo?" Without moving her hips she drew me in and forced me almost out several times. "Speak up, cowboy. Is this new?"

"Yes."

"And this?" She drew me in deeper and began to pulsate around me. Softly. Like butterfly kisses.

"Oh, yes."

She went from butterfly kisses to jackhammer. A spectrum of sensations I had no experience with. It just about blew my ears off. She threw back her head and laughed her magical laugh. "I can climax three times for every one time for you."

"You'd better hurry."

She clamped down on me like a vise. "Or I can not let you climax at all." She almost lifted me off the ground to demonstrate the strength of the grip she had on me. Then she went back to the butterfly kisses and ran from one end of the spectrum to the other again.

I held on for dear life. I was right where I wanted to be. Holding on to Kalina and Kalina holding on to me. It was like this all night.

WHICH WAY? RIGHT OR LEFT?

"Wake up, cowboy."

My eyes popped open and Kalina was sitting beside me ready to hit the road.

It was a typically beautiful day with clear blue skies and a gentle breeze. But I didn't mention it. That was self-evident.

"Gaje sure sleep late," she said.

"Last night I was your Gajo."

"Today you have to earn it again." She laughed teasingly. "Let's go. Move. *The day is dying if you aren't moving.*" She laughed softly. "Think Gypsy Gajo."

I reached for her and she moved away. "That was last night, Cowboy. We need to move. I need to find my father—among other things."

I got up and began digging my jeans out of my pack, looking around to see what others were doing.

"No jeans," she said, "dress Gypsy." Kalina walked over to the old faded yellow Citroen station wagon. "And don't look around." She opened the rear hatch and took out a faded red shirt—faded between the gaudy red it once was and the cool pink it was becoming—and tossed it to me.

I put on the coarse, gray wool slacks and the faded red shirt. I buttoned the cuffs and collar, and then examined the shirt. "Found, no doubt."

"Papa Two prefers faded reds." She opened the passenger door and climbed in. "Let's go. You can drive can't you?"

"What about your motorcycle?" I asked.

"A temporary trade," she said. "Get in."

I slid behind the wheel. I had driven Formula Two racing cars in two races. Could I drive? Of course! But any driver was only as good as his wheels. I hit the starter. The car staggered to life sounding like everybody's worst automotive nightmare. "Where's your motorcycle?" I said, meaning it as a joke. But her mind was elsewhere.

"I told you, we swapped for a day or two. Let's go, Cowboy."

I drove to the campground gate. A couple of young boys opened it for us. They smiled and waved at Kalina as I drove out onto the ancient asphalt highway. "Which way? Right or left?"

"Always a good question to a Gypsy. Left or right?"

"Well if we are looking for your father, which way should I go?"

"He's Gypsy."

I thought for a moment. "Which way to Lourdes?"

"Right."

I cranked the wheel to the right and put the pedal to the metal. We lurched into motion, slowly building up speed. This certainly wasn't a Formula Two car.

Kalina broke into song. *"Head 'em up. Move 'em out. Move 'em up. Head 'em out. RAWHIDE."*

We sang Frankie Laine songs for the next half hour. Of course we sang 'Green Leaves of Summer,' 'Ghost Riders in the Sky' and 'I Believe.' Then we segued into Jan and Dean and Beach Boys and every other one of my old hootenanny songs. She knew the words to all of them.

The interesting thing was that I never sounded so good.

But that's what happens riding with Kalina.

"I love singing," she suddenly said on a serious note. "Some of my fondest memories are singing with Papa One when we were traveling in his caravan. In fact, I'd rather sing than eat."

"I know what you mean," I joined in. "Unfortunately, most people would rather hear me eat than hear me sing."

"Bad joke, Cowboy."

We were approaching a fork in the road.

"Slow down," she said. She was studying the trees that lined the road. "He went left."

I cut the steering wheel and took the left fork.

"And stop!" she said.

I pulled over to the edge of the road and braked. But, obviously not soon enough because . . .

"Back up."

I did, slowly.

"Good."

"How in the world do you know he went this way?"

"The *vurna*. He's using a red rag. He likes red—but you know that. He tears off a strip of red cloth and ties it to a tree branch on the road he takes. He marks the trail and we follow."

She opened the car door and got out. She went to the rear of the Citroen and climbed up onto the roof. I could hear Kalina walking across the roof. She stopped for a few seconds and then it sounded like she was kneeling down.

Just as I started to get out to see what she was doing, she peered in through the windshield from the roof and stuck her tongue out at me. Then she clamored off the roof and back into the Citroen. She smiled and waved a strip of a red rag at me.

"Now you know what to look for and I can nap if I want to."

"Everyday is a new adventure with you."

"You like that?"

"Yes I do."

"Good," she said and kissed my cheek. "Was last night good for you?"

"The best ever."

She laughed her laugh. "Then try to do the same for me tonight."

"But I thought . . ."

She put her fingers on my lips to silence me. "Last night was about you. Tonight should be about me. Tomorrow night, who knows? Gypsies don't make plans. But you know that."

I did know that. I was beginning to think Gypsy. And tonight would be about her. But, wasn't that making plans?

ABOUT HER

We stopped at two campgrounds that afternoon as we pursued Old Bohemius. As always, he was one or two jumps ahead of us. And, as with every stop we made, the current residents of that camp approached Kalina individually and seemed to consult with her. Sometimes she made notes in her blue notebook. Other times, she would look up things in the notebook and read her findings to them.

Naturally, I asked about these little confabs. She said it was Gypsy business. When I asked to join her so I could understand, she said: "No. They will speak more precisely in their own tongue—which they won't speak in front of you because it would be impolite."

I understood. As much as these people went out of their way to include me, I was still the outsider. Always would be. It was the new kid syndrome all over again. I knew it well. But that didn't diminish my desire to be one of them. My desire to be included. My desire to be accepted. But there was no use in fretting over it—that wasn't the way the world worked. Besides the only productive fretting occurred on a guitar.

The sun was a soft yellow, low in a faded blue sky, as we pulled into the third campground. The little boys at the gate, who let us in, were excited to see Kalina and guided us to a choice site.

While Kalina consulted with her people, I went about setting up our campsite. I began by gathering wood for a fire. As I did, I noticed a little nine or ten-year-old boy watching me. As soon as I noticed him, he approached, smiling.

He pointed at the wood I had gathered. "For Kalina's fire?" he asked.

"Yes."

The little boy turned and made a "come here" gesture. I looked in the direction he had turned and saw half-dozen boys about his same age hurrying toward us, each with an armload of firewood. They dumped it all in a pile and stood back, looking at me.

"You've made Kalina very happy," I said.

They beamed a chorus of smiles and the first boy put out his hand. "Kalina's Gajo, I am Lasaros." He had a killer smile that was destined to leave a wake of broken hearts.

"Kelly," I said, shaking his hand.

He pointed nonchalantly at the sky. "Light rain tonight. Are you going to make a shelter?"

"I was thinking maybe a canvas lean-to," I said. "There's a tarp in the back of the Citroen."

"We are familiar with it." He gave me his best smile. "May we be of help?"

"Of course," I said.

Lasaros snapped his fingers and the boys descended on the Citroen like an Indianapolis pit crew in mid race. In a couple of minutes we had shelter from the coming rain. The car was the back wall of the lean-to. Two four-foot tall wooden poles were the front corners and it was all held in place with ropes and pegs.

I was amazed at their speed and precision.

"Tell Kalina that Lasaros and his men were here," he shouted as they all rushed off together, chattering with pride.

I resisted the impulse to thank them. My Gypsy instinct, I guess.

*   *   *

The sun was setting behind black-green mountains when Kalina returned. There was a very light mist in the air. The droplets refracted and reflected the orange and purple sunset. Kalina was exhausted. She handed me a bottle of Scotch whiskey and sank down on the sleeping bag I had spread out under our lean-to.

I went to the open tailgate of the Citroen, got two tin cups, came back and sat down beside her on the sleeping bag. I poured a splash into each cup, reexamined Kalina's weary look and doubled the dose.

We sat there watching the sun vanish behind the distant mountains. I could hear a couple of guitars having their strings stretched as a couple of musicians began to noodle. Somewhere a violin was softly being tuned. I could hear the hiss of the mist settling on the fire and smell the sweet smoke of our campfire's fresh, damp wood. It was a nice smell.

Kalina snuggled up to me and the best smell in the gathering night was her.

We sipped our drinks as we watched the last glorious deep reds and purples of the sunset being swallowed by the black sky. The mist sizzled and fumed against the fire. The distant guitar noodling became music and was joined by an equally faint violin.

I gently massaged Kalina's neck and shoulders. They were wound tight with the days' tension.

"If I knew what you were doing, I might be able to help," I said.

"It's Gypsy business. Today was just getting ready for tomorrow." She leaned back into my hands and I worked her neck and shoulders harder. Firmly, but gently.

If today was "getting ready," then tomorrow she would turn to stone. I worked her neck and shoulders more soothingly and I could feel her begin to relax. I continued my massage over her shoulders and down her arms. Kneading her muscles. Driving the tension toward her fingertips. And, out through her fingers.

She drew her arms in through the sleeves of her blouse so that her blouse was more of a serape. I slid my hands up under the back of her blouse. Worked my fingers across the silky skin of her back. Putting love into each touch. Hoping my touch said what I couldn't find words to express.

My lips found the back of her neck. Gently teasing.

She pulled her blouse up around her neck and lay down on her stomach. The dark gold of her skin glistened in the warm firelight. I continued massaging and kissing her neck, back and arms. I kissed and stroked her to the rhythm of the guitar and violin music. I was playing the Kalina. The music was magical.

Kalina rolled over and held out her arms to me. My lips found hers. It was a long pleasing, teasing kiss. My kisses teased their way lower. Down her neck to her breasts. I made her squirm with pleasure before drifting lower. I raised my head and read her eyes. They said: Don't quit.

I didn't.

ON THE ROAD TO LOURDES

In the morning we headed toward Lourdes under a dark threatening sky. We stopped at every Gypsy campground on the way.

It was my job to inquire about Kalina's father. He was always about an hour, or a day, ahead of us, depending on the age of the person telling me. If the person was our age we had missed Old Bohemius by an hour or so. To the older folks we had missed him by a day so.

While I was making my inquiries, other Gypsies always drew Kalina aside. Usually the conversations seemed to be serious. As always, Kalina would make copious notes in her blue book. Or, she would page through her notebook and read something to them. In either case they seemed happy and pleased to have spent this time with Kalina.

She never hurried these stops. Listening to and talking with these people seemed to be as much of our reason for being there as searching for her father. She had a way of treating everyone like they were special and it was obvious that she made them feel special. It was a magic that she had.

When she was ready to move on she would give me some sort of sign and we'd both head for the car. As we left a campground, the conversation was always the same. I'd ask what she'd talked about. She'd say: "Gypsy business." Then she would ask me: "What did you learn?"

"He's still ahead of us," I'd say.

But in typical Gypsy fashion, Kalina was in no hurry to catch up with him. We would find him when we found him. All roads led to the same place.

We rode in silence for a while after leaving the second campground. It was mid-morning. The sun was trying to break through the gray clouds, but you could tell it wasn't going to happen today. I was driving and studying the landscape. She was reading a book on Roman history.

"All the campgrounds look alike," I said.

"To the ignorant eye," she said, distractedly paging through the book. It had been in the Citroen and had occupied her most of our drive time.

"Thanks." I feinted feeling hurt.

She saw through it and smiled. "Poor tender cowboy." She finished what she was reading and closed the book. "The size of the grounds is determined by what our people could afford to purchase at the time. Generally between one and four hectares."

"I knew a Hector back in Kansas," I wise-assed. "He had a brother named Jeckle."

"Yeah, yeah," she said. "They were crows. Only it was *Heckle* and Jeckle. Here we are talking about a hectare. A measure of land from ancient times. Do you really want to know? Or are you just bored with the silence?"

"I'd like to know."

"Good, because silence is the breeding ground of thought. Only the stupid don't realize that." She smiled her best and slid the history book on the floor under her seat. "A hectare is ten thousand square meters. Approximately two point four seven acres in a cowboy's limited understanding."

I had always been a quick study at math. I've always been able to jump to an answer without knowing how I got there. Math genes, I guess. But *a cowboy's limited understanding* was a slight I couldn't let ride.

"That means there are approximately two hundred and fifty-nine hectares in a section based on *a cowboy's limited understanding.*"

She thought a second—but only a second. "Are all cowboys wiseasses when they know something?" she asked.

That meant Kalina knew how many acres were in a section. And other than farmers and ranchers, I didn't know many people who did. I just decided to shut up and drive.

*   *   *

Traveling with Kalina was a constant history lesson. She was a major history buff. She told me things about the little towns we passed through that I would have never even thought to ask. And when I did ask a question that she couldn't answer her response was always the same. "I have to learn that." And out would come her blue notebook and she'd start writing.

We had just passed through a small village and there was a campground up ahead.

"Pull over," she said.

I did.

"What do you see?" she asked.

It was late afternoon. The sun was slanting in from the west, getting ready to slip behind the mountains. Ahead, in the far distance, were mountains, a hundred shades of brown, tan, gray and shadow shades of all three colors. The land around us was a hundred shades of green with ancient trees as accent. It looked like the work of an impressionist painter. I could have stayed forever. If Kalina were with me.

I felt an elbow in the ribs. "What do you see?"

"A beautiful piece of land. A Gypsy campground," I said.

"Self evident," she said.

"But, of course."

She shook her head in exasperation. "Are all cowboys this thick skulled? Take away the fence and the facilities and what do you see? Why would you want this land?"

Now I understood the question. "There's a stream at the back. You have water. The land is rolling, you have drainage. It's close to town, you have supplies and medical help."

"Ah, it thinks."

I knew we would be staying here tonight because Kalina didn't like to travel at night. I threw it in gear and slowly motored toward the campground gate. There were already children there waiting for us. They had seen us coming. They opened the gate.

"Kalina," one of them shouted.

She waved back.

It hit me that in many ways this scattered community of Gypsies was like a small town. Everyone knew everybody else. They knew all about each other. And if you ever did anything wrong it stayed with you the rest of your life. Just like living in a small Kansas town. For the first time I had underpinnings.

It wasn't totally strange ground anymore. I could relate. This was an important epiphany for me.

Inside the campground, people watched us from their campfires, but maintained a distance. I figured it was because of me. But something seemed different.

The air was without a breeze and the sweet smelling smoke hung in the air. Kalina climbed out of the Citroen. I followed. She had her notebook in hand and people approached her as usual. Curiously, I was left alone. I wondered if I had committed some faux pas at a previous camp. Word did travel awfully fast.

Finally, a very young couple came forward. It was obvious that the others in the camp were encouraging them. I sensed that this was why people were acting differently. The couple nervously asked me, in English, if we would like to join them for dinner. I glanced over at Kalina and she nodded yes. I accepted their invitation and they hurried off.

*   *   *

It was a very pleasant dinner and the young couple seemed to relax as the dinner progressed. The conversation ran the gambit. French police. French politics. What did I think about France and where else had I traveled.

At Kalina's urging I told them the story about the end of the beer strike in Copenhagen. A short way into the story I heard chuckles from the dark outside the campfire light and I realized I was story telling to a group again. I spoke a little louder and got a little more animated. They all loved it. They couldn't imagine the Danes going that long without beer.

After I finished the story, I saw movement in the dark and knew we were being left alone with the young couple.

Then conversation moved to Viet Nam and I realized what this was all about.

Yasel, the young husband, asked what I thought about Viet Nam. I told him I had several friends serving there and that I was number one on the draft list back home but there were so many volunteers from my area that no one had been drafted in over a year. I told him that in one year I'd be twenty-six and over the draft age. I was wrong about that. Actually, the law was that your twenty-sixth year was the *last* year you were eligible. But I'd discover that later.

"The reason I asked," Yasel said. "is because the French army is going there in support of the Americans. We were there before you, you know?"

I nodded yes, that I did know.

"I'm thinking about enlisting," he said. "What do you think?"

I studied him closely. He was handsome and strong looking. Although he was married, he didn't look old enough to enlist.

"Two things," I explained. "First, France doesn't have an army there. No European country does."

"There's talk of it," he said defensively.

"And, secondly, I think you should stay home with your lovely wife. It's not your fight. I'm not even sure it's ours. I *really* think you should stay home." I glanced at Kalina and she nodded agreement.

"Where's the honor in that?" he asked.

"Where's the honor in dying?"

He got up and left the fire.

I looked over at Kalina. "That obviously wasn't what he wanted to hear. I hope I wasn't too blunt."

"You were perfect." She winked. "You did *my* job."

Yasel's wife got up to go with him. I was never sure of her name. "That was good for him to hear," she said. "Bahtalo drom." She started away, stopped and looked back. "Have you lost any friends in Viet Nam?"

"Two so far."

As she followed her husband into the night, she said, "The answer is always in the music. Isn't it?"

I looked over at Kalina. "What did she mean by that?" I thought I knew, but I wasn't positive.

"You sing music. But you don't listen to it." She smiled and shook her head at me. "Gypsies know how to listen to the music. The music asks questions of the times and tells truths. We don't travel with baggage on our backs like the Gaje do. Baggage not only weighs you down, it leads, based on past decisions. Baggage insists on being right. Music doesn't. Music is free to question."

"It sounds to me like you're showing *Gaje prejudice*," I said.

I saw anger flash in her eyes.

"Are you saying *I'm prejudiced* . . . against Gaje!?!"

"Are you saying *I* can't hear the ideas in music merely because I'm Gaje?" I gave her my best smile and saw the anger leave her eyes. And she laughed.

While I had her I went on. "Before I left Kansas City I lived in a place called Folk House. There were seventeen of us. Fifteen were musicians. They all wrote their own songs." I laughed thinking about it. "You have no idea what listening to music entails until you have fifteen songwriters living with you. I'd get off work and have a herd of roommates wanting to know what I thought of the songs they'd written that day." I laughed louder. "Listen to the music? That's all I did for two years."

"What did your one roommate who wasn't a musician do?"

"He managed the club where our roommates performed."

She laughed. "And they asked questions with their music?"

"They questioned everything. It's just that most people didn't want to hear the questions they asked."

"People never want to hear the hard questions." She kissed me. A gentle brushing of lips. "Were you good at it?" she asked. "When you were a reporter? Good at asking tough questions?"

"Asking questions was what I did for a living."

She kissed me, teasingly. "I love inquisitive men." She kissed me more seriously this time. "Ask me anything, Mr. Question Man. What do you want to know?"

"Tell me about the King of the Gypsies."

She jerked back. "Man, you sure know how to ruin a mood, Mr. Question Man. I like my cowboy much better. He can read between the lines."

It was a shame I was so Gaje-slow at moments like this.

She saw the look in my eyes and laughed again.

Just then two people came out of the night carrying two thick eiderdown blankets.

"Later," she whispered.

"For you," they said, offering the blankets to us. "For tonight. For comfort. Warmth." Their English was halting. But they were working hard to show respect for Kalina's Gajo.

Kalina acknowledged their generosity and offered them a drink from a bottle of Scotch that appeared from nowhere. They declined and melted back into the night, smiling.

We spread the first eiderdown on the ground, laid down on it and pulled the second one over us. The night was beginning to cool and the eiderdowns were toasty. We laid on our backs and looked up at a million stars. It seemed romantic to me. I got no hint from her. So I tried picking up our conversation where it had been a couple of eiderdowns ago.

"I asked about the King of the Gypsies."

"Don't you have a more important question to ask, cowboy?" she asked, snuggling into my arms.

That question didn't need to be asked, to be answered.

I NEARLY BLOW EVERYTHING

When I awoke, Kalina was nowhere in sight. I grabbed my towel and headed for the showers. It was late for the Rom. There was no line and even one showerhead was vacant. I stripped, hung my clothes and towel on a hook and took the unoccupied shower.

I soaped up and in doing so stole glances at the women's side of the showers. I couldn't help sneaking a look. One woman caught my eye. She was a dark skinned beauty with long raven black hair. She winked. It was the woman who had winked at me a couple of times at the wedding. The one who had angered Kalina. I turned away and noticed that all the men were leaving. Gypsies certainly know when to give you personal space.

I turned back toward the woman. She was making her way across the showers with a big smile on her face. She was gorgeous. I was aroused. By the time she reached me, we were the only two people in the showers.

She grabbed hold of my convenient handle and pulled me to her.

Suddenly another hand grabbed my testicles.

Kalina.

They stood face to face and both of them squeezed. I would have dropped to my knees but they were both holding me up by body parts I wanted to retain. So. I just stood on my tiptoes and took it.

Then Kalina let go of me and threw a haymaker right that landed flush on the other woman's nose. I heard bone pop. Blood splattered. The woman released me and staggered back a few feet from the force of the punch. She wiped at the blood, turned and started away.

Kalina grabbed me by the personal area previously controlled by the other woman and forced me to the shower floor, with her on top. She kissed me. I was surprised. Then she rolled us over so I was on top of her.

I glanced up at the retreating woman. Coming toward me she had looked like a mature, voluptuous woman. Going away, she looked like a skinny-ass teenager.

"How old was she," I asked. I shouldn't have.

Kalina looked up and saw where I was looking. I never saw the punch coming. A right cross to my left eye that would have made Mohammed Ali proud. It really rocked me. It's the punches that you don't see coming that hurt the worse. I toppled off her.

She rolled on top of me, pinned my arms to the shower floor with her knees and slapped me about a dozen times. Not pity-pat slaps. WHACKS! Then she grabbed me by the hair and pounded my head on the floor three or four times.

Finally she climbed off and stood up. "That's today's lesson, Cowboy." She leaned down and tapped me on the chest. "Time to go." She headed toward the women's entrance/exit.

I got up slowly. Shaky. My ears were ringing. My head hurt like hell. I staggered to where my clothes and towel hung on a hook beside the door. My eye was already swelling shut. I'd never taking a beating like that. I was still stunned but I toweled off quickly and dressed.

As I left the shower, I walked past a line of men who were politely waiting to go back inside. They had been too polite to enter during the confrontation. There were a few chuckles. Someone said: "Look at that eye." He said it in English so I would understand. There were more chuckles as they filed back inside.

Making a fool of myself hurt worse than my eye.

When I reached the Citroen, wondering if it would be there, it was and it was packed. Kalina was in the passenger seat. By then, my eye was almost swollen shut.

"Wow! What happened to you?" She asked and patted the driver's seat. I climbed in.

"How old was she?" I asked again.

"Fifteen or sixteen. She has a reputation. She only goes after other women's men."

"I'll bet she'll think twice next time," I said.

"I doubt it. Most people don't change. Drive."

I did.

THE ROAD AND THE
NEXT CAMPGROUND

We rode in silence through beautiful countryside. It was an old road with ancient trees growing alongside it. I drove following directions, not knowing our destination. There was nothing new in that. I could tell we were headed east. The sun filtered through the trees. It hit the windshield of the faded yellow Citroen and my eyes as only an early, rising sun can. I should say *eye*—singular. One was completely swollen shut now.

What was new was the silence. It was not the angry silence of an American woman who had chanced upon you while a naked lady had your dick in hand. It was a silence born of Gypsy disappointment. I knew better than to break it.

After a while she reached over and snapped on the radio. She tuned it for a moment and zeroed in on a rock and roll station. It was faint at first. Faint and static ridden. It was a low powered local station.

The voices of the D.J.'s were young. The format was unstructured. I recognized it immediately as a university radio station because I had done a short turn at the University of Kansas Radio station (KUSA) my sophomore year in college. I loved it—but I didn't have the voice for it.

"Listen to the music," she said.

I snapped back from nostalgia.

"Listen up you dumb, tone deaf, Gaje." She laughed.

I quit wandering in my memories and listened. "Bigot," I murmured.

She laughed again. We were healing.

It wasn't the usual pop stuff coming out of the radio. Not what we called the feel-good stocking-stuffer music. This had more of an edge to it. Think-about-it music. Like the stuff my old roommates were writing, but couldn't get anyone to listen to or record.

Most of the songs were new to me. So were the groups. Of course, last year we'd gotten the British Invasion groups. And they all wanted something. Dusty Springfield *Only Wanted to Be With You*. The Beatles wanted to *Hold Your Hand*. The Kinks *Really Got Me*. The Rolling Stones couldn't get no *Satisfaction*. And, Petula Clark wanted to go *Downtown*. Naturally this student station played all those songs. But most of what came over the radio was totally new to me. It was new music with an edge. Music to make you think.

Listen to the music.

Last year Dylan had told us *That The Times They Are a-Changing*. And they certainly were. Although at the time I was standing too close to see it. One of those forest-for-the-trees things. The programmers at this station were really into Dylan's *Changing* album. In addition to *The Times*, they played two other of his early warnings. *With God On Our Side* and *Only A Pawn In The Game*.

Occasionally they slipped in a feel-good song from last year
like **The Girl From Ipanema**. But for the most part, the
music was new, now, raw, hard and edgy. And, as we rolled
east the reception became stronger.

Suddenly **Satisfaction** exploded through our radio's
speaker. It wasn't new to me. And, I had never been a big
Stones fan—until I saw Kalina rocking with that song. She
would have made Pat Boone a Stone's fan if he had seen
her.

                    *   *   *

About an hour later we passed through a medium-size
village. It was built of fieldstones. A picturesque fantasy
village. Mezieres-sur-Issoire. Population, a couple thousand.

As I continued driving, I realized that Kalina was studying
me. She probably didn't think I was aware that she was
watching me because my eye closest to her was swollen shut.
But a good newsman can see what's behind him.

"Beautiful country," I said to break the silence.

"Yes," she agreed. "But I envy the vastness of your
country."

"And, I envy the proximity of your languages." I looked at
her with my good eye.

She nodded. "You are doing good at being Gypsy . . . for the
most part." She smiled. "But how is it for you?"

"I'm liking it," I said, my eye back on the road.

"I'm talking about how it feels to be Gypsy with your
Midwest upbringing."

Man, she had a way of putting her finger on a problem before I had identified it. "I'm not sure. I love your friends. And, I guess you're okay . . . for the most part."

She punched me playfully in the shoulder and then the music reigned again. *I Want to Hold Your Hand*. And we sang with it.

*   *   *

A few kilometers down the road we encountered an even quainter village. Les Landes. Again it was built of fieldstones and fantasy. Population, a few hundred.

Leaving the village, we ran into road construction. It slowed us down considerably. The road crew alternated the right of way on the one open lane of traffic. Kalina took a great deal of interest in the roadwork and the traffic. First the eastbound cars moved, then the westbound cars. The two-lane road we entered town on was being widened to four lanes on this side of town. Ah, progress—even in France.

When we cleared the construction area there were a bevy of signs. The usual directional, highway and cautionary signs, and one huge informational sign. Kalina pulled out her ever-present blue spiral notebook as she read the big sign.

"What's that sign say?" I asked.

"They are widening the road to four lanes from here to Bellac."

"Ah, progress," I said aloud this time.

"At who's expense," she asked and cocked an eyebrow.

There was obviously a lesson to be learned here. So, I shut up, paid attention and drove. I noticed that the land being used to widen the highway was on the south side of the existing road. For two kilometers the raw, graded earth lay open and waiting for the road crews to pave it over. The grading stopped at a beautiful stone and wood bridge that crossed a wide shallow stream named *Ruisseaur De La Planche De Saint-Bonner*.

"Pull over," she said quietly.

I drove off the paved road onto the graded raw earth. The Citroen's tires threw dirt and stone rattling up into the wheel wells. Dust rose as I braked slowly and stopped about twenty yards from the bridge. Kalina got out and walked toward the bridge, observing the land around her. I followed suit.

The landscape was breathtaking. The clear stream rolled lazily over the gray and tan, rocky streambed. It was surrounded by multiple shades of green shrubs and flanked by weather-ravaged old trees. The stream itself was about ten yards wide. The streambed was maybe forty yards wide and, over time, the rushing water had cut eight or ten feet deep into the surrounding landscape.

The bridge appeared to have been built in stages as the stream meandered and widened its bed. The center span was twenty yards long. It was the crudest segment and no doubt the oldest—maybe two or three hundred years old. Who knew what it replaced? The nearest and farthest segments of the bridge had been added maybe a hundred years ago. The bridge was a patchwork of utilitarianism. I wished I still had my camera. But it had found a new home in Copenhagen sometime during the celebration ending the beer strike.

"This would make a beautiful photograph."

She looked over at me and nodded. "You see it now—and maybe as it once was. But I see it tomorrow."

I took another look. I saw tomorrow. The quaint old stone and wood two-lane bridge was gone. A four lane-bridge of modern steel construction carried traffic from one bank of the stream to the other—the flowing water below unseen by motorists. Progress.

We walked back to the Citroen in silence.

"You saw what will be?" she asked.

"I did. It's a shame."

Kalina opened the passenger's door and slid inside. I slid in the driver's side and fumbled the key into the ignition.

"And, what of the people?" she asked.

My head jerked up and I looked at the bridge. But I saw no people. I looked at Kalina questioningly.

"You see the bridge and the stream as they will be tomorrow," she smiled sadly. "But you don't see the people on the other side. No one does."

Now, I saw it. A campground on the other side of the bridge and the stream. A Gypsy campground.

"Drive," she said.

Before I started the car I took a good look. I saw the existing road and how the campground had been built to conform to it. I saw how the new road had been planned without consideration of the existing campground. The new road would cut off a huge portion of the campground. Almost half.

*   *   *

We were met at the campground gate by a pride of young boys who unlocked the gate and yelled and waved at Kalina. Other people began to appear, standing back until Kalina selected a camping spot. She pointed to an empty place beneath a tree and beside an unused fire pit. I parked there.

"You are in charge of setting up our camp," she said. "I have other obligations."

We both got out of the Citroen. I stood beside the car and watched.

Kalina went to the crowd of Gypsies waiting for her. A few came forward smiling and shook hands with her. The majority held back, watching. It was as though she were a visiting dignitary.

Several of them stole glances at the Gaje. Kalina's Gajo. They had heard about me. I could tell by their reactions and brief smiles that word of my eye had not reached here. But I was sure that they knew who gave it to me. And, that I had it because I deserved it. And, by the time we reached the next campground those people would have heard about *The Gaje's Eye*.

*　　*　　*

Later that night, as I sat alone beside a campfire, a man appeared out of the dark carrying two large, pottery coffee mugs. He was a big man—not in height but in mass. His skin was the color of the night if the night could have shaded itself with cobalt blue. His smile revealed more gaps than pearly whites. His suit pants were charcoal gray. He wore no coat. His shirt was iridescent yellow with a spot of blood showing at the bottom of his shirt pocket.

He thrust one of the coffee mugs at me. "Scotch whiskey, Kelly. Very civilized, say what?" He sounded exactly like the gap-toothed English comedian, Terry Thomas. He looked at me, lowered his eyes and chuckled. His buffalo-shaped shoulders bounced when he chuckled. "You never saw it coming, did you now?" He pointed at his own eye, indicating mine.

"Nope," I said. "She's fast and good."

"She always has been," he smiled. "Caught me the first time as I was reaching for her comb. Just teasing. But she put me on my butt." He laughed again. It was obvious that he loved to laugh. It put people at ease.

"My names is Ayashah, don't you know?" he Terry Thomased. "Quite. But they always tell me to tell the English that my name is *Putty Tat*."

I shook his hand. "Because it's less threatening," I said.

"Quite." He studied my eye, shook his head and smiled again. "No one will ask you *why*." He sat down, knocked his mug against mine and we both drank.

He was one of those few people that you are at ease with from the moment you meet them. He was weathered and battered by life and unaffected by his journey through it, if you didn't count the scars on his eyebrows, cheeks and chin. I guessed his age to be mid-thirties—maybe a little older. Later I discovered that he was a year younger than me.

"Has she mentioned me?" he asked. "No, of course not," he answered himself. "We're lovers, don't chew know. I love her like there's no other. She loves me like her brother." He laughed. "Think there's a country song in that, cowboy?"

He broke into song, strumming an imaginary guitar.

"I love her like there's no other.

"She loves me like her brother."

He laughed and took a big slug from his mug. I noticed that the red spot on his shirt pocket had grown.

"You probably won't see much of what's-her-name tonight," he said.

"You mean Kalina?" I asked.

"Quite. What's-her-name?"

Did this mean Kalina had yet another name? Then I saw his smile and knew he was toying with me. It was his way of being friendly. His way of saying I know you are *in* on our ways.

"So, she'll be spending the night with you?" I said.

His guffaw was explosive. "Quite right!" He slugged from his mug. "Don't I wish?" From nowhere he produced a chrome flask that danced colors in the firelight. He poured more whiskey into my mug and then his.

With his flask he pointed to a distant campfire. I could see a half dozen people gathered around the fire. "She has business over there with George and the others. About the road and the campground. They will be at it most of the night. Get a good night's sleep. She will sleep tomorrow while you drive."

He topped off my mug with his flask, turned to leave, stopped and turned back to me. The flask was no longer in hand. He produced a lump of butcher paper from his blood stained pocket. He flicked it open with one hand. It was a small lump of raw meat. "Almost forgot," he said. "For your eye. Later you can cook it or leave it on the ground beside your bedroll and make friends with a dog. Maybe the dog will sleep with you and keep you warm. It won't be Kalina. But . . . beggars and all that rot, don't cha know." He walked off into the night.

"Nice meeting you, Ayashah *Putty Tat.*"

"Quite right, Old Bean," Terry Thomas said from the night. "It was a two-way drom."

* * *

Later that night as I slept, a dog snuggled up close to me. I petted it for a while. I heard him/her eating the meat.

I slept fitfully, dreaming about this new life and the people in it. Their realities—the realities of their life here and now. My realities—the realities of where I was from. The differences between the two realities. I dreamed of roads and campgrounds and bad guys and uncles and new friends and Old Bohemius and the road.

Mostly I dreamed about the road. It was always about the road. The realities of the road.

At some point I woke myself up talking and moaning in my sleep. Kalina kissed my eye, cuddled closer and said everything was all right. "Listen to the music," she whispered.

In my mind I heard the music in the car from earlier in the day. It wasn't the music she meant. That music had been edgy. The music I heard now wasn't.

"Do you believe in the magic of a young girl's soul?
Do you believe in the magic of rock and roll?

BREAKFAST WITH GEORGE

The smell of frying bacon woke me early. It was actually the smell of potatoes frying in bacon grease with some sort of campground-grown tuber and garlic. Always garlic. Ah, Gypsyland. A Gaje in Gypsyland. Every day was an adventure.

I opened my eyes and saw Kalina by the fire, cooking. God, she was beautiful! She was with a tall, dark and strikingly handsome man in his forties. They were laughing and very relaxed with each other. The rising sun was still hidden behind the eastern mountains—yet it painted the early morning sky gold. Kalina and the man were backlit by the golden sky. Again I wished I had my camera.

It was a portrait of fresh love—even though he was too old for her. Still it was a picture of two people who were in love—whether they knew it or not. In my head, I could hear Mick Jagger and the Stones.

"I can't get no
I can't get no
I can't get no . . .
Satttisssss-fact-tionnnnnn
Cause I try and I try and I try
I can't get no . . .

"The prince awakens," the man said.

Kalina walked toward me, her arms wide. "Just my luck," she laughed. "With a world full of princes, I get a one-eyed prince."

"But in the land of the blind I am all seeing," I said.

"We could use a visionary like you," the man said, coming toward me with his hand outstretched. "Kelly, I am George." He was a dark skinned Cary Grant. Just my luck.

We shook hands and I could tell he was trying to read the look on my face. The words from one of yesterday's songs came to mind. The Fortunes'.

"I see that worried look upon your face
She's found somebody else to take your place
You need some sympathy, well so do I
You've got your troubles, I've got mine."

I'm sure that's what he saw because he smiled and pointed at a gorgeous, lanky woman, who could have been Kalina's sister, approaching from behind me. "And here comes my better half. Petshiva, meet Kelly. Kelly, meet Petshiva."

It was a very proper, formal introduction. That's the way George was. If there was a proper way of doing things, that's the way George did it. In the short time I had known him I had already learned to like him.

"Howdy, podner," Petshiva said, affecting a cowboy twang as we shook hands. "Nice eye."

She was taller than Kalina. Hell, she was taller than George, who was taller than I was. Her eyes were similar to Kalina's. Except where Kalina's eyes were a golden tan with emerald green flecks, Petshiva's eyes were emerald green with golden tan flecks. I wondered if they were sisters or related.

Petshiva leaned forward as if to kiss me and then jerked back. "Awakk!" she shouted and turned toward Kalina. "Kalina, your cowboy's got morning breath." She started walking toward Kalina. "I'm starved. What cha' cooking, Baby Goods?"

"I'm cooking what you're smelling," Kalina said.

Petshiva stopped, looked back at me and cocked a hip. "The answers to your unasked questions are: 'No and Yes.'" She continued toward the cook fire where Kalina, was holding out a plate for her. "Of course," she continued, without looking at me. "I don't know you well enough yet to know if I have **your** answers in the right order."

"What questions," I asked.

They both smiled at me and said in unison: "Are they sisters? No." They laughed and then in unison: "Are they related? Yes." They laughed again and looked over at George. Then the three of them said in unison, "The Gaje are so easy."

It's nice to be teased. When people are comfortable enough to tease you, it's because they like you.

I looked at George. "How do you put up with the two of them?"

"I've learned to never cross them and I try to keep them separated," he said. "One more thing," he added. "Always keep your chin tucked against your shoulder and your right hand in front of your right eye."

They all laughed.

*   *   *

After breakfast, I drove while they slept. They had been up most of the night. I had guessed what the big confab last night had been about. It was about the planned highway cutting through the Gypsy camp.

I picked up most of this information while we ate breakfast. It was early morning chatter generated by the excitement of their all-night planning session. They were exhausted but still fueled by the promise of last night's plans and dreams.

For the most part I listened and kept my mouth shut. At the University of Kansas' William Allen White School of Journalism I had a journalism professor who had won a Pulitzer for investigative reporting. He was an aggressive little guy with big ears and a pompadour. Without a doubt, he was my favorite reporting professor. Man, talk about a guy who had the natural ability to cut through bullshit and go to the heart of the matter. That's how he won his Pulitzer. Anyway, he constantly reminded us that you learned twice as much, twice as fast, with your ears open and your mouth shut. A good life lesson.

The Highway Commission (or the French equivalent) was trying to invoke their equivalent of eminent domain on the campground. George and Petshiva were the legal leaders in the battle. Kalina was sort of the overseer. I also learned that she was the overseer/go-between on several issues that the Gypsy community was dealing with.

After breakfast we all climbed into the Citroen. The University at Poitiers was our destination. It was the second oldest university in France, although not in continuous operation. It had voluminous records concerning land transactions.

I drove. Kalina rode shotgun. George and Petshiva crawled into the back seat.

"Sleep fast," Kalina told them.

They pulled blankets over their heads and that was the last I saw of them until we reached Poitiers. *Sleep fast.* I loved Gypsy terminology.

"Where to?" I asked Kalina.

"Down the road," she said hooking a thumb to the right. "Then left and straight on 'til learning." She pulled her blanket over her head.

"Any other clues?"

"Follow the music."

*   *   *

The radio reception continued to improve as I drove east. Same station. Great music. Like yesterday, most of the music contained a message of some sort. And most of the music was completely new. I was enjoying it and turned the volume up a little.

"Turn it down!" Petshiva bellowed from beneath her blanket in the rear seat. "Or I'll plug your ears with my thighs until you suffocate."

That created an interesting image in my mind.

"It's not an idle threat, Kelly," George said from beneath his blanket. "She kills for sleep."

Still, it was an interesting way to go.

"Don't even think about it, Cowboy," Kalina said from beneath her blanket. "It would be your last rodeo." I turned the radio very low.

"Good choice," Kalina whispered.

*   *   *

A little later I turned left on a road that was heading north. The radio signal grew louder and I cut the volume again.

The second song that I heard after turning north was familiar. I couldn't believe my ears. It was by an old roommate from Folk House. Barry MacGuire. He'd been my roommate for a couple of months after leaving the Christy Minstrels at the end of last year. His big solo with the Christy's had been **Green, Green.** He'd sat on our big, tan, U-shaped couch for days working on the song that I was now listening to. When he had finished it, none of the club owners in Kansas City would let him play it at first.

Then it became an issue with Barry. "If I cain't play it here, I ain't singing here." The owners recanted. But no one would record it.

I had sat in my living room in Mission, Kansas, and heard this song being born. Now, I was listening to it on French radio. *The Eve of Destruction.*

"The eastern world it is explodin' violence flarin', bullets loadin' you're old enough to kill but not for votin' and even the Jordan river has bodies floatin' but you tell me over and over again my friend, ah, you don't believe we're on the eve of destruction."

Barry had moved to New York in February and here I was in France listening to him. Wow, what a rush! I wanted to wake everybody up so they could hear it, but decided they'd rather be sleeping.

After listening to a few more songs I could see the spires of medieval churches on the distant horizon. The town itself sat on a raised plateau between valleys and streams.

As I drove into the ancient section of the town, my passengers began to stir. First, Kalina peeled back her blanket and began a history lesson on Poitiers. How the buildings along the winding streets I was navigating were all built during Roman rule. After the Romans came the Visigoths and on and on. Joan of Arc had been subjected to a formal inquest here in 1429. Three years later the University had been founded.

When Kalina got into the University's history, was when I got interested. It seems that at the time of the French Revolution the University lost its accreditation. Some say it was because it was a hotbed of hotheads—but what university isn't? Some say it was because of anti-Christian elements. Some say the University was haunted.

Bing! Ghosts. Spooky stuff. Hauntings. Things that swoosh in the night. Mention that sort of thing and you've got me hooked. They don't even have to go bump in the night to hook me. A simple *creak* will do. You develop a natural fascination for things like that when you grow up with a mother who is psychic.

Yes, I know, that sounds weird. But try growing up with a mother who has dreams that really come true. Not just occasionally—but all the time. Dreams that were, as she put it: "So vivid they had to come true."

Like the time she had a dream that the plane my dad was booked on was going to crash. She called my dad, who was in New York on business, and told him that she had one of her dreams. The plane he was booked on was going to crash and there would be no survivors. She begged him to take a different flight. Dad, an aeronautical engineer who believed only in "*solid science*," didn't believe in Mom's dreams. But because she was so upset, he took an earlier flight just to calm her down. His original flight crashed. Everybody was killed.

I could go on about her other dreams, but that isn't what this story is about. Still, try growing up with a mother whose dreams come true and then try not to be intrigued by the "*other science*" as she called it.

By the time I parked in front of the ancient, stone library, Kalina had me totally caught up in the occult legends of the University. However, once inside the library, the three of them headed for the Hall of Records while I found the history wing.

Luckily, I found an ancient librarian, who took a liking to me. She appeared old enough to have been present when the library was originally christened. She spoke English and brought me occult books I would never have found otherwise. She even bookmarked the pages I needed in each.

Kalina found me at a corner table surrounded by the books the librarian had selected. She told me that they were going across the street to grab a bite to eat and discuss their findings. After which, she added, we needed to get on the road. George and Petshiva were staying.

I told her I'd like to keep researching while they ate. She tousled my hair and took off. After Kalina was gone, the old librarian came over to gather up the books I was finished with. While she did, she reaffirmed her conclusions that I was from the U.S. and that I was interested in becoming a writer.

"I can always spot a future writer," she told me. But I could tell that there was something else she wanted to ask. Finally, she did.

"You have to be careful of her kind," she said, obviously meaning Kalina. "They aren't always doing what they appear to be doing." She winked to punctuate her warning, tapped her eye as if to say: *you have been warned* and retreated to her desk.

In what seemed like no time, Kalina was back.

"Come with me," she said. "They have written a song about you."

"About me?"

"It sounds like you," she smiled.

We left the library and crossed the street to a student hangout. *The Shared Table* was the best that I could translate its name. It was a cavernous hall populated with long tables lit by chandeliers. Most of the tables were half filled or better. As the name implied, the students shared food and drink here. But more importantly, they brought in their records and shared their music. There was a special camaraderie that you felt from the moment you walked in the door and the music was the driving force.

Kalina pointed at a half-filled table. I sat and she continued on to the bar. A large black woman was tending bar and holding court there. And, I mean large. She stood six-feet-four if she was an inch. That did not include the biggest Afro hairdo I'd ever seen. She tipped the scale at around two hundred and seventy-five pounds and I doubt if you could have found an ounce of fat on her. She was just plain big.

She and Kalina chatted and laughed at the bar as the black woman poured two glasses of red wine. Kalina reached for her money and the black woman waved her off. As Kalina carried the wine back to our table I wondered if she ever actually paid for anything. If so, I hadn't seen it yet.

Kalina put the wines on the rough wood table and sat down beside me. We were both facing the bartender. With a dramatic flourish the black bartender pointed at us, then she bent behind the bar. The song that was playing abruptly stopped. A new song began to play. But it wasn't a record. It was a tape. Something that someone had recorded live.

I heard the harmonica and I knew who it was.

It was that little skinny rich kid from Minnesota who had driven his parents' Mercedes over his new jeans to make them look old and battered before setting out for New York with his Martin guitar to become famous—or so the story went.

He hadn't needed to distress the jeans and act down and out because he could write. He was a prophet with a grasp of poetry. I was already a fan. But this was new, different and wonderful.

The guitar on this recording was electric and so was his backup. What a departure!

The funny thing was that in the background of the recording you could hear boos. Obviously, wherever this was recorded, some people didn't appreciate his switch from acoustic to electric.

But that wasn't the case here. Suddenly, everybody in the place was on their feet, moving with the music. Later, Kalina told me they had been playing it all day. And it had been this way all day.

It was the first time I had ever heard this song. All six minutes and nine seconds of it. An extraordinary length for a song at the time. Nobody who wanted his or her song broadcast recorded a song that long. The unwritten rule was that a song couldn't exceed three minutes. Some of the Brit bands were pushing the four-minute mark. But six!?! This song was *the* trendsetter.

"This is about you," Kalina said. She touched her glass to mine and I listened to Bob Dylan rasp out what was to become my favorite song.

"Once upon a time you dressed so fine
You threw the bums a dime in your prime, didn't you?
People'd call, say, "Beware, doll, you're bound to fall"
You thought they were all kiddin' you
You used to laugh about
Everybody that was hangin' out
Now you don't talk so loud
Now you don't seem so proud
About having to scrounge for your next meal.
How does it feel?
How does if feel?
How does it feel . . . to be without a home?
How does it feel . . . to be on your own?
With no direction home
Like a complete unknown
Like a rolling stone . . ."

*   *   *

Kalina was exhausted. She dozed off and on as we drove away from Poitiers. But most of the time she was awake. Running on nervous energy. Driven by the excitement of what she, George and Petshiva had discovered. And that was that legal precedent was on their side. The French Highway Commission could not just seize the campground for the "public good" and pay what they wanted.

I learned that both George and Petshiva had law degrees. They predicted an easy win. In the end, they believed it would be their choice to stay or sell. They felt they were holding all the cards. They believed they could swap their campground for a new one plus a bundle of cash.

We had left George and Petshiva behind to finalize the research. I'm sure they were just as wired as Kalina was.

Finally she dozed off. I drove with Dylan's voice in my head. "How does it feel?"

Just before sunset we found a campground. As usual, kids were eager to build us a fire and set up our camp. We rolled out our sleeping bag and skipped dinner.

I massaged Kalina's neck and shoulders to relax her. At first her muscles were hard and tight with excitement and elation. But, as I worked on her, I could feel the tension washing away, the muscles relaxing. Her whole body was going limp. Earlier in the day, I had been hoping that we would celebrate their legal victory a little more vigorously tonight. But, a couple of hours ago, I realized that wasn't going to happen. So, I let my fingers do the talking.

She began mumbling to me and I knew by her voice that she wasn't much longer for this waking world.

"Tomorrow," she mumbled. "I want . . . you to . . ."

Her voice trailed away and I kept massaging. I knew the moment I stopped she would say: *Don't quit.* A couple of minutes passed. I thought she was asleep—but she was trying to put her thoughts into words.

Finally: "I know with your Midwestern background it is hard to be Gypsy." There was a pause and I thought she'd gone to sleep. Then: "To do as Gypsies do." Another long pause. The muscles in her neck and back were turning into warm taffy. It felt good to me. It must have felt great to her.

"I have to know if you can be Gypsy, Cowboy."

"I can be anything for you."

She chuckled softly. "Yeah, yeah. Pillow talk, Cowboy."

"Are you saying a cowboy can't be Gypsy?"

"It's like sending a marshmallow in to put out a bonfire," she quoted from the movie **Pillow Talk**. That was the last thing she said that night.

She didn't have to say *don't quit.* I didn't. She got a full body massage, and although she was asleep, I could tell that somewhere in there she was enjoying it.

In my head I kept hearing Dylan: *"How does it feel . . ."*

JILLING DROM

Jilling Drom is as close as I can come to saying 'on the road again' in Rom. As usual, we were on the road early—following her father, more or less. But today was going to be different. Today, Kalina was going to test me to see if I could really be Gypsy. A black eyed Gypsy. Actually my eye was purplish today. But I was still pretty much a one-eyed Gypsy.

A one-eyed reluctant Gypsy. Reluctant because, like Kalina, I didn't know how well I was going to cope with really being Gypsy. I was having a hard enough time being a Kansas Cowboy when I wasn't even a farm boy. I mean, in reality, at best I was an urban newsboy. Gypsy?!? Who was I kidding?

We traveled down a straight-as-a-string highway across flat land with mountains on both sides. This was unusual because most roads were picturesque and wound around like they were following medieval routes. This one must have been newer. It was probably like the road they were planning on running through the campground behind us.

The sun was breaking through the low multi-gray clouds, painting the folds silver, as we came to the little, postcard town of Arlanc. The houses and stores were like fairytale gingerbread houses. Elaborate curtail and pastel paint. I really felt like I was in fairytale land until I saw a big, ugly, gray concrete box of a store. It was completely out of touch with its surroundings. It was Mono Prix. The French version of a K-Mart.

Kalina pointed at it. "There," she said. "It's a big chain. They can afford us." She laughed her magical laugh. "Remember, Cowboy, what we take isn't for us. It's for others. Think: The James boys; the Daltons. The Younger brothers. Think: Kansas."

She smiled at me and I smiled back.

"The Daltons were just low-life thieves and Kansans aren't thieves."

She studied me, a frown on her face. "I thought Frank and Jesse James robbed from the rich and gave to the poor."

Strictly speaking, the James boys gave to the poor so the poor would hide them. But I didn't want to bust her balloon. "A better way to put it is: Frank and Jesse robbed from the rich and *shared* with the poor. And I always thought the Youngers were cool. They were the good outlaws."

"But not the Daltons?"

"Scum."

Her laugh lit me up. "Okay, Cowboy, we are going to rob from the rich and *share* with the poor. Are you ready to be an outlaw?"

I nodded. I was about to become an outlaw. I felt chills. God, she was good at pushing my buttons.

GYPSY NOW

I pulled into the parking lot. There were only four other cars in the huge paved and lined lot. Paved and lined. So out of place here. It sort of made it easier.

"Park with the nose of the car facing the store."

I did. We got out of the faded yellow Citroen. Not exactly my idea of a getaway car. I left the keys in it. My modern equivalent of not tying the horse's reins to the hitching rail.

We started walking toward the Mono Prix. Funny how an ugly box of a building gets uglier once you decide to rob it. And that's what we were about to do. We were going to rob the rich and give to the poor. We were outlaws. E-haaa!

I hoped I didn't wet my pants.

We went inside.

Kalina grabbed a cart and we began to cruise the aisles. It was mainly a food store with rear sections for clothing, hardware and sporting goods. There was a small section for stereo equipment and there was an enclosed pharmacy area.

The store manager was on us from the get-go. He reminded me of the balding, fat Frenchman in the Saltine Cracker logo. I could almost hear his unspoken P.A. announcement to his staff. *"Alert! Alert! Gypsies on aisle four!"* It *was* exciting. A major rush. Everybody in the store was watching us. And I just followed Kalina's lead.

We started for the back of the store. Employees flanked us one aisle away on each side. They tried to go unnoticed. But that just made them painfully obvious.

Kalina pointed at a hibachi. I retrieved it and put it in the cart. She pointed at a bag of charcoal. I got it and put it in the cart.

"Inspector Cousteau and his men are watching us," I whispered. I was having fun. I was being an outlaw. Kalina smiled at me. She had known she had the right button before she pushed it. Nothing new there.

"They always watch us. You are Gypsy now, Cowboy."

She pointed at what she wanted. Like a good dog, I retrieved. A package of bologna. A baguette. Several kinds of cheese. A bottle of red wine. A bottle of A-1 Sauce. Some horseradish. I fetched and deposited the items in the cart. She nodded and we headed for the checkout counter.

Kalina put a credit card on the checkout counter and the rotund Saltine manager rattled off something in French. "They don't take credit cards from Gypsies," she translated for me. "For Gypsies it is cash only. Very rude."

What a surprise, I thought.

I started to reach for my money—she kicked me so subtlety he could never have noticed. Still, it was hard enough that I grunted.

The grunt drew his attention to me. He was really checking me out now. He wasn't sure what that grunt meant. Had he pissed me off? Gypsies are, for the most part, non-violent toward the Gaje. Yet, look at my eye. I didn't get this eye being non-violent. Maybe I was part of a hot-headed clan. I could see it in his eyes. His eyes were easier to read than mine. He fidgeted and raked his hand through his thinning hair. He didn't want any trouble. He just wanted us out of his store.

Kalina pulled cash from the pocket of her skirt. Counted it. Pointed to the hibachi, the charcoal and the A-1 Sauce.

He rang those items up and she paid.

I carried them out to the Citroen. Kalina raised the tailgate door and I put the three items inside. Kalina glanced back at the store to see if we were being watched. We weren't. They couldn't have seen us anyway. That's why she had me park with the rear of the Citroen away from the store. Then from the folds of her skirt she pulled out three T-bone steaks, three potatoes, some scallions and some mushrooms. The steaks were big enough to feed six.

"You stole those steaks while they were watching you?"

"What'd you think the A-1 Sauce and the hibachi were for?"

Kalina took three forks and three hunting knives out of the folds of her skirt. "These will have to do for steak knives. The real steak knives were in a boxed set and it was too cumbersome. And it is hard to leave pregnant when they know you didn't come in that way."

I laughed. "Well, if anyone could pull that off, I'd bet on you."

She kissed me, leaned against the open tailgate and gave me an evaluating look.

"So, how did I do," I asked, glancing at the store. "Was I Gypsy?"

"Well, since we aren't in jail, I'd say you made your eight-second ride, Cowboy."

"I love it when you talk cowboy, Gypsy girl." I gave her an excitement-charged smile. I had passed her Gypsy test. "Let's go before they count the steaks," I added. I saw her almost grimace. Why couldn't I learn to keep my mouth shut?

She looked at me sadly, shook her head, closed the tailgate, walked over and slid her arms around my neck. "We don't see them, but they are watching us. If we hurry off, they will count the steaks." She kissed me, straightened the collar of my jacket and casually walked around to the passenger side of the Citroen. "Now we go, Poncho."

Ouch! I was supposed to be Cisco—not the second banana. She was really good at blind-siding. I saved a little face by not asking who the third steak was for.

We climbed into the station wagon and I crept out of the parking lot.

ANOTHER CAMPGROUND

We rolled on until we reached a fork in the road. The highway went to the left; a secondary road went to the right. A strip of faded red rag led us to the right.

Another strip of faded red rag guided us into a campground. Gorgeous, ancient forest surrounded the grounds. The late afternoon sun filtered golden light through the multi-shaded greens of the leaves. It was getting to the point that I could picture these campgrounds without looking. They all looked alike. And, the strange thing was that they were all starting to look like home. Was I becoming Gypsy?

We parked and got out.

I stood there hypnotized by the sunlight filtering through the trees with the mountains in the background. A dozen campers, vans and trailers were scattered around. People were starting campfires. Children were playing hide and seek. It could have been anywhere—but it wasn't. It was the Gypsy camp Norman Rockwell had always been looking for. And, once again I was without a camera.

A fortyish, stocky Gypsy approached us. He barely looked at me.

"Bin-Bin," Kalina said. "It is good to see you." She indicated me. "This is Kelly. My Gajo. He only speaks English."

Bin-Bin smiled and offered his hand. "Welcome, Kelly." His brown-toothed smile was insincere. Forced was a better word choice. Not insincere. Worried and forced.

We shook. But his focus was on Kalina. A sad concerned look clouded his deeply wrinkled face. At first Kalina didn't notice. Eyes, pinched, downcast, he gave her the keys to her NSU in exchange for the Citroen keys.

"Hey, Bin-Bin," she said. "I just taught Kelly how to fool the Gaje."

"You fooled them good, I bet." He winked to show me that he wasn't discounting me with his lack of warmth.

I wasn't being my usual dense, Gaje self. I was reading between the lines. Something was wrong.

"To celebrate," Kalina continued, "I'm cooking dinner for you and your family tonight. I've got steaks and potatoes and . . ." She finally noticed his sad demeanor. "What's wrong?"

"I have bad news for you," he said. "Your father was here last night. Old Jumpy saw him and said to tell you Old Bohemius is very sick. Coughing up blood. He went to Lourdes but he wasn't cured. He's lost a lot of weight."

"Where's my bike?"

He pointed. "Over there. Gassed and ready."

Kalina pulled her daypack out of the Citroen. She took her jeans out of her pack and tossed the pack at my feet.

"Put that in the left saddle bag on my bike. And tie your pack on over the saddle bags like before." She was all business. No emotion. She could cry on the road. She looked at Bin-Bin. "Everything in the back of the Citroen is for you and your family."

She stalked off toward the showers on long purposeful strides, her red skirt twitching from side to side.

Bin-Bin continued to stare at the ground. "She has a temper like her mother." He took a good look at me for the first time and saw my purple, swollen eye. "But I can see you know that." He laughed. "She caught you looking at another woman, right?"

"How did you know?"

"They always hit you in the eye when they catch you looking at another woman. And because you are looking at the other woman you never see the punch coming." He laughed again. "The Tsuhrara women are more than a handful, Gajo. Beware."

I nodded. "Do you know where Old Bohemius was going?"

"I think he was going back to Lourdes."

I looked up and saw Kalina coming out of the showers wearing her jeans. I could tell by her purposeful stride that she wasn't planning on wasting any time. I got a move on. Stuffed her daypack into the left saddlebag and tied my pack over the saddlebags.

She handed me her red skirt. "Stuff it in the right bag."

I did.

She climbed onto her bike and slapped the seat behind her. I climbed on and held onto her. She popped a wheelie and we were off.

"Bin-Bin thinks he knows where your father was going," I said as we swung out onto the highway.

"Yeah, yeah. He's headed back to Lourdes."

"How did you know?"

"Because he's pig-headed. It didn't work the first time so he'll go back and give it another try."

It's hard to carry on a conversation when you're on the back of a motorcycle. So I just shut up and hung on to her.

I held her tightly. It was the only comfort I could offer. I couldn't hear her sobs over the roar of the bike and whoosh of the wind—but I could feel them. It almost made me cry, too. But I had to cowboy up for her.

THE VILLAGE OF BARTRES

Kalina pulled her bike to the side of the road a few kilometers from Lourdes. There were maybe a dozen cars parked off road here. She pointed her bike at a small stone shack about twenty yards away. It was lop-sided with double wooden doors in front. There was a third wooden door above those two. If it had once been a barn, and it had all the earmarks of having been a small one once, the second story door would have accessed the hayloft.

"What do you know about Lourdes?" Kalina asked.

"Not much. A farm girl saw the Virgin Mary appear and I don't know if the girl was sick and was cured. I don't know. I think her name was Bernadette."

Kalina's harrumph told me I was certainly not up to speed. And the history lesson began. I knew that the history lesson was more of a way for her to build a defense between her and what was happening to her father than it was about giving information to me. If the situations were reversed, I doubted I would be handling it as well.

"That shack over there," Kalina said, pointing. "That's where Bernadette was wet nursed by Marie Lagues. Her name was Bernadette Soubirous.

"Her family was desperately poor. Her father failed at everything he attempted to do. He sent her here in November of 1844. It was one less mouth for him to try to feed. By some accounts she had five siblings. Some say nine. The church has its version. Pick a version—they were dirt poor.

"Marie nursed Bernadette through the winter and sent her back to her family in the spring. Thirteen years later her family sent Bernadette back to Marie. And, that's where the legend, or myth, or whatever you choose to call it began."

I could tell by the tone of her voice and her demeanor that she wasn't really buying the story. But it was *history* and she was a history buff. It occurred to me that the reason she was such a history buff was that history stabilizes. She had been on the move all her life. She had no home. No roots. Where ever she went she learned the history. That was her form of roots. And right now she needed roots.

History was Kalina's roots. Being from the Midwest, I knew about roots. If your family hadn't lived in the area for fifty years or more, you were considered a newcomer. You weren't ever going to be anything but a newcomer. I understood the concept. I'd never been anything but a newcomer all my life. While I knew my family history, both my mother's and father's sides, they were always on the move, too. I really understood her need for roots.

No matter where they traveled, Gypsies were always newcomers. Or, more accurately, they were always outsiders who were not to be trusted. But in their campgrounds they were family. Even I was family in their campgrounds.

She nosed her bike around so I could get a little better look at the stone shack. "Bernadette worked for Marie as a farmhand, a baby sitter and goat herder. Because of all her duties, Bernadette didn't have time to learn the Catholic faith. Marie, who was very religious, thought it was her responsibility to teach her. She tried but Bernadette wasn't all that bright and had trouble retaining the information. So, Marie sent her to Lourdes to prepare for her first communion. That was January 21st 1858."

Kalina pointed at a dirt path that led south from the stone shack. "That's the path Bernadette took. Pilgrims who come to Lourdes follow her path. That's why all these unattended cars are sitting here. Their owners are either on the path or already at the Grotto. Hang on."

Kalina began motoring slowly down the path, sort of ground surfing with her feet to maintain balance as she continued her story.

"From here, Bernadette walked to Lourdes. It wasn't just once that she saw the Virgin Mary, like most people think. It was *eighteen times* and it was witnessed by other people."

We motor-surfed past a family of four who gave us dirty looks. Kalina could care less. We motor-surfed on.

"The first apparition was on Thursday February 11th 1858.

"Bernadette went to Massabielle on the banks of the Gave to gather bone and firewood with her sister and a friend. Did you know bones burn like good firewood?"

I didn't. But it was a rhetorical question. Kalina was using the story to build a barrier between her and reality. My role was that of a masonry's hod carrier.

"As Bernadette was crossing the stream she heard a noise like a gust of wind. She looked toward the Grotto and saw a lady dressed in white. A white dress. An equally white veil. She also wore a blue belt. There was a yellow rose on each foot. Bernadette made the sign of the cross and recited the rosary with the lady. When the prayer ended the lady suddenly vanished.

"On her third visit the lady spoke to her for the first time. Bernadette gave her a pencil and paper and asked the lady to write her name. The lady said, 'It is not necessary. I do not promise to make you happy in this world—but in the other. Would you be kind enough to come here for a fortnight?'

"Word spread. Each time Bernadette returned more and more people came with her.

"By the seventh apparition one hundred and fifty people accompanied her. All of them saw the lady materialize and vanish.

"On the eleventh visit there were one thousand people present." Kalina's voice was building.

"The twelfth time, one thousand five hundred people witnessed the apparition. Or, so the story goes." Sarcasm.

"It was on this visit that Catherine Latapie, a friend from Lourdes, plunged her dislocated arm into the spring. Her arm and hand regained their movement." Kalina's tone of voice was evangelistic.

"On the fifteenth time about eight thousand people witnessed the apparition.

"On the eighteenth and final time, when Bernadette arrived at the Grotto the police had it blocked. Bernadette had to view the Grotto from the far side of the Gave. And the lady appeared above the water of the Gave. They said the Rosary together and the lady vanished. No one knows how many witnesses there were. But all told the same story." Kalina's presentation had gone from evangelistic to dramatic.

A group of eight or ten pilgrims, who were coming back up the path, began shouting at us. They obviously didn't appreciate us being on their path with a motorcycle. Or maybe they didn't like the sarcasm in her voice.

To let them by, Kalina eased her bike off the path and across the tourist trash-littered land to a two-lane road.

LOURDES

We cruised slowly along the main road into town through increasingly heavy traffic until we spotted a campground ahead.

"This is ours," Kalina said. "But it's different from the others."

At the gate several boys were charging for parking. They waved us through the gate. We were in a Gaje parking area. We passed fifty or so parked cars before we got to a second gate. Another group of boys again waved us through . . . and into the Gypsy parking area.

As we passed, the boys, shouted Kalina's name. Not as a greeting to her—but as an announcement to the half a dozen caravans parked there. People began to appear before she cut the motor on her bike. They were smiling, happy to see her. Almost anxious.

"Wait here," she said climbing off the bike. "I have business." She took her notebook from the left saddlebag and met the approaching people. There were lots of smiles, hugs, fast conversation and nodding of heads. Then Kalina was on her way back to the bike, followed by all the people.

Kalina stashed her notebook in the saddlebag and climbed on the bike while people introduced themselves to me and shook hands. There were too many hands, too many faces, and too many names, delivered too fast to retain them.

"Papa was here," she said firing up her bike. "Here and gone." She waved to everyone and we were off. Out of the Gypsy camping area, through the Gaje parking area and onto the road.

It was easy to see why the Gypsies could charge for the parking. We were on the edge of town about a kilometer from the Grotto and every possible parking space was occupied. The traffic on the street was stop and go. Kalina threaded the bike between the traffic and the parked cars.

Lourdes was a small village. Maybe 17,000 people. We came into Lourdes through its older area, which were mostly stone walled structures. Some were wood framed. I got the flavor of what it might have been when Bernadette came through here.

But now the street was a mixture of storefronts and open-air stands catering to their newly found industry. The little shops' and stands' merchandise was almost exclusively religious artifacts and trinkets.

I hung on tighter than I needed to and said to the ear hole of her helmet: "Back there you said you had business. What kind?"

"Does the Gaje smell money?" She laughed. "The Gaje are good at smelling money."

"Not always. The Indians still have the beads and all we have to show for that deal is Manhattan."

"A developer wants to buy our campground."

"Of course," I said waving at the crude little street. "It's a commercial mecca waiting to be developed."

"Waiting?" she chuckled to herself, or maybe at me. "You haven't seen anything yet."

We motored along observing the shops. Foot traffic increased as we got closer to the Grotto.

"Don't take his first offer," I said, being a fountain of knowledge.

"I didn't. Nor the second. Nor the third."

She obviously didn't need my limited expertise. She was obviously quite good at negotiating. Why would I expect otherwise?

And then we entered the section of the city that had grown up after Bernadette's apparitions. Hotels. Lots of hotels. They were making money hand over fist off the sick and dying who were praying desperately for a miracle.

I understood Kalina's distain and I gave her a tight hug to let her know I was in tune with her feelings. This was where her father had chosen to come and she was pissed at his decision. I would have been, too. Back home my grandmother had cancer. But I never would have brought her to this tourist trap in hopes of a miracle. It was a waste of money, hope and energy. Mostly, it was a waste of precious time.

Thinking about my grandmother and the intentionally deceptive false hope this place represented, I teared up. I pretended it was the wind in my eyes. I think Kalina knew better. I had told her about my grandmother and she had to know what I was thinking.

Kalina stopped a good distance from the Grotto. We couldn't get any closer. She parked next to a fireplug. All the street parking was taken. The parking lot here was full. And beyond the lot were rows and rows of thirty-foot-long park benches full of praying people. My heart went out to them.

We walked the rest of the way, looking at the faces. Faces full of hope. Memory was my camera. I recorded many faces. Lined faces. Dirt creviced faces. Hope filled faces. Hopeless faces. Faces that were so life-eroded that they were almost no longer faces. Mostly they were sad, disappointed faces.

Kalina was looking for only one face. And it wasn't there.

It was obvious by all the sad faces that the Virgin Mary wasn't showing up today. Maybe this was her day off. Virgins do have days off, don't they?

Well, the Lady hadn't appeared for Old Bohemius either. And he wasn't cured. He was gone. We needed to look for him elsewhere.

"This is where the myth began," she said. "Very spiritual, huh?"

I heard the skepticism and anger in her voice. She knew everything about this place—but it wasn't creating a miracle for her father. And she wasn't a believer anyway. Gypsies don't believe in mysticism. They believe in sleight of hand and misdirection.

I could read her anger and frustration as she paced around looking at the faces of all these people who were here hoping, wishing and praying for a miracle. Why had Bohemius been like them!?!

Kalina stopped in front of a newspaper kiosk. She studied the front pages looking for a clue. Anything. And then the date line on the newspaper caught her eye. Time and dates don't mean much to Gypsies. But this did.

"We have to be in Paris in two days. For Fawn and Charlie."

I didn't know why. I didn't care. We walked back to her motorcycle, climbed on and sped off. I was happy to be holding onto Kalina. I was in heaven. How could you not be in heaven if you were holding onto Kalina and going some place? Who cared where? Paris sounded good.

THE MARCH

France isn't that big. Traveling from the south to Paris took us about ten hours road time. Four hours that day. Six hours the next, which included several stops.

When we set out the second day, it was a glorious, cloudless, blue-sky day. Naturally I said nothing about it. It was self-evident. But on the way north clouds began to build up. At first, they were white cirrus clouds. Then they began turning dark and still darker until they were thunderheads. Finally, turning into black cumulonimbus and I could smell the coming rain.

Fortunately, we arrived at Fawn and Charlie's place before the deluge. I call it *their place* because it wasn't an apartment. It was a space in a warehouse. It was what they could afford. They were ecstatic to see Kalina. I realized that she was their roots. Fawn and Charlie were merely gracious to me. We were offered a blanket and floor space for sleeping. It wasn't a very big room and, already about twenty other people were sharing the floor. In Kansas it would have been intolerable. But I was learning to be Gypsy. You could be six inches from another couple and yet miles away. Outside, the rain broke loose. It beat down with a fury. It was loud, sounding furious.

"Is there an agenda for tomorrow?" Kalina asked.

Fawn was the talker. "More people will start showing up here in the morning, with signs. We will march."

"March about what?" I asked.

"Against the Untied States being in Vietnam," Fawn said. "My country."

It wasn't a hard sell for me. Like I've said, I had already lost two really good buddies there. And, if I didn't have asthma, I'd probably be in a body bag, too. There had been a couple of accidental deaths on the live ammo training range at Fort Reilly, Kansas. A couple of guys with asthma had gotten choked up on the range and couldn't breathe. They had raised their heads to get a breath and were shot. Until things cooled down, the Army didn't want anyone with asthma. So, I was on hold. At the top of the draft list—but on hold.

"I'm in," I said. I didn't mean it to be as self-serving as it probably was.

"We're honored to have the Gypsies with us," Fawn said, shaking my hand. Then Fawn hurried off to make more preparations for tomorrow.

I stared after her. Did she really not recognize me from our first meeting? Had I really changed that much? I looked at Kalina.

She had been observing my reaction and smiled at me. I was Gypsy—at least to a Vietnamese girl.

I smiled back at Kalina and winked. I liked being Gypsy. It was a new world.

*   *   *

Kalina woke me in the morning with hot sex. I am a slow-to-awake person. It was over before my eyes were open. But really good, if not great. I'm only good for two things in the morning. Writing and sex. My new typewriter was outside in the motorcycle saddlebag. And who in their right mind would trade writing for Kalina. Hopefully I'd never write in the morning again.

"Time to march," she said.

It was my first anti-Vietnam march. But not my last.

It was on the Left Bank. People just materialized. Slowly. One by one. In the beginning there were, maybe, a hundred people. That number grew kept growing slowly. At first there were more people watching than marching. Then the watchers started joining in, once they determined it was safe. Before long we numbered a couple hundred. Then hundreds. As much as possible, we stuck to streets that did not allow cars.

By mid afternoon, the speeches started. By then there were probably two thousand marchers or more. That's when the police started showing up. And they were pissed off about being there. We were ruining their weekend.

Coming from Kansas I wasn't used to protesting against anything. I didn't understand the rules. When the police show up, you sit down. Or, as we say in Kansas, you hunker down.

I didn't sit or hunker. So, I got clubbed. Head wounds bleed a lot.

Kalina led me out of there. Cops chased us because we were moving. Never move during a riot or protest. If you do, you become a target. It was a lesson that served me well three years later in Chicago's Lincoln Park during the Democratic

Convention riot. I didn't run. I didn't get clubbed. I stood my ground there.

Kalina led me to her motorcycle and we climbed on. "Hang on tight, Cowboy." I was happy to obey.

The French cops were right behind us and when we took off, they jumped into a police car and came after us. "Why us?"

"You're Gypsy now."

I realized what it was to have a target painted on you. I wasn't in Kansas anymore where only rabbits, squirrels and deer had targets painted on them. Here, Gypsy was a target, too. Sometimes I was painfully slow in realizing a truth.

But Kalina was gleeful about the chase. From the left bank we went across to the Ile de la Cite then to the right bank. The cops were right behind us. And then a second cop car joined in. Sirens screaming. And then a third. We were very popular.

"We've become a parade," I shouted into the ear hole of her helmet.

She laughed. "Ain't it grand!"

We skidded around corners at speeds I didn't think were possible. Sometimes she'd stick out her foot on the road to keep us upright. She was loving it. I was scared shitless. But I was hanging onto Kalina and that was cool.

We raced up Rue Du Montmartre a half a block ahead of the cops. Kalina skidded to a stop below the Montmartre Basilica. Probably the highest spot in Paris. Below us were hundreds and hundreds and hundreds of stairs to Place Pigalle. The evening lamplights were just coming on, lighting the stairs. What a photo!—if you had a camera and if you had time to set up the shot.

The cop cars skidded to a stop behind us. No time for photography. We were caught. Or so I thought.

But this woman always had a trick up her sleeve. It was very Gypsy.

The cops started climbing out of their cars. They were smiling. They had us.

Kalina threw back her head and laughed. She gave them the finger. Obviously she thought she had them where she wanted them.

"Hang on," she said.

I was happy to hang on.

She stood the bike up in a magnificent wheelie and down the stairs we went. Hundreds and hundreds of stairs. Kidney jarring stairs. But there was no way they could follow us. No way could they get to the bottom of the stairs before we were gone. Yep. Kalina had them right where she wanted them. She was truly an amazing woman. And I was lucky enough to be hanging onto her.

"Hoo-haa!" I shouted.

"What's hoo-haa?"

"That's cowboy for 'Holding onto Kalina.'"

She threw back her head and laughed like she did when she knew she had suckered the cops into the chase. "You are in love with me."

"Getting there."

"No. You are *definitely* there."

She was always one step ahead of me. And I loved it.

"Hang on," she said again as we reached the bottom of the first flight of stairs. "We're almost home." She did another wheelie. She loved doing wheelies. And I was learning to hang on. I loved hanging on . . . or did I say that before?

We hit the bottom of the second flight of stairs, crossed a street, and plunged down a third flight. And a fourth. And a fifth.

Then we were on a steep cobbled street. Finally, flatland. I breathed a sigh of relief. Kalina cut down a shadowy street. Although I didn't know it at the time we were in the Eleventh Arrondissement. Old. Run down. Shops and warehouses were mixed with apartments. The moonlight was brighter than the infrequent streetlights.

Kalina cut the engine on her bike and coasted up to two big weathered wooden doors that once had been painted blue enamel. She turned and looked back at me. "The world is changing, Kelly," she said.

"I know it is," I said, fingering the scab on my head the cops gave me.

"We will be safe here tonight. Get the doors."

I climbed off the bike and groaned. I was not used to riding a motorcycle down five flights of gray stone stairs. Or was it six? I'd lost track. I opened the huge doors and Kalina straddled-walked her bike into a dark passage.

"Where are we?"

"Shhh. We mustn't wake anyone." She dismounted her bike and quietly put down the kickstand. She put her helmet on the seat and started off. I put my helmet behind hers, dug my fedora out of the saddlebag and followed.

"Will it be safe here?"

"Of all places."

Then she led me off into a large open courtyard. There were five or six small nondescript tents, a dozen caravans and one large gold tent. It was a very strange scene in the silver moonlight and deep shadows. The walls held in the smell of smoke.

"Wait here," she said and walked toward the gold tent.

I watched her scratch on the side of the tent. She waited a moment and scratched again. Then she ducked inside. I looked around at the tents. Where the hell was I?

As best as I could make out I was in a walled, open-air compound smack dab in the middle of Paris.

I only had to wait a couple of minutes before Kalina returned with a double sleeping bag under her arm. "Shhh," she said as she spread it out on the ground and climbed inside. I climbed in with her. I took one last look around. Where the hell was I?

We made love as silently as possible.

ANOTHER LESSON IN GYPSY

I awoke the next morning to the sounds of running water, crackling fires, soft footsteps, whispers and the smell of brewing coffee. I sat up with a groan. My back was stiff and sore from the jarring ride down the endless Montmartre stairs. Kalina "shushed" me.

I glanced over to where she was crouched beside a small cook fire heating a four-cup pot-metal coffee pot. I started to glance around to assess where I was.

"Eyes down," she whispered.

I looked at my watch. Six a.m. I stole a few quick glances around the compound. About half the tents I'd seen the previous night were gone. The gold colored tent was still there. Kalina handed me coffee in a light brown clay cup and motioned me off the sleeping bag, which she rolled up. She tucked the rolled sleeping bag under her arm and strolled toward the gold tent. It gave me a chance to study the place.

In front of each tent there was a small cook fire burning. Women were tending them. Children and dogs were hanging around.

On the closest wall, there were about seven water spigots, head high, above a urinal-like trough. Much like the enclosed showers in the campgrounds. Only these were out in the open.

Cookie-cutter style men were washing up. All dark. Mostly stocky. All strong looking. All naked to the waist. Their eyes were downcast. No one looked up. They were just lined up, each waiting his turn at the showers. None of them spoke. In fact, no one in the courtyard was speaking.

On the opposite wall was an identical set up for the women. They, too, were lined up waiting their turn at the showers. Naked to the waist. Their eyes were downcast. All were dark. But unlike the men, they came in a variety of shapes and sizes.

I glanced over at Kalina, as she returned from the gold tent, and saw that she was giving me a hard look. I looked down. A couple of minutes later she was standing in front of me, blue jean legs spread in a defiant stance. I looked up. Her fists were on her hips.

"You want another fat eye?"

I lowered my head to give her less of a target.

She knelt down beside me and chuckled softly in my ear. "I know it's hard not to look. I steal glances, too. Just don't stare." She poured two more cups of coffee and handed me the light brown clay cup again.

As I raised it to my lips, over the rim of the cup, I saw an attractive woman in her late thirties to mid forties come out of the gold tent. She was wearing a bright green skirt and white blouse and was carrying a tray. She came directly to us.

Kalina leaned back from me.

The woman offered the tray to Kalina. It contained several biscuits. Kalina took one and said nothing. The woman offered the tray to me. I took one.

"Thank you," I said. Damn it! I'd done it again.

The woman gave me a disgusted look. Almost a sneer. "Gaje," she whispered.

"My Gajo," Kalina said. "He's American and learning. Slowly."

"Welcome," the woman whispered to me in English. Then the woman looked at Kalina and bowed her head in respect. Quickly, she held the tray out to me again. I looked at Kalina for guidance. She nodded yes. I took a second biscuit.

The woman returned to the gold tent, proud and dignified.

"You never say, thank you. I told you that," Kalina whispered.

"I know, I know. It just slipped out."

"Don't let it happen again. It is embarrassing to me." It was obvious that she was more than a little pissed off. Here she was, stuck with a slow learner. She paused a moment, regaining her composure. "Don't look around or speak until you have finished your coffee and biscuits. It's rude," she whispered.

"I know. You told me," I whispered back.

"Yes," she whispered. "I did tell you, but it didn't take."

I shut up, ate the biscuits and drank the coffee.

Voices drew my attention. The first I had heard that morning. They were voices of children running and playing. I hurriedly finished my biscuits and coffee and struggled to my feet, groaning softly. I'd tried flexing and twisting my back to loosen it up. But it was still stiff from the ride down the stairs. But not nearly as stiff as it had been yesterday after the ride. Thus proving the value of a firm bed. And you don't get much firmer than the hard ground.

I looked around the courtyard, still trying to decipher where I was. I was in a campground in the middle of Paris—but where? The ground was hard packed. No vegetation. What happened here when it rained? Was it a field of mud?

I noticed that the ground slanted slightly toward the front wall where the wide wooden doors were. Then I saw the drainage pipes in the base of the wall. I pointed at the drainage pipes and turned to Kalina. "I see how you deal with the gentle rains. But what about the hard rains?"

"If you have a tent," she pointed at the four large stacks of two-by-twelve wooden planks. "You create a floor and sit on those and sleep sitting up. But, generally, you will be invited into someone's caravan."

Made sense. If there was one thing these people excelled at, it was taking care of each other.

The men and women were beginning to wander around and talk to each other. The women wore loose, full skirts in a palette of colors. Usually their blouses were white. The men wore dull colored suits and hats with bright colored shirts. They spoke to each other in a strange guttural language, which I was beginning to recognize as Rom. I was beginning to recognize some of the words, too. The conversations were punctuated with laughter. They were happy people with not much to be happy about.

Except . . . they were family!

"Wait here," Kalina said and walked off toward the gold tent.

I watched a man make his way across the courtyard shaking hands. "Bahtalo drom," I heard him say as he neared me. He was leaving.

When he reached me he bowed slightly. "Bahtalo drom."

I smiled and nodded. "Bahtalo drom," I responded.

He rattled off something in Rom.

I smiled, nodded my head in agreement and laughed.

He stuck out his hand and we shook. He started to turn away. But he stopped. He cocked his head at me, studying me. Then in English: "You're Kalina's Gajo, aren't you." It wasn't a question.

"Yes," I said. "How did you know?"

He threw back his head and laughed. "You fooled me. At first. Good for you." He slapped me on the shoulder. "But then we shook. Your hands betrayed you. You have very soft hands." He laughed and walked away. "Bahtalo drom," he called back over his shoulder.

"Bahtalo drom."

Kalina came out of the gold tent carrying a string bag with two brown-paper wrapped items in it. "We go." She headed toward her bike.

I followed. "Where in Paris are we?"

"You figure it out. It will make you smarter."

She donned her helmet, climbed on her bike and slapped the seat behind her. I donned my helmet and climbed on.

The children were watching us now. She motioned at the large wooden doors and the children raced to open them. She popped a wheelie and we were off again.

IN SESRCH OF BOHEMIUS

We sped through the streets, around corners, down allies. I had no idea where we were. I had only a vague idea of where we'd been. I knew it wouldn't do any good to ask again. I'd already been told to figure it out. So I just hung on and enjoyed the ride.

A gentle breeze made the air crisp and clean. It blew away the emission smells and the smells of dog shit, which were always present in Paris. The clouds were clearing, the sky above was azure. The sun beat down warm. *Jilling drom.*

We reached the thinning outskirts of Paris and Kalina pulled into the parking lot of a mom and pop food store. She turned off the bike. "Wait here. Keep it upright." She climbed off and went inside.

"Keep it upright" seemed simple enough. But it was heavy. Much heavier than I thought and it was a struggle to keep it upright. If Kalina could do it, so could I. I think she was just showing me how strong she was.

She came out of the store carrying a baguette of bread. She tucked it into one of the saddlebags and climbed on. "How was it?" she asked.

"Heavy," I said.

She laughed. "It's a bike."

And we were off again.

THE BIRTHDAY *PATSHIVA*

An hour or so later we drove into a campground along with a flood of caravans and cars.

"What's this, another wedding?"

"No. It's Uncle Bias' birthday celebration. Gypsies live from *patshiva* to *patshiva*. From ceremonial celebration to ceremonial celebration." She dropped the kickstand. We climbed off. She took the string bag and the baguette from the saddlebags and we merged into the crowd flowing toward the center of the campground.

"Well, it's certainly a beautiful day for it," I said without thinking.

Heads began to turn in my direction. There were hard stares and frowns. I realized what I'd done. "Damn it, I've done it again."

Kalina laughed, then said to everyone, "This is Kelly, my American Gajo. He knows better. He's just a slow learner."

That drew laughs and I got a few smiles. And the progression continued toward the center of the camp. I realized the deference I was getting because I was with Kalina. And, the pressure I was putting on her. I had to start thinking more before my mouth motored.

When we reached the center of the camp, which was lush and green with that sweet smell of foliage, there was a line of people leading up to Uncle Bias.

Uncle Bias was seated in a canvas lawn chair just as dignified as he had been at the wedding. Standing behind him was his statuesque wife, expressionless as before. Beside her was the youngest son.

People handed the son gifts, then spoke for a few seconds to Uncle Bias, laughed, and moved on. He was surrounded by gifts, which a young man was picking up and carrying to Uncle Bias' caravan to make room for the gifts that were yet to come. I recognized the young man from the wedding. He was now Uncle Bias' oldest unmarried son.

A couple of guitars and a violin started tuning up somewhere. The notes drifted on a light breeze that seemed to be swept into the campground with the arriving vehicles.

"The gifts are in appreciation of friendship," Kalina said. "And the few words are a remembrance of joy they shared at some important time."

The line moved up and finally we reached Uncle Bias.

"Uncle Bias!"

"Kalina!"

"I'm surprised anyone came," she said.

They laughed and hugged.

"May I use your knife?" she asked.

He withdrew a wicked looking knife and handed it to her butt first.

She took the first package from the string bag and cut it in half. It was a sausage. She cut the second package in half.

Cheese. She cut the baguette in half and handed the three halves to him. "Half of everything I have is yours."

He smiled his appreciation and handed the three items to his oldest son, who scurried off to Uncle Bias' caravan.

"The only thing I don't know how to split is him." She motioned at me.

They both laughed. I felt my ears redden but I laughed, too. Kalina shot me a look that said this wasn't my show. Butt out. I did. I wasn't doing anything right today.

Uncle Bias winked at me, fingered his mustache and goatee and nodded at me. "Gajo."

"Do you remember, Uncle Bias?" she asked. "When I was going to ride my bike over the Pyrenees? And it broke down? And I needed help? And you came?"

"I must not have had anything else to do."

"I can always count on you."

"I'm often caught with nothing to do."

She took his hands. "I love you."

"Don't go sentimental on me."

She kissed his cheek and started away. But he held onto her hands.

"Old Bohemius was here earlier. He's gone now."

"How did he look?"

"Not well."

She nodded. "Any idea where he was going?"

"Well, he's been to Lourdes twice. So, I guess the next stop is *Saintes Maries De La Mer.*"

He released her hands and we walked away.

I studied her for a moment. She was fighting back tears. "What's *Saintes Maries De La Mer?*"

"Where a lot of Gypsies go to die."

"I guess you'll want to go find him."

"No." She shook her head. "He'll be found when he wants to be found."

"But how will you know where to look?"

"All roads lead to the same place."

A HISTORY LESSON

The *patshiva* was seamless. It ran from shortly after we arrived into the late afternoon and evening, as continuously and smoothly as a flatland brook. It had a bit of carnival atmosphere, yet with the relaxed ease of old friends at play. A harmonica and a Jew's harp joined the guitar and violin music. Then several kazoos joined in. It seemed that everybody could play something and did.

The setting was like a fairytale. A large dinner-plate moon was suspended overhead. I hadn't seen it rise because I was too busy singing and dancing. The warm breeze carried all the sweet bewitching smells of summer. It was all very intoxicating.

People were dancing. I saw Bahtalo and Reservoria. Of course they would be here. It was traditional for newlyweds to live with the grooms family the first year or until they could afford to set off on their own.

Most of the music was American, which illustrated how dominant American music was at the time. Still it all had a Gypsy sound. A lot of the songs I knew and sang. Others joined in. **Louie Louie** and **Sugar Shack** drew the largest chorus. I sang and danced until Kalina led me to a surrounding group of people. I thought I had overdone it but, I was wrong. She wanted me to meet these people. For the most part they were older. Their eyes fascinated me. Wise eyes with stories to tell.

"Ask anything you want," she whispered. "You have curiosities. They have answers." Then she introduced me to them and said I had some questions and they should feel free to answer them honestly.

"Honestly?" someone said. "What's that?"

A lot of chuckles from around the circle. A Gypsy joke.

"How long have you been coming to these campgrounds?" I asked.

The oldest man in the circle leaned forward on his knees. Otimus was his name. "Since my grandmother was a child. Maybe longer."

"It's beautiful," I said. Immediately wondering if I should have said that because, after all, it was self-evident.

Agreeing nods and murmurs all around erased that fear.

I asked cultural questions interspersed with inane ones. Finally I got around to what I really wanted to know. I prefaced the questions with: "I'm a writer and a student of history. So, I hope these questions aren't too personal."

Not a sound back. I glanced at Kalina and she nodded to go ahead.

"Were any of you here when the Nazis occupied France?"

"Most of us," Otimus said. He was a skinny man. But in no way frail. Blotchy skin made more so by the flickering firelight.

Several of the men and a few of the women spit on the ground.

"I take that as a yes," I said trying to lighten things up. I could tell by their looks that there was no 'lightening up' of this subject. "If it's not too personal, what was it like?"

Eyes darted to Kalina. Out of the corner of my eye I saw her nod. I was really beginning to realize how much power she had. They had all deferred to her. These elders were deferring to her. I wondered how many other such incidents I had missed. But I went with my reporter's training. Stick with what you want to know. I waited for an answer.

"When the Nazi's first invaded Europe," Otimus began. "They captured the cities one at a time then moved to the capitol. One country after another. It was always the same. Then they swept through the cities and arrested the people who were the most removed from society. The ones least likely to cause trouble because they were not well connected. The Gypsies. They put us in concentration camps. Those of us in France thought it couldn't happen here. The French would stand up to them. But they didn't. The French don't stand up well.

"We warned the Jews that we knew that they would be next. We told them we were going to flee into the countryside. They could come with us if they wanted. Most didn't. Some did." He pointed to a man about his age.

"Albert Katz," the man introduced himself. He was balding. Stooped. But with a winning smile I'll never forget. "I was living with my grandparents. They encouraged me to go. I did."

"Some," Otimus continued, "sent their children with us."

A young man four or five years older than me leaned forward. "My parents sent me. I was ten."

Otimus cleared his throat. "The Germans didn't come into the countryside very often. When they came through these mountains they came in convoys and it was only a route for getting from city to city. We knew when they were coming. Kalina's mother was in her teens and she was a born leader. W called her 'The Sparrow.'"

Several people reverentially whispered '*The Sparrow.*'

"The Sparrow would have us scatter throughout the mountains. Men and women. Each with a rifle and one bullet. The Sparrow was one of our better shots.

"It was her idea that we only fire once so they couldn't get a fix on us. Make each shot count. At first, shoot to wound. Kill those who rescue the wounded. Afterward, we would go down and retrieve their rifles, their bullets and their winter clothes. That's how it went."

Albert Katz poured whiskey into a tin cup and passed it to Otimus. He took a big slug, and passed the tin cup to me. The history lesson was over.

Later, alone, I asked Kalina what happened to her mother.

"They caught her," was all she said.

TAKING CARE OF THEIR OWN

Kalina took my hand and led me back to the main party. Heavy clouds were beginning to blanket the sky but you could still see the silver moon through the black clouds. We sang and danced for another couple of hours.

When the moon was directly overhead the music abruptly stopped. People began to drift away. I looked at Kalina questioningly.

"His birthday is over."

Someone I'd never seen before came forward and handed us two thick eiderdowns. One to lie on. One as a cover. I was beginning to understand that these people always traveled with extra bedding because they always took care of their own. No one else would do it for them. I liked their way of life. Not an easy life. Hard-earned. As different as it was, somehow it felt like home.

Kalina had once asked me to describe life in Kansas as succinctly as possible. I had said: hard-earned.

We snuggled into the eiderdowns and in moments I was asleep, even though I had other things on my mind.

Sometime during the night I felt rain on my forehead. Kalina was completely under the eiderdown and didn't notice.

This was going to be a wet night. I pulled the eiderdown over my head and cuddled up to her.

Someone tapped on the eiderdown. I pulled back the covers. It was a woman I'd seen at the party, but I didn't know who she was. She smiled and motioned for us to follow her.

I awoke Kalina and we scooped up the eiderdowns and followed. The woman led us to the open tailgate of an old Fiat station wagon. We crawled inside. She shut the tailgate behind us.

Minutes later the clouds opened up. Lightning. Thunder. A major downpour. Rain was drumming on the car like the music that was drumming in my brain. The space was tight but it was dry and warm. And I was cuddled up to Kalina. Who could ask for anything better?

ANOTHER HISTORY LESSON

We were on the road early. The morning air was damp and chilling, but as the sun rose it killed the chill and dried the air.

We stopped at the first Gypsy campground we came to. Kalina was warmly greeted, almost as if she were a celebrity. Almost? Why was I having a hard time getting it through my thick skull? She was a celebrity. Everyone knew her. Everyone was always glad to see her. She introduced me and the language changed from Rom to English. How considerate. How very Gypsy.

Quickly, after the greetings, the people withdrew and an elder came forward. He was very old and hunched. His hawk face was deeply lined and his hair was long and snow white. He had a slight limp. He had a cane but didn't use it.

"Uncle Dalaus," Kalina said, throwing her arms wide.

They hugged long and with much history. He held her at arms length and studied her. Then they hugged again. She didn't need to ask anything.

"He was here yesterday," Uncle Dalaus said. "His health is very bad. He is going on will power."

"*Saintes Maries de la Mer?*"

"Of course. One last chance. He will wade into the sea and if it doesn't work, he's there." He looked over at me and nodded. I nodded back. "You need to check each campground on the way. Even his will power could give out at any time."

He hugged her again and looked over at me. "She's going to need support, Gajo."

"I'm here for the course," I said.

"I read that in you," Uncle Dalaus said to me. Then to her, "Old Jumpy said he'd have what you asked him for when you get to the *Saintes Maries patshiva*. We will all wade together." He kissed her cheek and started away. Then turned back. "My heart leaps mountains to be with you."

"Bahtalo drom," she responded.

Kalina walked over to me. "Hold me. No one can see me cry."

I held her to me as I watched the old white haired man walk away carrying his cane. I could feel her body shake as she cried. But she made no sound. I looked over her shoulder at the people to see if they noticed. But they had turned away or were already leaving. No one wanted to see her cry either.

"What is this celebration and wading in the sea about?" I asked, trying to get her mind on something else and not knowing what else to say. I never know what to say at moments like this. Why couldn't I come up with such beautiful lines as: My heart leaps mountains to be with you? Or, something even half as poetic, maybe even cowboy lame? Just something.

And the *Saintes Maries de la Mer* history lesson began as I held her close and tears ran down her cheeks and down my neck.

"The story goes," she began, "in 42 A.D. two Biblical 'sisters' of the Virgin Mary, Saint Mary Jacob and Saint Mary Salome, the mother of Saints John and James, drifted in a small boat without oars, or a sail, from the Holy Land. They landed on the shore where we're going." She stepped back from me and wiped away her tears, regaining her composure.

"With them was an Egyptian servant girl. Sarah. She is the patron saint of the Gypsies," she said, starting for her bike.

I started to follow. But she stopped, pulled me to her and hid her face again. She cried some more—quietly. Even though I was holding her, she was alone.

"Once a year," she continued, talking into my shirt. "There is a five day *patshiva*. Gypsies travel from all over to be there. On the next to last day, statues of the three are paraded down to the sea and dipped into it.

"While the statues are in the water, sick Gypsies wade into the sea with the hope that Saint Sarah will cure them. They dip tarot cards in the sea. Things like that. Old ways."

"I didn't think Gypsies believed in that sort of thing." I said.

"My generation, and the one before it, and the ones before that, don't believe, but we honor the 'Old Ways'," she explained.

"Finally, on the last day, a coffin containing the statue of Sarah is waded out to sea as far as we can take it and then we push it out to sea. The current at that time of day will carry the coffin out to sea."

She paused to take a deep breath. Regaining control, she wiped her face against my shirt, erasing tears and tear tracks.

"I wish there were something I could do," I said. "Maybe talk him into going to a hospital."

"Never," she said. "First Lourdes and now *Saintes Maries de la Mer*. That's Daddy Two. Trying for double bahtalo. The old fool."

She stepped back. She was dry-eyed now and there were no tear tracks. "How do I look?"

"Beautiful."

She smiled. "Time to check the next campground, Cowboy."

In minutes we were on the road.

As Kalina liked to say: "Wind in our hair! Bugs in our teeth! We don't have to stop to eat."

ON THE WAY TO SAINTES MARIES DE LA MER

We hit campground after campground in our pursuit of Old Bohemius. At first, we were about eight hours behind him. At each stop we got closer and closer. My read on that was: he was losing energy and going slower and slower. At least, if I were tracking a wounded animal, that would have been my read. The same is true of a politician when you have them cornered. I don't know why I thought of that. But it is true.

We'd stop and schmooze a little. Kalina would do a little business, notebook in hand. Everybody wanted to say "hello" and wish her Bahtalo drom. These stops kept us from catching up with him. But it was important to check each campground—just in case this was the one where he ran out of gas. And once there, it was important for her to fulfill her role as Kalina for *her people*.

Night fell two campgrounds before we reached *Saintes Maries de la Mer*. I've already mentioned that Kalina didn't like to travel at night. "It's not Gypsy," she once told me. "Gypsies camp at night. Socialize. Make new friends."

So, that's what we did.

We were invited to dinner by the camp's elder. I had finally realized that the camp's elder/spokesman/chief changed every day because the make up of the camp changed every day. In this case 'elder' wasn't a good description. Chief was a better title.

His name was Alvon. He was in his early to mid-forties. Dark and off beat handsome. His features were out of round. Everything leaned to one side. And yet . . . he had a very commanding presence. The type of guy women are drawn to and don't know why.

His wife was willowy and just as gorgeous in an off beat way as he was handsome. A Picasso pair. Katral was her name.

They spread a coarse wool blanket on the ground and we ate picnic style. Ham and beans and cornbread. All delicious. *Cowboy food* they called it.

Alvon, Katral and Kalina knew each other but hadn't seen each other in a year. The evening was mostly personal catch-up. Business came later.

Alvon was a short story writer, specializing in sci-fi and the supernatural. "They can't tell I'm a Gypsy from the written page. That was very important at first. Now I have a small following. *Small* being the key word," he laughed. "Most of my stories sell. But no one knows I'm Gypsy."

"Why don't you write about Gypsy life?" I asked

Everybody laughed.

I thought about my question and realized how dumb it was. But he answered it anyway.

"First of all, they would know I was Gypsy and if they did, as you say in America, that would be two strikes against me. Other prejudices start with one strike. Gypsy is an automatic two strikes to start. And why would I want them to understand Gypsies? We spend our entire lives making them believe what we aren't."

"That was really a dumb question," I said.

Everybody laughed in agreement.

"You're a writer," Alvon said. "You must write short stories, too."

"I've written a couple. But I couldn't find the right magazine for them."

"That's an okay approach for a novelist but not for a short story writer," he said. "You are going about it backwards. As a short story writer, the first thing you do is find the kind of magazine you like and study it until you come up with the perfect story for it. You write to match the editorial make up of the magazine. You don't create and then try to find a home for your story."

It made perfect sense. But I hadn't seen it before. This dinner could change my writing life, I thought at the time. Later it did.

"Short story writing is the perfect genre for travelers," Alvon said. "I assume you use American Express as home base for your news and feature stories."

"Yes I do," I said, surprised that he knew that much about me. Word had sure gotten around on Kalina's Gajo.

"You should consider short stories. It is the perfect medium. Eight pages. No more. In those eight pages you create a world of sights, sounds, smells and touch. Not easy, but fun."

Katral laughed: "You unlock this door with the key of imagination. Beyond it is another dimension . . ."

Alvon chimed in: " . . . a dimension of sound, sight and mind . . ."

"*The Twilight Zone.*" Katral concluded.

They all laughed. Friends, happy and safe behind the walls of our home. Our home was the world. The walls were our minds.

Katral was a painter. She took some photographs from her purse. I realized that she was the first Gypsy woman I'd seen with a purse. As she pulled out the photos I saw that the major contents of her purse were acrylic paints and brushes. It was more of a traveling art studio than a conventional woman's purse.

She passed the photos to Kalina first. Then Kalina passed them to me. They were good. Excellently rendered surreal paintings. I wished I could afford one. But I knew better than to ask price. She probably would have given me one. That's the kind of people they are when you are on the inside.

After dinner we lazed around on the blanket in the firelight and drank a couple of bottles of wine.

It turned out that Alvon was the *front figure* in the negotiations with the developer who wanted to buy the campground outside of Lourdes. They talked strategies. I made suggestions at first. Then I realized that, while the last traveler to board the bus may have good ideas, he doesn't know what ground has already been covered.

I lapsed into silence, listened and learned. They were quite astute in their planning. The developer's original proposal was a fifty-fifty deal. Bear the development costs fifty-fifty. Share the profits fifty-fifty. The land was their buy-in, the expertise was his.

They figured that they could maneuver the developer into making an offer of five million francs with equal ownership and him bearing all the development costs. Of course the back half of the campground would belong to Gypsies for their personal use. It was, after all, sacred land that had belonged to the Gypsies for multiple generations. You couldn't put a price on that.

If they sold that land, the other Gypsies would skin them alive and nail their hides to the wall. It was just too emotional of an issue to be dealt with. An emotional chip that couldn't be played.

Kalina, Alvon and Katral calculated that selling the *emotional chip* would result in a sale of the campground for ten million francs and sixty percent of the profits.

"Not a bad deal," Kalina said, "for land we have no use for."

Finally, Katral got up and left. She returned with two eiderdowns and dropped them on the blanket. "Sleep here."

Then she took Alvon and they left us.

Kalina and I made love.

It was a beautiful night.

But that is self-evident.

SAINTES MARIES DE LA MER

We rolled into *Saintes Maries de la Mer* passing a dozen or so ranch-style motels. It was early morning and cars were parked side by side in front of the motels. The day was warming quickly. A gentle on-shore breeze carried the smell of salt water with it. Stillness hung over everything.

We motored past a sign that said: Population 2,250. And the concrete highway turned into a cobblestone street. A visual declaration that we were stepping back in time. Old stone buildings lined the street. A gray stone church that looked like a 16th century fortress dominated the landscape.

Gypsy vans, caravans, trailers and campers were parked everywhere along the street. We passed a huge field that was full of Gypsy vehicles. Hundreds and hundreds of them. Some were beautifully carved golden-oak caravans that had once been drawn by horses and now were mounted in beds of trucks. Some were ancient Airstreams. Some were modern canvas pop-ups. I really couldn't guess how many.

"Good Lord," I said. "How many Gypsies come to this *patshiva?*"

"Eight to ten thousand. And then there are the tourists who come to see us."

People seemed to materialize on the sidewalks. Hundreds at first. Then thousands.

"How will we find your father in all this?"

"It won't be hard. He knows we are looking for him and so does everyone else." She patted my arm that encircled her. "It will be easy."

I found that hard to believe. There were just too many people. And it was still morning. There would be hundreds, if not thousands more by noon.

"Will the King of the Gypsies be here?"

Kalina laughed.

"For years I've heard about the King of the Gypsies," I began. "But every place I've gone with you, all the Gypsy campgrounds, the wedding, the birthday party, not once have I heard anyone even mention the King of the Gypsies."

A small, field stone hotel up ahead had a green neon sign hanging over the sidewalk in front of it that said: St. Sarah's. Below it was a flashing red neon sign that said: Rooms. She parked the bike between two parked caravans in front of the hotel and climbed off. She had a big smile on her face.

"There is no King of the Gypsies."

"No?" I couldn't believe it.

"Yes." She laughed, truly delighted. "Any male can claim the title whenever it works to his advantage. It's just another way to fool the Gaje and particularly the police. It's sort of a crown on the road. It goes where it is needed." She laughed again. "Think Gypsy, Gajo. Think Gypsy.

"Say, you have to go into a hospital for some kind of treatment. I tell the nurses that you are the King of the

Gypsies. Or at your age, the King to be. To them you are an important person. So, you get better care. Like that."

I should have seen it coming. It was the logical reason I hadn't heard any of the Gypsies mention their king. He didn't exist. Kalina was chuckling to herself and shook her head. Us Gaje were so gullible. She grabbed her pack from the saddlebag on the bike as we started toward the hotel. She also took the string bag with the remaining sausage, cheese and bread.

"Leave nothing you want to keep."

I grabbed my pack and we went inside.

THE SAINT SARAH HOTEL

The lobby was small and ancient, but extremely clean. Yellow and brown, of course. There was a faint odor of Pine Sol. Behind the reception desk stood a very attractive older French woman. Her long hair was an intriguing blend of gray and blonde. Her skin tone was peaches and cream. She smiled and asked: "Une chamber pour deux?"

She and Kalina rattled back and forth in French for a while. The French woman plucked the only key visible from a boxed mahogany bracket that was home for the room keys. She motioned for us to follow her.

Kalina turned to me. "We may have found something rarer than hen's teeth. A queen sized bed."

We followed the French woman up the stairs to the first landing. She unlocked and opened the first door. We went in.

It was small. We didn't need big. It was old—but clean. The queen-size bed occupied most of the room. There were a table, two straight-backed chairs, a dresser, a coat rack and a corner sink. The bathroom, no doubt, was down the hall. After living outside for months, it looked like the Presidential suite in the Waldorf Astoria.

Kalina looked at me. I smiled. We took the room. The French woman handed Kalina the room key and left. We plunked our packs down on the wooden table.

Kalina went to the only window and looked at the foot traffic below. I could sense that she wanted to be alone. She was being Gypsy. Taking her personal space where she could find it. In her head she was alone right here, right now. I turned away, giving her more privacy.

After several minutes I heard her turn from the window and I turned around. Tears were streaming down her cheeks.

"I took the room for two days," she said. "By then we will find someone we know who will invite us to sleep outside their caravan. In the meantime," she motioned at the bed. "We should make use of this luxury."

We did.

FINALLY THINKING GYPSY

A couple hours later we went out. The sidewalks were packed with people like they were sardines—or anchovies. I prefer anchovies. There was a pretty even split between the tourists and the Gypsies flowing past us. Mixed in among the human current was an occasional cop, propelled by the drift of the crowd.

The tourists were obvious by their gawking and the Gypsies were obvious by their outfits and their strut. The tourists were obnoxiously taking pictures of the Gypsies and the Gypsies were obnoxiously badgering the tourists into having their fortunes told. It was all a game to the Gypsies. And they were having fun.

"I just realized," I told Kalina. "That since I've been with you, this is the first time I've seen Gypsies telling fortunes."

"I've told you, we don't believe in it. It's just a fun way to take the Gaje's money." She laughed. "It's a carnival. Celebrate. Enjoy. Have fun. It only happens once a year."

I totally understood. Why not take advantage of all the Gaje who were trying to be taken advantage of. I was thinking Gypsy. Finally.

Kalina spotted someone she knew and waved. The man, who was in his fifties, waved back, smiled and made his way though the crowd to us. He and Kalina hugged. He was taller than most Gypsies, lean and even his craggy features couldn't hide his homeliness.

"Bati," Kalina introduced us. "This is Kelly. My American Gajo."

"Proud to meet you, Kelly. If you are Kalina's Gajo, you are all of our Gajo." He seemed to talk from the right side of his face as though his left side didn't work. He extended a hand and we shook. Before I could say a word he turned back to Kalina. "You look worried."

"Have you seen Old Bohemius?"

"No. Is there something wrong?"

"He's very sick and here to wade for a cure. I'm trying to find him."

"I will pass the word. Where are you staying?" His eyes got watery.

"At the Saint Sarah's Hotel. Tonight and tomorrow night." She pointed down the street at the hotel sign. "By then I'll find a Gypsy place."

"My caravan is in the middle of the park. You know it." A tear ran down his misshaped face. "I have eiderdowns and sleeping bags."

"Bahtalo drom," Kalina said.

"Bahtalo drom," he responded. He turned away and went to the closest group of Gypsies, maybe five in all. I noticed he had a slight limp. He talked to them briefly and motioned at Kalina. The five nodded at Kalina and then split up, each heading in a different direction.

"See," Kalina said to me. "It won't be hard to find him." Then: "Bati is Old Bohemius' true cousin. They are like brothers."

THE LOWERING OF
THE THREE SAINTS

Just about everyone seemed to know Kalina. As we wandered the streets of the ancient town, Gypsies were constantly stopping her either to hug her or shake her hand. She told them she was looking for Poppa Two. They all said they would help. As soon as they wished her a lucky road, they split up in search of Bohemius.

We wandered the streets for several hours and there was no doubt that the word was out that Kalina was looking for Bohemius. She'd been right. Finding him wasn't going to be hard.

We talked to at least twenty people in less than an hour. If each person we talked to, told four more people, that would make eighty people looking for Old Bohemius. And if each of them told four . . . Remember, I said I had this math ability/thing? Well, three more retellings like that and we'd have over five thousand people looking for him. My guess was that in less than two hours Old Bohemius would know that Kalina was here and looking for him.

We found a little bistro and had a leisurely, late lunch. We both had a grilled cheese sandwich with pommes frites and we shared a bottle of red. We sat in the window and watched the crowds flow by outside. Some of the Gypsies in the crowd noticed Kalina and waved at her. She always smiled and waved back.

At five before three Kalina stood up. "Time to go."

I followed her out of the bistro and about a block down the street. She stopped in front of the *Saintes Maries de la Mer* church. A large crowd of tourists and Gypsies were watching as a special ceremony began. The lowering of the saints. The reliquary of the two Marys was lowered by rope from the high chapel. Kalina and I watched from the back of the crowd.

From the corner of my eye, movement on the other side of the square caught my attention. A policeman had Old Jumpy in tow and he looked miserable. I looked around. Cinderella and Mateo were nowhere in sight. What was going on?

I could stand by and do nothing. That was probably Gypsy. But doing nothing wasn't me. I started across the square to intercept them. Although I didn't know what I was going to do when I got there.

Kalina saw where I was going and was right behind me. "Careful, Gajo," she said, laying a hand lightly on my shoulder. "They don't like us Gypsies."

Before I could get to them the cop pushed Old Jumpy up to a narrow, open-front food store. The cop pushed him toward a man wearing an apron, no doubt the owner of the store, and said something. Old Jumpy just stood there rubbing his out-sized nose. The owner studied Old Jumpy, not sure that he was the right man. Just as I got there, the owner nodded at the cop.

"Excuse moi," I said to the policeman.

He turned icy eyes on me and sized me up.

"I am from the United States. My French is not very good. I'm trying to learn but . . ."

"I speak English," the cop said, his voice cold and officious. His face was as hard as his eyes and voice. This was a man who had dealt with hard things.

"I am here representing the King of the Gypsies in the United States. He was too ill to travel."

"So?" His voice remained icy and cold. He was sizing me up.

"I know this man. What is he supposed to have done?" I was trying to be pleasant, non-confrontational. I produced my best smile.

The cop continued to study me. As he studied me, he fingered some of the apples that were on display in front of the store. Then he glanced questioningly from the apples to the owner. The owner nodded okay. What was the owner going to do? Say no? The cop took a bite out of the apple as he continued to study me.

I asked: "What has he done?"

Kalina rushed up and took my arm, trying to pull me away.

"Victor, stop! We never confront the police here." She turned to the policeman. "You have to excuse him, please. He is my cousin from America and doesn't know any better."

The cop continued to study me as he munched on the apple. A crowd was beginning to form around us.

"I still want to know what he's supposed to have done," I said. I was not about to back down,

"He stole a chicken," the cop said. "The store owner here saw him."

I laughed. "It couldn't have been him. He is the King of the Gypsies here in Europe. He doesn't have to steal. He is given whatever he wants."

"He's the second King I've run into today," the cop said with a sneer.

"There are four tribes," I explained. "All four tribes are here. And all four of their Kings are here."

The cop eyed Old Jumpy suspiciously. Old Jumpy smiled back and nodded. Yes, I am the King of the Gypsies. The cop glanced at the crowd surrounding them. Mostly Gypsies.

"Also, because he is the King of the Gypsies, if he had stolen the chicken, the store owner would never have seen him." I smiled and winked at the storeowner. "He's too good."

Several of the bystanders chuckled at the logic. Even the cop smiled. Then he looked over at the storeowner and spoke to him in French.

Kalina translated for me. "Are you sure you saw *this* man take your chicken?"

The storeowner responded in French. Again Kalina translated for me. "Well, I thought it was him. They all look so much alike."

The cop rolled his eyes. This was becoming ridiculous.

"That's an excellent eyewitness you have there," I said.

The crowd chuckled.

I smiled and offered my hand. No harm, no foul.

The cop shook my hand. "Okay, run along. But don't let me catch you doing anything."

"I don't understand," I said. "Like doing what?"

"Gypsy things," the cop said. "Stealing. Picking pockets. Begging."

Kalina took my arm, trying to lead me away. I pulled my arm away. I gave the cop my best smile. We were having fun now.

"We have an old saying," I said. "A begged apple tastes the best." I motioned at the apple he was holding. "You tell me, is that true?"

The cop looked at the apple he was holding and smiled. Touché. Snickers and laughter from the crowd.

The cop turned to Kalina. "American Gypsies are just like regular Americans. Pushy pains in the butt."

Kalina laughed and nodded. "Isn't that the truth."

There were laughs and chuckles from the crowd. The cop walked through the crowd smiling. Face saved. Old Jumpy patted me on the back and said to Kalina:

"You have a good Gajo. By tonight everybody will know how he kept me out of jail. Of course you will join me for dinner tonight."

"What's for dinner?" she asked.

"Chicken," he said.

Before he walked away, he pulled an envelope and a small box from a coat pocket and gave them to Kalina.

OLD BOHEMIUS FOUND

We had just returned to our hotel room after chicken dinner with Old Jumpy, Cinderella and their family. They had prepared a delicious chicken stew to celebrate the evening. Actually, Old Jumpy had taken two chickens and had just handed them off in the crowd when the cop had apprehended him.

I was getting ready to open a bottle of red that he had given us with the parting words: "Stolen wine tastes best," when there was a knock at the door.

"Yes?" Kalina said. "Who's there?"

"Bati. I have located your father."

Kalina opened the door.

Bati, Old Bohemius' cousin and two other men entered. All three bowed to Kalina. Bati looked even more frail and haggard than before. The other two were strangers to me. "He is in the camp on the other side of the hotels," Bati said. "Closer to the sea."

Kalina began stuffing the few things she had taken out of her pack back into her pack. I did the same. It only took seconds. A Gypsy never completely unpacks. A Gypsy is always ready to leave in a hurry. Maybe because of an opportunity—or maybe out of necessity.

We climbed on Kalina's motorcycle and followed Bati and his friends in their caravan. They drove to the campground where Old Bohemius was staying. They stopped in front of Bohemius' campsite, pointed and then drove on.

It was dark and getting late, the grounds were lighted by maybe a hundred dying campfires. Old Bohemius was sitting in a red and white canvas lawn chair in front of his fire, looking very regal with his deep maroon dunha (eiderdown) around his shoulders, drinking from a tin cup, eating stew from a gold-panning pan. Behind him was his caravan.

It was the first time I'd seen his caravan and it was a beauty. It was a 1950, robin's-egg-blue, flatbed Ford truck with what looked like a hundred coats of hand polished wax. It glowed in the firelight. An ornately carved vardo was mounted on the flat bed. Later I learned that the wood was golden oak and the carvings were all his. Every carving was a piece of his life. People, places and pets. The story of his life's journey in smoothly sanded, highly polished golden oak. Only the wheels were gone from the original vardo that was once pulled by a horse. Actually, several beloved steeds all of whom were immortalized in golden oak around the vardo.

We climbed off her motorcycle. Kalina went to the vardo and took two tin cups from a ring, which hung on the side of the vardo just like they had in the past. She handed one to me. Then she went over to Bohemius and kissed him on the cheek and sat down beside him. I sat beside her.

The smell of the sea rode in on a gentle breeze. No one spoke or acknowledged anyone.

Finally, Old Bohemius smiled and nodded at us. He looked like he'd lost twenty pounds since we last saw him.

"We did have good times, didn't we?" he said to Kalina and passed Kalina his bottle of Scotch whiskey.

"The best," she said, pouring Scotch into her tin cup. Then she passed the bottle to me.

"I really wasn't angry when you went to school."

"I knew that."

"Actually, I was proud of you. You fooled the Gaje school good."

Kalina raised her tin cup to him as a salute. He raised his. I raised mine. We all drank. This was all personal stuff and I was feeling out of place. Like a stranger at a wake of someone you barely knew—which was true.

"Why don't I leave you two alone so you can . . ."

"Nonsense," Old Bohemius interrupted. "I want to get to know my little girl's Gajo. See what makes him tick. I heard about today. Everybody's heard about you today. You sure fooled that Gaje policeman." He started laughing.

But the laugh became a raging, hacking cough. Finally, he turned his head and spit up blood. Kalina sat there staring into the fire as if nothing had happened.

"What do you do, Kalina's Gajo?" he asked.

"Right now I'm a newspaperman. A reporter. But some day I want to be a novelist."

"Is there good money in that?"

"To be honest, probably not."

"I've known a lot of honest fools in my time." Old Bohemius smiled at me.

"He loves what he does, Daddy."

"Good man." Bohemius refilled his cup and passed the bottle to Kalina. She waited for him to continue before passing the bottle to me. "I understand you are pre-occupied with things that are self-evident, Gajo. Like the weather." He continued. "Why is that?"

"In Kansas we have a saying, 'If you don't like the weather wait fifteen minutes. It will change.' You learn to pay attention to the weather."

"Tell me about your Gajo, Kalina."

She refilled her cup and passed the bottle to me.

"Well," she began. "He's a slow learner. Not as smart as he could be. His hands are soft. He's barely strong enough to hold my bike up. And, as you can see. Not much to look at."

Old Bohemius nodded as he evaluated her words. "Yet, he interests you?"

"I'm trying to decide," Kalina said.

"Okay, Gajo. Your turn." Old Bohemius smiled and the knife scar down his cheek seemed to wink at me. "What's so special about this Gypsy girl?" He laughed. "Other than the obvious fact that she's just plain fly-popping hot?"

I had never before heard a father refer to his daughter as *fly-popping* hot. I smiled and nodded my agreement.

"Well, there's that," I agreed. "And, she's frugal. In fact, now that I think about it, I've never seen her spend a franc on anything. She always gets someone else to pay for her. She's got a great personality, all the girls love her, she sews her own clothes—and she's pig-headed and neurotic."

"Neurotic!?!" Kalina almost yelled, ah . . . neurotically.

"Neurotic?" Old Bohemius asked, smiling, knowing there was a punch line.

"That's not necessarily a bad thing," I explained to them. "In Kansas there's a saying: 'Neurotic sex is the best.'" I figured he could handle that if he referred to her as *fly popping*. But it was a risk.

Bohemius raised his cup just short of his mouth. Over the rim of his tin cup he said/whispered: "Tell me about yourself, Kalina's Gajo." His mouth smiled just before he sipped. But his eyes were cold and serious.

"I'm from Kansas," I began. He waved me silent.

"I mean. tell me things you haven't told others. Anything you've told them, I already know." He smiled again.

I read him loud and clear. This was cut-to-the-chase time, without a lot of chase time. "What do you want to know?"

"Are you a man who has nothing to hide . . . or are you a good liar."

"When it comes to Kalina, I have nothing to hide. But if I need to, I can lie like the devil."

He laughed, more polite than humor. "Tell me about your mother's parents."

"Her mother is part Irish and part Cherokee Indian—hard working and honest. Mom's father is Irish, a printer by trade and a drinker by nature."

"Tell me about your father's father."

"He came from Scotland."

Bohemius waved a hand to cut me off. "Then I know about him. What about you father's mother?"

"Her family came from France and . . ."

Again he cut me off. "What's her family name?"

"I'm not sure," I said. "I think it was Plan-something or . . ."

"Of course it was," he interrupted. "And her given name?"

"Gypsy," I said and got the silence and the disbelieving stares I had expected.

Bohemius looked at Kalina and chuckled. "I believe the part about him lying like the devil." He held out the whiskey bottle and poured into my tin cup. "What did you call her?"

"I never knew her," I said.

"What did your father call her when he spoke of her?"

"Mother."

"And what did your father's father call his wife?"

"I don't know. I never knew him either."

Bohemius studied me for a brief moment before pouring more scotch into Kalina's cup. "Your Gajo seems pretty iffy to me."

"At best," she replied.

"But relatives are pretty iffy anyway, any-how, any-who," he said.

Kalina banged her tin cup against his. "Case in point," she said.

He laughed, handed me the bottle and looked over at Kalina.

"I should have relied on The Mule," he said and pitched part of his drink on the ground.

"The Mule," Kalina said and pitched part of her drink on the ground. Then she looked at me.

"The Mule," I said, not knowing what I was talking about, and pitched part of my drink on the ground.

They raised their cups in the air. So did I. "The Mule." We all drank. I handed the bottle back to Bohemius. He refilled his tin cup and passed the bottle to Kalina. She refilled and passed it to me. I refilled.

"The reason I didn't go to the clinic is because they steal your dignity," he said to Kalina.

"I understand," she said.

"Good," he said and drank. "We did have good times didn't we?"

"A lifetime's worth," she said. "Sometimes Number Two is Number One."

Bohemius fought back tears. "Bullshit," he said and took a big drink. "Old Jumpy said he could make a hole on our land outside Marseille," Bohemius said.

"That's a good place," Kalina said. "Always one of my favorites, too."

"I always wanted to go out to sea."

"Then that's what it will be."

He raised his cup and we all drank.

"It will be good to travel with your mother again."

"I'm sure she can't wait," Kalina said.

Bohemius raised his tin cup. "To good times past and good times coming."

Kalina raised her cup. "To all the good times."

We all drank. I don't know how Kalina was able to remain dry eyed. I was on the verge of tears.

BOHEMIUS' LAST WADE

The next day we took Bohemius down to the beach for the annual parade to the sea. First came the Camargue Cowboys on white horses. A hundred of them. Exactly one hundred. They are the ranchers and cowboys who raise the witty and wily bulls for the bull games that date back to Roman times.

After the Cowboys came a white rowboat carried by a dozen well-dressed Gypsy men. Lying in the boat were the statues of the two Saint Marys and one statue of Saint Sarah. Six Gypsy pallbearers followed the rowboat carrying a pine coffin. Behind them came thousands of Gypsies. And behind them came thousands of tourists, cameras clicking.

Kalina, Bohemius and I were right behind the coffin carried by the pallbearers. Obviously, a place of honor. Bohemius was wobbly but any time Kalina or I offered support, he shrugged us off. He didn't want help. He wanted his dignity.

Just short of the waters' edge, the Camargue Cowboys formed an aisle for the boat and its carriers and the coffin and its pallbearers. The boat and the coffin were transported down the aisle. Everyone else spread out along the shoreline.

The smell of the sea was the strongest I had ever experienced. My senses were probably heightened because of the situation. I could smell the horses. They smelled very clean. I could smell some of the people. They had probably skipped their morning shower knowing they would soon be chin deep in the Mediterranean.

The boat was carried a couple of feet out into the water. The coffin was set down on the sand equidistant from the sea. The three statues were taken from the boat and placed standing upright in the sea. And thousands of Gypsies waded out into the sea.

Babies were christened. Tarot cards were dunked. And the sick waded out, taking a long shot at a miracle. All of this came from people who didn't believe in mysticism or magic.

Bohemius waded out a few feet and turned back to Kalina. "Aren't you coming in?" he asked her.

"I don't swim."

"This isn't swimming. This is wading."

"I don't wade either."

Bohemius started laughing. It became a racking cough. He waded further out.

"He's teasing me," Kalina said. "One summer I nearly drowned in a lake. Later that year we came here. I waded out and stepped in a hole. I went in over my head and sucked in a lot of seawater. I panicked. I thought I was going to drown and I caused quite a scene. He has been teasing me about it ever since."

I laughed. I wish I had known him longer. He certainly knew how to have fun right to the end.

"What was that about The Mule last night?" I asked.

"The Mule is all your ancestors who have passed on before you. In the old ways you asked them for help with any sickness. Papa Two went to Lourdes instead. Now this."

Shortly, Bohemius waded back to shore. He was very wobbly. Both Kalina and I offered support. He proudly shrugged us off. Dignity first.

He leaned over to Kalina and whispered. But I could hear. "I think it's time," he said.

Kalina whispered to the Gypsy next to her, passing the word.

BAHTALO DROM BOHEMIUS

We were just a short walk from the beach to Bohemius' vardo. It was a good thing, too. He had to rest twice on the way back. He should have rested one more time, but refused to. When we reached his vardo he pulled down the back steps, climbed them haltingly and opened the rear door. He took a long last look around, stroked his magnificent woodcarvings on the vardo and then went inside. He lay down on his bed and placed his hat on his chest.

"Wait here," Kalina told me. Then she went up the steps and inside.

From where I stood I could see most of the inside of his vardo. It was neat and orderly. Each inch of space was utilized like on a boat.

Kalina went to him and kissed him. They hugged. It was a long and tender moment.

"You can't marry the Gaje and be Queen," he said. I was sure I wasn't supposed to have heard that. But I did.

"I know," she said. Then she erected a tent over his bed using a rope and a sheet.

"Don't mourn for me longer than a week or two because I will be impatient to travel again."

"Bahtalo drom, Daddy." She poured him a scotch in his tin cup and sat it beside his bed.

"Bahtalo drom, Kalina."

She came down the steps and walked up to me. "Your turn."

As I watched her walk away I realized that I was at the head of a long line of people. No doubt all here to pay their last respects. I went up the steps and inside.

Bohemius held up his hand for me to take, which I did. His large, once strong hand, was now surprisingly weak.

"I told her that she couldn't marry you and become Queen."

"I heard. But I didn't think there was a King or Queen of the Gypsies."

"There is no King. But we Tsurara are a matriarchal tribe. She probably told you it was one of the other tribes. But we have our Queen. The title goes to the one best suited to lead and govern the tribe. You've seen the notebooks she keeps. You've seen how people come to her for advice and guidance. She is the best prepared. She is the most respected. She's next in line." His coughing racked him.

"She will not tell you this—but you need to know it if you love her." His coughing stopped him again. "Her mother was our Queen. When we fought the Nazis, her mother led us. Her father and I were like brothers. When the Nazis killed her mother, many of us became Kalina's uncles out of respect to her mother. The Sparrow. When her father died, I was selected to become Papa Two. I was very lucky to be so honored." Again the coughing stopped him.

He squeezed my hand. "Don't try to talk her into marrying you. She will make up her own mind and let you know."

I nodded.

He squeezed my hand again. "If she chooses you, it will be a good choice. I like you . . ." he smiled and coughed " . . . as Gaje go. Now go be with her. She will need you."

"Bahtalo drom," I said.

"Bahtalo drom."

I came out of the vardo and stopped half way down the steps. A sea of familiar and concerned faces stretched out in a long line. Old Jumpy and Cinderella. Mateo and his family. Bin-Bin and his wife. Bati and his family. Uncle Bias and Ithal Lee with their wives. Reservoria and Bahtalo. And all the uncles. Otimus. Dalaus, Uncle Stan and Uncle Ollie. And many more.

One by one they filed into Bohemius' vardo to pay their final respects.

THE SET UP

I found Kalina sitting beneath a giant oak tree. She was crying and making no effort to hide it. I sat down beside her and put my arm around her. She snuggled close to me and cried freely.

"Is there anything I can do?"

"No. Just stay with me. Follow my lead and don't mention his name. It is bad luck."

"I'm here for you," I said.

"I know you are," she said and kissed me.

About an hour later Old Jumpy came up to us. "He's traveling," he said.

Kalina nodded. She took a deep, calming breath and stood up.

Old Jumpy stepped aside and behind him Uncles Stan, Ollie, Bias and Otimus were holding a pine coffin. It looked exactly like the one used in the procession to the sea earlier.

Kalina inspected it. She nodded approval. Then we followed the coffin bearers back to Bohemius' vardo. They carried the coffin through a crowd of people and into the vardo. They opened the hinged lid. Then they picked up Old Bohemius' body, placed it in the coffin and closed the lid.

Seven tall candles were passed from the crowd to Kalina inside the vardo. She placed three on each side of the coffin and one at the foot. Someone passed her matches and she lit the candles. She climbed out of the vardo.

Three scarves and a roll of silver tape were passed to her. She walked around the pickup and wrapped the two side view mirrors of the truck with the scarves and taped them in place. She did the same with the interior rear view mirror.

She climbed the stairs back into his vardo and I could see her sit on his bed. She put her face in her hands and uttered a cry of anguish like I'd never heard before. Then she cried.

I started to go to her but Cinderella stopped me with a hand on my shoulder. "It is her time to be alone," she said.

I stood there feeling helpless and useless. I watched the sun sink lower in the sky. The on-shore breeze picked up a little, fluttering the scarves that covered the mirrors.

Eventually she came out the back of the vardo carrying two of Bohemius' eiderdowns. She closed the back door, descended the steps and raised the stairs into traveling position.

"He travels," she said in Rom.

"Bahtalo Drom," the crowd said. Not a shout. Not a whisper. But a heart-felt farewell.

Kalina spread the eiderdowns on the ground and sat down.

Cinderella gave me a little nudge forward. I was supposed to join her now. I went to her but before I could sit down, she stood up.

"Too short a time, Ole Shining Star," Old Jumpy said loudly. "Too short a time."

Kalina threw her arms wide and almost shouted, "May the road ahead of him be as good as the one he traveled on this earth." The crowd murmured agreement and she sat back down. She drew me down beside her.

One by one the people in the crowd filed by behind her, each patting her gently on the shoulder. Shortly we were alone and the sun was gone. Kalina continued to cry.

Much to my embarrassment my stomach began to growl.

She laughed through her tears. "The grocer where Old Jumpy found the chickens makes a great submarine sandwich. Go find a couple of them and a bottle of my daddy's favorite beverage. He would like that."

FOR THE ROAD

When I returned from the grocery store, Kalina was sitting on the eiderdown with three tin cups in front of her. I handed her the two paper-wrapped sandwiches. She placed one beside each of the two outside cups. I handed her the bottle of Scotch whiskey. She motioned for me to sit down with her.

She poured scotch into the tin cup on the left, hers, half full. She poured into the one on the right, mine, half full. She poured a splash into the center cup. Then she picked up the center cup and pitched its contents over her shoulder. "For the road," she said. We picked up our tin cups and toasted each other. "For the road," we said.

I don't remember eating the sandwiches. I do remember drinking a whole lot of Scotch. We continued the same ritual with virtually no conversation for what seemed like hours. People seemed to drift by. I'm not sure. It was a blur.

I don't remember if we went to sleep or if we passed out. It doesn't matter. The results were the same.

ONE LAST TRIP TO THE SEA

The procession down to the sea the next day was the same as the day before. First came the one hundred Camargue Cowboys on white horses. Exactly one hundred. They formed an aisle for the white rowboat and the dozen well-dressed Gypsies who carried it. In the boat were the statues of the Saints Marys and Saint Sarah. They sat the boat down at the edge of the water.

Behind them came the pine coffin and the six pallbearers. Old Jumpy. Uncle Stan. Uncle Ollie. Uncle Ithal Lee. Uncle Dalaus. And Uncle Bin-Bin. They sat the coffin down behind the rowboat.

Surrounding this were thousands of Gypsies. Surrounding them were thousands of tourists, camera shutters tripping.

At the back of the gathering were six policemen. One was the cop I had the encounter with yesterday. I caught his eye. He smiled. I nodded and smiled back.

One of the policemen in that group started weaving his way through the crowd toward the procession. When he reached the coffin, he tapped on the lid with his baton.

I looked questioningly at yesterday's cop. Was this normal? He nodded "yes."

One of the pallbearers, white-haired distinguished-looking Uncle Dalaus, raised the hinged lid. The cop looked inside. It was empty. Two of the men at the rowboat picked up the statue of Saint Sarah, carried it back to the coffin and put it inside, while the cop watched. Then Uncle Stan closed the lid. The cop, who had inspected the coffin, withdrew to the edge of the crowd.

Kalina nudged me with her elbow. "Time to be Gypsy," she said. "Occupy their interests."

I nodded and crossed through the procession between the coffin and the rowboat. The cop, who had withdrawn to the edge of the crowd, now had his eyes locked on me, I had his attention. He was watching my every move. So was everyone else. I walked past him and patted the cop on his shoulder twice. With the second pat I gave him a little squeeze. I figured that would piss him off. It did. He spun around and came after me as I headed for the five policemen on the far side of the crowd.

The Gypsies in front of me parted, giving me a clear path. They closed behind me obstructing the cop's pursuit of me. By now I had attracted the attention of the other five cops. I smiled and waved at yesterday's cop. He gave me a slight wave. A cautious wave.

When I reached the cluster of cops, I held out my hand to yesterday's cop. He shook it. But I could read in his eyes that he didn't trust me.

"I'm glad I got to see you again," I said to him. "I'm not sure if I made it clear how courteously and professionally you handled that situation yesterday. You are a credit to the uniform." He smiled and raised his left hand as if to block something.

I looked. It was the cop who had chased me through the crowd. His baton was raised. He was getting ready to whack me.

"Alain," the cop from yesterday said. "This is . . ."

"Kelly," I supplied the name.

"He is representing the United States' King of the Gypsies, who was too ill to travel to this celebration."

"Sir," I said to the cop from yesterday. "Alain, here, was very thorough and professional in checking the coffin and all. I patted him on the shoulder in recognition of his good work. It's what we would do in the United States. I think he misunderstood my actions."

"You never touch a policeman here," the cop from yesterday said.

I turned to face Alain. "Sir, I apologize. It was meant to be a compliment."

He didn't know whether to believe me or not, but he held out his hand and we shook. Then I shook the hand of the cop from yesterday again and headed back toward the procession. The tourists and Gypsies parted so I had a clear path. All eyes had been on me. I had been the center of attention. I hoped it was what Kalina had wanted. Who really knew?

When I got back to the procession the pallbearers were no longer holding the coffin up. It sat on the sand.

But Kalina now stood at the head of the coffin.

"The times they are a changing."

Old Jumpy patted the coffin, turned away from it and entered the following crowd.

The strikingly handsome George, his beautiful wife Petshiva, the lawyers who were opposing the French Highway

Commission on the campground right of way issue, and their friend Ayashah stepped to the perimeter of the crowd.

George shook hands with Old Jumpy and took his place as a pallbearer.

Bin-Bin wiped a tear, turned away and was replaced by Ayashah.

Uncle Ollie shook his big head sadly, turned away and was replaced at his pallbearer's handle by Petshiva.

Uncle Stan snapped a salute and backed away. As he reached the crowd Alvon, the shorty story writer, and his artist wife Katral emerged. Uncle Stan and Alvon gripped each other's arms as they passed and Alvon took Uncle Stan's place.

Bati blew a kiss to the coffin, backed away and was replaced by Katral.

And, Ithal Lee walked away and was not replaced. The sixth handle was unattended.

Kalina motioned for me to take the sixth handle. "You did good Gajo. No one saw the switch." Tears were running down her cheeks.

Instantly tears started down mine and I quickly wiped them away. And took my place.

She stood straight and made eye contact with each new person around the coffin.

"Friends, the guard changes."

"The times they are a changing."

A small bouquet of flowers was passed forward through the crowd and finally given to Kalina. She wiped her tears away with the bouquet, raised the coffin lid slightly and placed the flowers on Bohemius' chest beside his hat.

At Kalina's signal we pallbearers lifted the coffin and followed Kalina out into the Mediterranean. When we were chest deep in the water and could feel the tide going out, Kalina kissed her fingers, rubbed them tenderly on the coffin lid and we released it.

The coffin quickly floated out to sea. Old Bohemius had gotten his final wish. Burial at sea.

THE LAST GOOD-BYE

We went back to Bohemius' vardo. Kalina lowered the stairs and opened the back door. She took the nearly empty bottle of Scotch from last night and a blanket from inside the vardo. She took three tin cups from the ring outside the vardo. She spread the blanket on the ground, sat down and poured the remaining Scotch into the tin cups.

Like yesterday, she pitched out the contents of the middle cup. Only this time she pitched it over her shoulder, without words. The words were self-evident. We toasted each other and drank.

Almost immediately Gypsies began trooping up to Kalina. Each gave her some sort of gift. Scotch. Wine. Dishtowel. Skirt. Blouse. You name it. They brought it. Reservoria and Bahtalo appeared from nowhere and stood behind her. After Kalina inspected each gift, and thanked the giver, she handed it to Reservoria and Bahtalo. They took everything into the vardo—except for a new bottle of Scotch. We put it to use immediately. And not just the four of us.

Each gift giver arrived carrying a tin cup. They all shared in the scotch. Each drink was a silent toast. But Old Bohemius' name was never mentioned.

The gifting continued for over an hour. Maybe two. Kalina acknowledged each gift and Resevoria and Bahtalo stored them in the vardo. Kalina's tears never quit flowing.

Finally, Kalina raised her hands. "Enough gifts. He wasn't that good of a man."

The people in the crowd laughed and drifted away.

"Reservoria. Bahtalo."

They came forward respectfully.

"Are you living with Ithal Lee and his family in their vardo?" Kalina asked.

"Yes, Kalina," Bahtalo said.

"Would you do me a favor?"

"Anything," Reservoria responded.

"Would you look after Papa Two's vardo for the next year or so?" Kalina asked. "It is too much of him for me right now."

Bahtalo and Reservoria looked at each other and smiled. Their own place! Privacy! You could see their hearts racing.

Kalina tossed the vardo's keys to Bahtalo. "Use it as your own."

"What should we do with Bohemius' gifts?" Reservoria asked.

"Spread them around. That is what they are for."

They thanked her over and over before walking off into the night.

I studied her closely. Even in her grief, *her people* came first.

She poured us more scotch. We sat in silence, drinking scotch. Then we laid back on the blanket and watched the stars, alone in our own thoughts. Very Gypsy.

"It's a new world, Kelly. It's our world now."

"It's always changing. Always will."

I have no idea who fell asleep first. I just remember cuddling together on the blanket.

I woke up once during the night and someone had put an eiderdown over us. We needed it with the cool ocean breeze. We were alone. But she was not unattended. Everyone was taking care of Kalina, their Queen to be.

MONT SAINT-MICHEL AGAIN

Kalina woke me in the morning. She was dressed in a red skirt and white blouse that I recognized as gifts from last night. "Go bathe in the ocean. Take clean clothes with you," she said. "We travel in half an hour or less."

In less than thirty minutes we were heading north. She didn't say where we were going. I didn't ask. I just rode behind her and hung on. We didn't talk much. She was deep in thought. But she said one thing that was very important to me.

"You were very Gypsy yesterday. You made me proud."

I started to say "thank you" but caught myself. That would not be very Gypsy. I smiled instead. She caught it.

And, while she was deep in thought, so was I. I was trying to figure out how to propose to her.

And, more importantly, *if* I should propose.

I wanted to honor my word to Old Bohemius, that I wouldn't influence her choice about being Queen or not. I really was at a loss. I didn't want to lose her. But I wanted to honor my word to her Papa Two. But to be honest, to hell with, Poppa Two. I wanted her.

After several hours of silence we arrived at Mont Saint-Michel. The tide was out, or it was one of those many days when the ocean no longer surrounded the abbey. She parked her bike in the lot and we walked out across the causeway to the abbey.

"You know," she said, breaking our silence. "Papa Two liked you."

"I liked him, too."

"Respected, is a better choice of words," she said.

"Word," I corrected.

Kalina looked at me, confused.

"*Choice of words* is a cliché," I said. "A cliché is a non-thinking response. You once asked me to correct you when you made that mistake in English."

She looked at me, analyzing what I had said. "So, you're saying that I should have said: 'Respected, is a better choice of *word?*'"

"Technically." Why in the hell had I made an issue out of something so unimportant?

She shook her head and gave sort of a *snort-chortle*—a new sound. I had no idea what that meant. I shut up.

We walked some then she stopped, looked out at the sea, then kissed me. "We can truly change things in this world. Make a difference."

"It's our world now, Kalina." I returned her kiss. "Ours to make of it what we will."

We held each other for a long, tender moment then continued walking toward the ancient stone abbey in silence. I didn't hear the birds circling overhead. I didn't smell the sea. I remember now that there was a stiff wind coming off the ocean. I wasn't aware of any of that at the time. The only thing I was truly aware of was Kalina.

I was aware of how deeply in love with her I was. I was aware of how much I wanted to tell her that. I was also aware of how wrong the timing was. I bit my lip and took her hand in mine as we walked toward the abbey. Taking her hand was the second best thing I could do. The best thing I could do still resided with *l'esprit de l'escalier*.

The interior of the abbey was incredible. Kalina gave me her walking history tour through the tomb, the aisles, the nave, and the choir south. It was the first time she had spoken in what seemed like hours. I loved hearing her voice. I loved being with her.

Finally she took me into an abbey building that she described as her favorite. It was easy to see why. Sweeping white archways, endlessly running into and overlapping each other. "Just look," she said.

I did. It was mesmerizing. I looked and looked while I tried to figure out how to propose to her. Or, whether I should. Or, whether I should wait.

Just let things play out. See if she wanted to be Queen more than she wanted me.

I knew in my heart that the choice was in hers. Old Bohemius was right. It was her choice to make. But for her to make her choice I had to let her know where I stood. How I said it really didn't matter as much as saying it.

So, I decided just to say it. To tell her I loved her. That I would always be there for her—whatever she decided. But when I turn to tell her, I was alone. I had no idea how long I'd been alone.

She had made her choice.

But the choice had been self-evident.

The Gypsies had their Queen.

The End

CPSIA information can be obtained at www.ICGtesting.com
Printed in the USA
BVOW021318121212

307622BV00001B/2/P

9 781479 734009